Eliza Redgold is an author, academic and unashamed romantic. She was born in Scotland, is married to an Englishman, and currently lives in Australia. She loves to share stories with readers! Get in touch with Eliza via Twitter @ElizaRedgold, on Facebook facebook.com/ElizaRedgoldAuthor and Pinterest: pinterest.com/elizaredgold. Or visit her at Goodreads and elizaredgold.com.

Also by Eliza Redgold

Enticing Benedict Cole
Playing the Duke's Mistress

Discover more at millsandboon.co.uk.

THE SCANDALOUS SUFFRAGETTE

Eliza Redgold

MILLS & BOON

All rights reserved including the right of reproduction in whole or in part in any form. This edition is published by arrangement with Harlequin Books S.A.

This is a work of fiction. Names, characters, places, locations and incidents are purely fictional and bear no relationship to any real life individuals, living or dead, or to any actual places, business establishments, locations, events or incidents. Any resemblance is entirely coincidental.

This book is sold subject to the condition that it shall not, by way of trade or otherwise, be lent, resold, hired out or otherwise circulated without the prior consent of the publisher in any form of binding or cover other than that in which it is published and without a similar condition including this condition being imposed on the subsequent purchaser.

® and TM are trademarks owned and used by the trademark owner and/or its licensee. Trademarks marked with ® are registered with the United Kingdom Patent Office and/or the Office for Harmonisation in the Internal Market and in other countries.

First published in Great Britain 2019
by Mills & Boon, an imprint of HarperCollins*Publishers*
1 London Bridge Street, London, SE1 9GF

Large Print edition 2019

© 2019 Eliza Redgold

ISBN: 978-0-263-08172-5

MIX
Paper from
responsible sources
FSC™ C007454

This book is produced from independently certified FSC™ paper to ensure responsible forest management. For more information visit www.harpercollins.co.uk/green.

Printed and bound in Great Britain
by CPI Group (UK) Ltd, Croydon, CR0 4YY

To my dear friend Anne in Devon,
with love and gratitude.

Thank you to the fabulous Nicola Caws, editor extraordinaire at Harlequin Historical in London, for her fantastic feedback and for agreeing that it was the right time to tell Violet's story. Thanks to my agent Joelle Delbourgo in New York, for her continued support and much appreciated advice. Thanks to Dr Rose Williams, for her insightful reading of the manuscript. While to Pamela Weatherill, for so many conversations about these topics, must be awarded purple hearts. Many thanks to friends and family, including those who joined us in France, especially to Marina Gillam, who brought the violet creams. To Nikki and Stefan Gasqueres, for the inspiring house-swap in Provence, *merci beaucoup*. I didn't expect to be writing fiction again, but I'm glad I did. And the biggest thanks to the suffragettes, for my vote.

Chapter One

'The Sun will run his orbit, and the Moon
Her circle. Wait, and Love himself will bring
The drooping flower of knowledge changed
to fruit
Of wisdom.'
'Upon my brain, my senses, and my soul!'
    —Alfred, Lord Tennyson: *'Love and Duty'*
                                    (1842)

'What the blazes are you doing?'

Violet peered down from the edge of the first-floor balcony and managed not to lose her footing. Her perch was precarious as she attempted to tie the banner across the balustrade. She hadn't knotted either end yet, the banner still clutched in her tense fingers. It would have been much easier by daylight, and from the inside of the balcony, but there was no hope of that. It didn't help being shouted at from down in the street.

'What are you doing up there?' he shouted again.

In the dim street lighting Violet couldn't make out the man's face. All she could see was a tall figure clad in a dark coat. 'It's none of your concern, thank you!'

'Of course it's my concern!' the man roared. 'That's my balcony you're dangling from!'

'What?' Violet let go of the banner and shrieked. 'Oh! My banner!'

The purple-, green-and-white-striped banner floated away. Leaning out to catch it, she lost her footing on the edge of the stone balcony and tumbled down.

Like lightning the man below jumped. 'Damnation!'

Violet landed in his outstretched arms. 'Oh!'

From the cradle of his arms she stared up at him. She saw him properly now, from the gaslight coming from over her shoulder. His hair was dark, falling over his brow. His eyes were a deep blue, so deep they seemed almost black. He was younger than she would have expected from the authority of his voice as he called up to her, but care grooved his mouth, shadowed his eyes.

None of it detracted from him being one of the most handsome men Violet had ever seen.

Time stilled. Clutched in his strong arms, her breathing slowed. Beneath her tight bodice her chest heaved. He, too, took her in, his gaze sweeping over her brown hair that had slipped free from her chignon in the fall, curls whispering around her neck. He scanned her wide brow, her full cheeks that she knew were too plump for fashion. His midnight eyes searched her blue ones that she knew must be wide with shock.

She parted her lips to speak. His gaze shifted from her eyes to her mouth.

Then he plonked her upright on the cobbles.

'No thanks, then, for rescuing you,' he said caustically.

'I've lost my banner!'

'Your banner! You nearly lost your life!'

Violet straightened her spine. 'I'd give my life for the Cause.'

'The Cause. You're one of those damned suffragettes!'

'I'm proud to be,' Violet said hotly. 'And there's no need to swear.'

'I'll do what I damned well like!'

'And so will I!' She stamped her boot.

'Is that so?' His eyes blazed into hers. 'Promise me you won't go climbing any more balconies. It's madness.'

'Who do you think you are?' she demanded. 'I'll make no promises to you.'

'What were you doing up there on the balcony at this time of night?'

'I thought it was the gentlemen's club…' Violet faltered. She'd chosen it as a prime target for one of her banners. Normally it was full of stuffy old men swilling port, or so she believed, but on a Sunday night it was empty, giving her a perfect opportunity to execute her plan.

'That's around the corner,' he said curtly. 'There are no signs on the club entrances. On purpose,' he added with a glare.

The tall stone mansions, with their columns and arched windows, were so similar. She'd been so pleased that the building appeared quiet that she'd quite forgotten to double check the address.

Violet's sense of humour got the better of her. She didn't know London well and she had carried out her reconnaissance from a passing carriage. She suppressed a giggle, felt the start of a smile.

The scowl on the man's face wiped it away.

She raised her chin.

'I must ask you to accept my apology,' she said with dignity.

'You had the wrong balcony. This is my home.' His jaw clenched. 'For the time being, anyway. I could have you arrested for trespass. For all I know you might be a burglar.'

'I'm not a burglar,' she protested. 'And you wouldn't dare.'

He raised a winged eyebrow.

'Try me,' he said grimly. 'How did you get up there?'

'That pillar.' Violet pointed at one of the Roman-style pillars on either side of the front door and the portico where she'd balanced on top. 'Then I climbed the drainpipe.'

A rather dirty drainpipe, she realised, by the state of her frock. The blue-striped taffeta was streaked with rust and dirt. Somehow she'd have to hide it.

His eyes followed the route of her climb. His hold on her arm tightened. 'Promise me. No more balconies. It's dangerous—surely you can see that.'

Violet shivered in the night air. She'd removed her cloak in order to climb more easily. Truth be told, the climb had been more difficult than she'd anticipated, teetering on the ledge, and her legs still trembled from her fall. If he hadn't caught her…

'Promise me,' he demanded again.

'How do you know I'm the kind of person who keeps her promises?'

He stared into her eyes. 'You keep your promises.'

She found herself unable to break his gaze. 'All right!'

Abruptly he stepped back. Beneath his coat his broad shoulders relaxed. 'Then I'll let you go without calling the constable. At least you won't go climbing any more balconies, even if I suspect it won't stop you tying more banners.'

Freed from his grip, Violet turned and ran.

'Don't worry,' she called over her shoulder as she dashed away. 'You can be sure of that.'

Adam Beaufort stared after the hourglass figure disappearing around the corner. Her fleeting footsteps clicked on the pavement as she vanished into the night.

He rubbed his eyes. What an extraordinary vision, witnessing the young woman stretched across the balcony, arms and legs spread like a spider. Her dress had hitched up as she inched across, clinging to the stone balustrade, using the columns as footholds, her banner clutched in one gloved hand. He had to commend her daring, even if it was sheer idiocy.

Then she had fallen into his arms. The feel of her as she landed right in them. Instinctively he'd leapt forward as she tumbled to where he guessed she'd land and caught her like a fish in a net.

He wouldn't forget how she'd felt in his arms.

He scratched his head. Her brown hair was glossy, her eyes bright blue. When she'd realised that she had the wrong address a smile had curved her full cheeks, filling her eyes with laughter. Not beautiful, but pretty.

And soft. That's what he'd felt, when he caught her. Frills and lace and, beneath it, soft, warm flesh. But her spirit—no softness there. She radiated strength and a cast-iron determination.

He had to admire that kind of female determination. His younger sister, Jane, had strength of character, too, although it was still developing. So did his elder sister, Arabella, but since their father had died the family relied on Adam for everything. Every decision, every penny.

Adam set his jaw. He didn't resent the responsibility, but he had to make some hard decisions now. Damned difficult, sometimes, being head of the family.

'There's no need to swear!' an irate voice echoed in his head. He frowned. She had an unusual accent. Northern, he guessed, beneath the carefully enunciated vowels. She wasn't, as some of the more unpleasantly snobbish acquaintances of his mother would have put it, 'one of us.'

His frown deepened as he stared at the shabby front door of their London home. Being 'one of us' took a lot of upkeep. The black paint was peeling on the wrought iron and the black front door needed a lick of paint, too. The marble steps leading up to the threshold were dull and dirty. The servants travelled back and forth with them, to and from Beauley Manor. He couldn't afford to keep staff in both homes. The London mansion needed much more than a good clean, never mind what a country estate like Beauley Manor needed. Then he had to add what his mother and Arabella and Jane needed, too. They would be back in London to attend a ball tomorrow night. Neither of them had asked for new ball gowns that could cost a fortune.

A fortune he didn't have.

From the corner of his eye he noticed something fluttering from the plane tree near the streetlight at the corner.

He strode over and pulled it down from the branch. It tore as it came free.

In his hand the banner unfurled. Purple, green and white. Under the streetlight he examined it more closely. It was made of silk, not cotton or sensible broadcloth. The tricolours were sewn together lengthways in somewhat imperfect stitches. In the corner of the white section was embroidered a tiny purple violet.

Scrunching up the silken banner in his fist, he shoved it inside his coat.

The sight of her, inching across the balcony, her suffragette banner aloft in her hand…

For the first time in months Adam laughed aloud.

* * *

Violet sighed over her embroidery as she unpicked a crooked seam. She'd been distracted ever since she fell off the balcony into the dark-haired stranger's arms the night before. He had held her only for a moment or two, yet she had felt so comfortable, so secure in that strong grip, though a tremor of danger had run through her veins. It had been the most peculiar sensation. Still, it was unlikely she would ever see him again. Her heart gave a strange squeeze of regret.

She poked her needle, threaded with purple, into the white silk and put it aside into the sewing pouch on its polished rosewood stand. She needed to make another banner quickly. The only advantage of being able to sew was that she used her skill to make her suffrage banners, not that her mother knew that to be the reason, of course. She'd wondered recently, though, what had happened to all the purple silk.

'I've been wondering if we should change your name.'

In astonishment Violet turned to her mother, who lay on the velvet *chaise longue* reading an illustrated fashion paper. 'What on earth do you mean, Mama? Change my name? What's wrong with Violet Regina?'

'Just the spelling,' her mother said hastily. 'We

could make it French-sounding. Vio*lette*.' She added a trill to the final syllable. 'French is quite the fashion.'

Firmly Violet shook her head. 'No, Mama. No. We are who we are. I love my name.'

'You're named after a chocolate,' her mother protested.

'And a pretty little flower,' said her father, coming into the drawing room and knocking over the porcelain shepherdess by the door, as he always did. The vast space was absolutely crammed with china ornaments. They, too, were the latest fashion, her mother insisted, whenever Violet suggested removing one or two.

'What's all this about, then?' her father asked, replacing the shepherdess on the stand and giving it a cautious pat.

'Oh, Papa.' Violet leapt up, ran across the room and hugged him tight. It was becoming harder to wrap her arms around his waistcoat, she thought with a smile. He'd always been shaped like a barrel, but now he was like a barrel about to burst. 'I thought you went up to Manchester, to the factory.'

Her father squeezed back. 'I put off the trip north until next week. Your mama has persuaded me to stay in London and come to this dance tomorrow night.'

'Ball,' her mother put in from the *chaise longue*.

Her father winked at her mother. 'Aye, we'll have a ball, my beautiful Adeline.'

'Reginald.' Her mother pursed her lips, but her cheeks flushed pink.

'So, do you have the most beautiful gowns money can buy?' Her father beamed. 'I want my girls to look fine.'

The final touches had been put on her own gown that morning at the dressmaker's in Bond Street. Even such a gown didn't alleviate the sinking in Violet's stomach. If only her parents weren't so eager. Still, she'd have to make the best of it.

'My dress is beautiful,' she replied. 'White lace with a violet sash.'

'The best Belgian lace,' her mother added.

'The best.' Her father rubbed his hands together delightedly. 'That's right. Nothing else for the Coombes. The best.'

Violet picked up her needle and smiled at him. Not for all the lace in Belgium would she have told her father just how much she dreaded the ball.

Only the thought of what she planned to do there spurred her on.

Chapter Two

'To alien ears, I did not speak to these'
—Alfred, Lord Tennyson: *'Love and Duty'*
(1842)

'What's wrong with these fellows, not asking my daughter to dance? Can't they see the prettiest girl in the room?'

Across the small table Violet squeezed her father's hand. Through her white kid gloves his hand was damp and hot.

From his evening coat he pulled a spotted handkerchief and wiped his brow. 'Upon my soul, it's stifling in here. Perhaps it's a good thing not to be dancing, Violet, out in that crush.'

Violet stared into the ballroom. Across the polished floor couples swirled, the men in black and white, the women in a rainbow of silks, taffetas, satins and lace. On a raised platform at the other end of the room the orchestra played a waltz by Strauss, one Violet had practised during her dancing lessons. Music and chatter filled the air, along with the tinkle of laughter and champagne glasses.

The three of them sat alone on fragile gilt chairs in a small curtained alcove off the dance floor. The red-velvet curtains were open wide, unlike some of the other alcoves, inviting visitors to their table. So far, no one had approached. Her dance card, lying on the linen tablecloth, remained empty.

Her mother blinked rapidly. 'I thought Violet would have plenty of partners. It was so fortunate for us to receive an invitation.'

'It's quite all right, Mama,' Violet said stoutly. 'I don't care to dance. Not tonight, in any case.'

She stilled her foot beneath the skirt of her voluminous ball gown. In truth, she loved to dance and her slippers had been waltzing under her petticoats ever since she arrived.

Her cheeks were warm. She sipped some champagne. It was the heat of the ballroom, she told herself. She refused to be humiliated by their obvious lack of welcome at the ball.

Biting her lip, she glanced down at her gown with a frown. Perhaps it suited her ill. It had more frills and furbelows than she would have liked— her mama had insisted on them—but they'd been to the best dressmaker in London, so it was perfectly cut. The sleeves were short, leaving her forearms bare to her gloves, the bodice dipped down to reveal the skin of her décolletage, but not in a vulgar way, her train draped beautifully and the violet sash emphasised the tininess of her waist. Her brown hair had been dressed by her mother's new French maid in a flattering style, swept up at the back into a high chignon.

In the glass above the mantel in the drawing room she'd seen her reflection before they left for the ball, her eyes cornflower bright and her cheeks rosy with unexpected excitement. Her chin, the same strong chin as her papa's, a feature that meant that she would never be considered a classical beauty, was slightly pink, too.

'You're a belle, Violet, just like your mama,' her father said proudly when she spun a pirouette, narrowly avoiding a porcelain trinket box crashing to the floor. Her first ball. Surely every girl longed to attend a ball. Perhaps it wouldn't be as dreadful as she expected.

It was, possibly, worse. Her trepidation about the ball had been justified. No one spoke to them. They weren't being cut, exactly, for they hadn't been formally introduced into society. But they were certainly not welcomed with open arms, or even an extended hand. One of the young ladies who had chatted with her at their horse-riding lessons in Hyde Park behaved as though Violet was invisible when she gave her a small wave across the room.

She didn't mind for herself, she told herself firmly. But she did mind for her father, with his high hopes, who'd beamed as they climbed into their new carriage drawn by four horses, and for her mother, too.

Upon their arrival, where she'd taken the opportunity to scan the entry hall, she'd stood near some disapproving Dowagers and overheard a snide, whispered conversation.

'The Coombes have come to London for the Season to try for a match for the daughter,' one of the Dowagers whispered. 'They don't seem to be having much luck.'

'Even with all those chocolates,' the other woman had tittered.

'My dear, no wonder. Have you spied the mother? Covered in feathers and weighed down with so many diamonds she rivals the chandeliers.'

Violet had turned hot with indignation. Why shouldn't her mama wear as many diamonds as she wanted to? They were newly cut gems, not the old, rose-cut kind that glinted in the dull unpolished settings slung around most of the other ladies' necks, but her mama loved her diamonds and her papa had been so pleased to be able to give them to her. Her parents had faced some hard times in the early days, before the chocolate business became a success.

Now, her mother picked up her huge ostrich fan. It was too big, by the unkind Dowagers' standards, but who were they to judge her beloved mama?

'What should we do?' her mama whispered from behind the feathers. 'Should we go home?'

'Certainly not!' Violet and her father spoke at the same time.

'Let's sit it out,' her father said.

Her mother's lip quivered.

'I'll take you for a turn on the floor, Adeline, cheer you up.' He glanced at Violet.

'We can't leave Violet sitting alone,' her mother protested.

Violet picked up her own fan, white lace trimmed with ribbon to match her sash. She'd stopped her mama from having peacock feathers added to it and she wore a simple pearl necklace like the other young women in white who appeared to be about her age, even if the pearls were perfectly matched and clasped with a first-rate diamond. 'I don't mind a jot, Mama. I don't care if I'm a wallflower.'

'Violets may grow in the shade, but they're never wallflowers.' Her father patted her shoulder as he stood and made an elaborate bow to his wife.

They made their way to the dance floor. The orchestra struck up another waltz. Her father took her mother in his arms.

The sensation of being held in the arms of the man who had caught her when she fell from the balcony came back to her. She'd relived it more than once, that sense of safety and danger, too, with his lips so close to hers. He'd even appeared in her dreams the night before, shouting something at her from the garden below as she leaned out of the first-floor window of a big house she didn't recognise.

She wondered what it would be like to dance with a man, held like that. She wasn't likely to find out. Tonight, she wasn't even going to dance.

Never mind. She jerked up her chin.

She'd made her secret decision long ago, when she first became a suffragette. Of course, she hadn't confided in her parents, any more than she'd told them about her suffragette activities. They wouldn't understand. But she would stick to her decision. She would put aside those hopes and dreams, her own desires, for the greater good. For the Cause.

Violet could so clearly recall the moment the Cause had seized her, body and soul. She had read about the suffragettes in *The Times* newspaper, which she much preferred to the fashion papers. A thrill of excitement had run through her as she learned about the women fighting to be allowed to vote, led by Emmeline Pankhurst. Like Violet, Mrs Pankhurst came from Manchester, in the north of England. 'Deeds, not words,' she urged her followers.

'Deeds, not words', Violet repeated to herself. In her own way, she'd vowed, she would make a difference, add her daring deeds to the Cause. She might not be able to join suffragette rallies, or go to meetings, or march in the streets, as she longed to. Her parents would never allow it. But she kept sewing her banners. No one would stop her.

'You keep your promises.' A deep voice came back to her. The man on the street had sensed she was someone who would keep true to her word and her deeds. She had sensed the same in him, too.

Her parents twirled past. Her father was surprisingly light on his feet and her mother was smiling now, to Violet's relief. She did so want her parents' happiness.

Sometimes she wished they had stayed in Manchester. They were happier there in their large house a few miles outside the town. But her mama wanted Violet to have everything and so did her papa, and that meant moving to London for the Season. They believed there were more opportunities.

Dancing lessons. Elocution lessons. French lessons. Riding lessons. Music lessons. To please her parents she took them all and it left precious little time to herself. So she sewed her banners and carried out her plans at night.

Deeds, not words.

On the way into the ballroom, she'd spotted another excellent target. Two targets, to be precise.

Violet rubbed her thighs together and heard the rustle of silk.

Adam Beaufort stared across the ballroom.

There could be no doubt. He narrowed his eyes as he studied the young woman who sat in the alcove opposite. She was accompanied, until they took to the dance floor, by an older man and woman, the man attired in a well-cut evening suit that nevertheless appeared to be straining at the buttons and the woman in canary-yellow satin.

He moved slightly behind the half-closed velvet curtain. He could see the young woman, but she couldn't see him. Yes. It was the climbing suffragette. Her hair had been loosened by her tumble when he'd last seen her and instead of a ball gown she'd been clad in smooth, slippery stuff that he could still seem to touch in his hands. Beneath it her flesh had been warm and soft.

He took the covert opportunity to examine her more closely. Her hair was a glossy chestnut colour that reminded him of a horse he'd ridden as a child, when the stables had been full at Beauley Manor. Most of the horses had been sold off now. Her white gown was understated, in contrast with her mother's, for he presumed the pair to be her parents. Its simplicity showed off her fine complexion that was possibly her best feature.

Yes, she was pretty. Though he might not have remembered her if he hadn't caught her in his arms.

He grinned to himself.

He'd been uninterested at the ball until he spotted her. The same faces, the same gossip. He couldn't think why he'd consented to come. But it was preferable to sitting at his desk and going through the family papers and accounts yet again, hoping the numbers would add up differently.

'Who is that in the alcove opposite?' he asked.

His mother lifted her lorgnette. 'I have no idea.'

'No one *we* would know,' said Arabella.

Adam winced. Arabella could sound snobbish and sharp, but he knew that his elder sister often sounded sharp when she was anxious and she was anxious now. She was intelligent, too. She'd guessed the extent of their financial straits, even though he'd shouldered the burden alone. There was no point in alarming them until it was absolutely necessary, though he guessed both Arabella and Jane had some notion. They'd seen him work on the estate accounts night after night, ever since their father died.

'Wait.' His mother peered through her eyeglass. 'She comes from somewhere in the north. Her father is Reginald Coombes. He makes some kind of confectionery. She's the sole heiress, I believe.'

'Oh, gosh,' said Jane. 'That must be Coombes Chocolates. They're delicious.'

A sweet heiress. Adam chuckled inwardly. Well, well.

'She's wearing a lovely dress,' Jane said rather wistfully. 'It's so much nicer than mine. I'm surprised no one wants to dance with her.'

Jane was wearing a debutante hand-me-down of Arabella's, bless her heart. A couple of extra inches of white trimming that almost matched had been added at the hem. Arabella wore a gown in a shade of mustard that did nothing for her complexion or thin figure, the unfortunate fabric a bargain buy at the haberdasher's. She hadn't attracted many partners, either.

'You're a Beaufort,' his mother said to Jane. 'It doesn't matter what you wear.'

'I think it might, Mama,' said Jane, with a sigh.

Indeed, being dressed in rags might matter, Adam thought grimly. He dreaded breaking the news of the extent of their diminished means to his mother and sisters. Telling them exactly what was left of the family fortune—precisely nothing—wasn't something he looked forward to.

Adam studied Reginald Coombes. Short and stout, he possessed the same bright blue eyes as his daughter. The mother, a blonde whose prettiness was almost overwhelmed by her yellow satin and more diamonds than Adam had ever seen on one person, gazed at her husband with obvious affection. It touched him that they seemed happier than many of the other married couples on the dance floor. Indeed, few married couples were dancing together at all. They certainly looked happier than he'd ever seen his own parents. Not that his parents were often together in the years before his father's demise.

He shunted the memories from his mind.

Adam moved his attention back to the lone figure in the alcove, watched how she straightened her back, stiffening her spine and jutting out her chin, as if daring anyone to pity her for being a wallflower. She appeared to be smiling.

But it must be hard, to sit there alone.

He slid on his gloves.

'Adam,' his mother hissed. 'What are you doing?'

'Miss Coombes?'

Violet jumped. In her mind she'd left the ballroom and begun to carry out her plan. She shifted on the gilt-legged chair and widened her knees so her thighs didn't touch. She couldn't risk anyone suspecting what she had wrapped like garters around her silk stockings. 'Yes? Oh! It's you!'

'Indeed.' A pair of midnight eyes found hers. 'We meet again.'

Violet's heart gave an unexpected thump. In her dream the night before, her rescuer appeared so impossibly handsome that she scolded herself in the morning. Surely her imagination had run wild. Now he stood in front of her in black-and-white evening attire he was even more attractive than in her dreams. In the dim streetlamp lighting she hadn't fully taken in the firm set of his clean-shaven jaw, the line of his strong mouth.

On the street after her tumble she'd been surprised that he appeared younger than his commanding voice suggested. He must be about five years older than she, rather than the ten she'd originally thought, perhaps close to thirty years of age, she guessed. The two forked lines between his dark eyebrows made it difficult to gauge. His shoulders were broad in the well-cut tailed jacket, which showed some wear.

'I wasn't expecting to see you here.' Violet shifted on her chair again. There was the faintest rustle of silk.

If he heard he made no sign. 'Nor I you.'

Violet cleared her throat. 'Actually, I'm glad to see you. I wanted to thank you properly. I ought to have been more grateful to you for…ah… catching me.'

It struck her later what a risk she'd taken. It could have ended very ill indeed if he hadn't been there.

A phantom of a smile glimmered in his eyes. 'To catch you was my pleasure.' He glanced around the ballroom. 'I didn't know suffragettes liked dancing.'

'I haven't been doing much dancing,' Violet blurted out, then bit her tongue.

'Perhaps we might remedy that.' He bowed low and held out his gloved hand. 'May I have the honour?'

'But I don't know your name.'

'My apologies.' He smiled. His teeth were even and white. 'We haven't been formally introduced. I know you are Miss Coombes.'

'Violet Coombes.'

'Indeed?' Some comprehension, almost amusement, flared in his expression. 'I'm Adam Beaufort.'

'Beaufort. I know your name. Then that means you are… There's a house…' Violet tried to simulate the society page in her mind. She'd read something about his family home, she was certain of it.

'The Beauforts of Beauley Manor. Yes.' He inclined his head. 'I recently inherited the estate.'

'Oh. I see.' It came back to her now. Their historic estate was in Kent, and the Beauforts were an exceptionally old English family. The kind of society family she'd never expected to welcome the Coombes.

'If you're at all concerned about my pedigree,' he said drily, 'that's my mother and my two sisters over there.'

He indicated a group in the alcove opposite. A grey-haired woman, straight-backed, dressed in black, was studying Violet through her lorgnette. Behind her stood a tall, haughty young woman, wearing a mustard-coloured gown. She looked down her nose at Violet. Seated next to the grey-haired woman was a big-boned girl with hair escaping from her bun. Violet had seen her laughing across the dance floor. She flashed a quick smile.

'My parents are here, too.' Just in time Violet remembered not to point. She nodded towards her mother and father. Her mother was tripping over her train, trying not to stare at the tall, dark-haired man in their alcove.

'Now we're introduced,' he said smoothly. 'Shall we dance?'

Violet stood up. Her head came just above his shoulder. 'Yes. Thank you.'

She took his proffered hand. Instantly the sensation of being in his arms returned. Even through their gloves she could feel it. Safety. Danger. Mixed into one.

Through the crowd he led her to the centre of the ballroom. The previous dance had ended and another was about to begin. A path cleared before him. Some of the men nodded in his direction, and more than a few pairs of female lashes fluttered. She sensed all eyes upon them, though he paid no attention to it.

They stood face to face. He released her hand. Suddenly she didn't know what to do with her arms. They hung awkwardly, by her sides.

'I presume you waltz?' he asked politely, as they waited for the orchestra to start up.

'I've had lessons,' she replied. Another thing she probably shouldn't have said. Then she recalled stamping her foot at him. She sighed. It was too late to pretend to be other than whom she truly was and she wouldn't have wanted to in any case.

Again she noted a flicker of amusement. 'Excellent.'

The music struck up. It was 'The Blue Danube', one of Violet's favourite pieces of music. He leaned close and whispered in her ear, 'I trust you dance as well as you climb.'

He swirled her into his arms.

Violet's breath surged up through her body. In an instant he swept her away, across the polished floor. Her lessons were nothing like this. She had never danced with such a partner—why, she never really danced before. In his powerful arms her feet glided over the floor as if she floated above it. The waltz started slowly, then became faster. The violins soared and shimmered, the horns played the beguiling tune as the woodwinds kept time. Her slippers chased his black-leather shoes, speeding with the melody as it rose and fell. His grip never wavered as he lifted her off the ground with every turn.

She'd wondered what it would be like to dance in his arms. Now she knew.

Violet threw back her head and closed her eyes. The music swelled. Now she wasn't following the rhythm, or his skilful feet. She stopped thinking about her steps, just allowed herself to blindly follow his lead as he looped her in circle after circle. The tune rippled inside her, sending her dizzy, as if she were spinning with her arms outstretched, the way she used to do in the garden as a child. Her lips widened. She wanted to cry out with the pleasure of it.

When she opened her eyes his were upon her. Hardened to impenetrable sapphire, they moved from her open lips to her bared neck, her head still thrown back.

He pulled her closer, his body pressed against her petticoats. Gripped by his eyes, his hands, she twirled, spun, twirled again.

Past his staring family in the alcove. Past her amazed parents. Past the girl from riding lessons, goggle-eyed. To Violet they became a blur. She could have danced for ever as he swept her across the floor, sending the other couples scattering in their wake.

All too soon the music ended. The final crescendo shattered in a crash of cymbals. He broke their gaze, let her go.

Violet put her glove to her racing heartbeat. 'Oh!'

Adam Beaufort, too, seemed to need to regain his breath. He bowed, but not before she'd glimpsed the dart of a smile. 'Perhaps you'd like some air, Miss Coombes. The balcony? I know you enjoy them.'

She laughed. 'Yes. The balcony. Please.'

As they passed a waiter Adam seized two glasses of champagne and led her through the French doors on to the empty balcony that overlooked the rear garden. She sensed eyes from the ballroom burning into her back. She raised her chin.

'Thank you.' Gratefully she grasped the stem of the glass he offered her and drank deeply. She was tempted to drain it. Instead she put the cool glass to her burning cheeks.

He, too, drank, surveying her over the rim. 'Your dancing lessons have been effective.'

'My lessons never taught me to dance like that,' she said frankly. 'It was wonderful. Thank you.'

He shrugged. 'There are certain skills in life that must be mastered.'

'Surely dancing is a pleasure, not a skill,' she protested.

One corner of his mouth curved. 'Most of life's pleasures become more pleasurable with greater skill, Miss Coombes.'

Violet removed the glass from her cheeks and stared out into the garden. Music wafted from inside the ballroom. Tiers of stone steps flowed down into a rolling lawn. Pale moonlight shone.

Her breath began to return to her lungs, but she still felt as if she were spinning. With her free hand she clutched the edge of the balcony. The balustrade was made of stone rather than cast iron, in thick pillars. Below was a sheer drop into a huge rhododendron bush.

Adam Beaufort raised an eyebrow. 'Assessing your descent?'

Violet laughed. 'No. I promised you I wouldn't climb any more balconies.'

Though she hadn't promised anything else. Her thighs brushed together, reminding her of her plan.

'I'm pleased to hear it.' He lounged against a pillar, sending his face into shadow.

'Tell me. What made you do it? Climb, I mean.'

'Isn't it obvious?'

He shook his head. 'Enlighten me.'

'It was for the Cause. I intended to drape a women's suffrage banner over the front of the gentleman's club as a protest,' she explained. 'You must know how long women have been fighting to be granted the vote. The women's colours are purple, green and white, you see. I sew the banners myself. Unfortunately I lost that one,' she added regretfully.

He fell silent for a moment, took another

draught of champagne. 'Is it the first banner you've hung?'

'No. I've hung others.' And it wouldn't be the last.

'What's your reasoning behind such an action?'

'Wouldn't any woman want to be treated as an equal?' she asked passionately. 'We're treated as children who don't know their own minds. Why shouldn't we have the vote, take a role in choosing the government of our own country? Deeds, not words. That's what we need now, for the Cause.'

'You're quite convincing, Miss Coombes,' he drawled.

She clenched her fist around the champagne glass. 'You're mocking me.'

'Not at all. Who can't admire such conviction? How did you become involved in…the Cause?'

'I'm only involved in a small way. I'm not a member of any organisation. I act alone. I'm just trying to do my part.'

'Do your parents know what you're doing?'

Violet sighed and shook her head.

He raised a brow. 'I take it they wouldn't approve.'

'It's a secret,' she said rapidly. 'I must ask you not to betray my confidence.'

'You have my promise. I, too, keep my word.'

Violet let out a sigh of relief. Somehow she knew he told her the truth, even if in the shadow of the pillar his expression was unreadable.

'There's more to it, isn't there?' he asked.

Violet's hand clenched on her glass. 'I'm sorry?'

His teeth gleamed. 'I suspect you have a more personal reason for your passion for the Cause.'

'How did you know?' she gasped.

He shrugged. 'Human nature.'

She took a sip of champagne.

'I do have a reason,' she said at last. 'You may know of my father's business. Coombes Chocolates.'

At his nod she went on.

'My father is a self-made man. He started the business and built it up from nothing. It's gone from a small enterprise to a national name. Thousands of people work for him now in the chocolate factory and many more thousands enjoy our wares. Why, someone is probably biting into a Coombes Floral Cream right now.'

'Indeed,' Adam Beaufort drawled.

Violet took a deep breath.

'I want to follow my father into the business,' she said rapidly. It was the first time she ever said it aloud. 'I have so many ideas, so many plans. Times are changing, a new century is here. There are new ways of doing things. Opportunities for social reform, for new methods. If women are given the vote…'

'It might make it easier for you to become a woman of business.'

He'd grasped it immediately.

She nodded.

'I've always admired my father and what he's achieved. The people in there don't see it,' she added with a jerk of her head towards the French doors.

'Surely you exaggerate.'

'Not at all. We should have stayed in Manchester where we belong, not tried to be part of London society,' she said fervently. 'It means so much to my papa, but they look down on him, despise him. Who knows? Perhaps you do, too.'

Startling her, he stepped out of the shadow of the pillar.

'My father was a drunkard, Miss Coombes, who lost our family fortune,' he said through gritted teeth. 'If you think I despise your father for being determined, hardworking and ambitious, you're very much mistaken.'

Violet's mouth dropped open.

Silence fell between them.

'Forgive me,' he said after a moment. 'I've been under some pressure of late. Such conversation is not fit for a ballroom.'

'It's honest conversation. I prefer it,' she replied quickly. 'And I ought to ask your pardon. You asked me to dance. No one else did.'

As she spoke she impulsively moved forward, raised her face to his. He stared down at her, an expression she couldn't decipher in his eyes. All she knew was that she took another step forward and lifted her chin higher, just as he moved closer to her and lowered his head, so close he surely felt on his lips the sigh that escaped hers.

From the ballroom came a crash of cymbals. Inside, the orchestra ended another piece of music with a rousing crescendo.

They leapt apart.

He retreated to the pillar. 'It seems this moonlight and champagne is having an effect on us.' His voice sounded deeper to Violet's ears. 'We've both revealed secrets tonight. Perhaps we ought to return to safer topics.'

Violet clutched the stem of her champagne glass so hard it threatened to snap. Her heart pounded.

He bowed. 'Would you care for another dance, Miss Coombes?'

'Oh, yes, please, I mean, thank you.' Suddenly flustered, she lay down her glass. 'Oh!'

Adam frowned. 'What is it?'

She froze. Beneath her petticoat she felt an unravelling.

She took a step.

A slip between her thighs.

'Miss Coombes...'

Another step.

A silken slide down her legs.

He stared at her face. 'What the blazes has happened now?'

'I can't dance with you. I'm sorry!'

Violet raced through the French doors and out of the ballroom.

Adam gazed after Miss Violet Coombes in astonishment.

She had refused another waltz with him.

Momentarily he felt affronted.

Then through the French doors he watched her scuttle across the ballroom. She scurried, crab-like, her knees held together, in a curious dance step of her own.

Once more he started to laugh. She was up to something. He'd stake his life on it.

He never expected to have such an extraordinary conversation with her. They'd both revealed more than they intended. The pressures of trying to sort out his father's estate wore him down, a constant worry, a permanent burden across his shoulders. He experienced a curious relief sharing it with Miss Violet Coombes. It lightened his burden, for a moment.

She preferred honest conversation, she'd told him. Her frankness disarmed him and she possessed a curious sweetness, too.

He grinned inwardly.

Like a Coombes Floral Cream.

He'd wanted to kiss her. It wasn't the first time. When he caught her in his arms in the square the instinct roared through his body, too. Tonight, when she stared up at him in the moonlight, her bright blue eyes full of understanding and concern, her pink lips parted, he wanted to take her in his arms and taste that sweetness. Hold that warm, soft flesh in his arms again.

Why the blazes had she fled from him?

It wasn't that near kiss. Such things weren't done on ballroom balconies, but he sensed she wasn't frightened by the honesty of that moment.

She'd wanted to kiss him back. Her soft, fast breath told him that.

Swiftly he followed her path across the ballroom and out into the entrance hall. There was no sign of her. The huge hall, with its marble floor, gilt-framed paintings and statues, appeared empty. Then a scuffling noise came from behind a column of marble.

A long, shapely leg clad in a white-silk stocking extended from behind the pillar, followed by a familiar tricolour silken banner.

It must have been under her skirt.

Stifling his chuckle, not wanting to alarm her, Adam backed behind another marble column. After a moment she appeared, glanced around furtively and raised herself up on tiptoe. One after the other she hurled the two billowing banners into the air.

Adam frowned. He couldn't quite make out what she was doing, but he could make a fair guess. He was about to reveal himself and remonstrate with her when her parents appeared and bore her off in a carriage.

He leapt out from behind the pillar and swore.

Her aim was excellent.

'Damnation,' he muttered below his breath.

The ballroom doors flung open. Before Adam could grab the banners a group surged into the hall.

A woman squealed and pointed.

All hell broke loose.

Adam groaned. Violet Coombes had no idea what she'd done.

Chapter Three

'Shall Error in the round of time
Still father Truth?'
—Alfred, Lord Tennyson: *'Love and Duty'*
(1842)

'Whoa.' Violet pulled the reins of the grey mare. All morning the mare had been frisky, playing up. It took all Violet's strength to stop her breaking into a gallop in the middle of Hyde Park. It was a day to gallop, the sun golden in the summer sky. Around her all the flowers in the garden beds were in bloom, their colours as bright as ball gowns and their perfumed scents heady. Instead, Violet slowed to a sedate trot.

A groom from the riding school rode up to her. 'That's it, miss. Give me the reins now. I'll lead you back to the others. That's probably enough for today.'

Violet passed them over with her thanks. Suddenly she felt exhausted. Dancing at night and riding in the morning was strenuous exercise. Her tight-fitting blue-velvet riding habit, trimmed with a lace jabot at the neck, suddenly seemed much too hot. She'd have something made in a cooler fabric for the summer and try to prevent her mama from adding too much trimming. The riding habits of the other young ladies, all in black, seemed to have marked signs of wear, as if to emphasise use.

While the groom led her to the group, her mind roved over the events of the night before. It had been so unfortunate that the banner had unravelled from around her thigh before she had a chance to dance once more with Adam Beaufort. She would probably never have another opportunity to dance with him, to be swept across the floor in those powerful arms, after running away from him so publicly. He must have been insulted.

She sighed. She owed Adam Beaufort another apology and yet another explanation, if she ever saw him again. He must have wondered what made her run off in such a peculiar fashion, but she had to move quickly before the banner fell to the floor from beneath her ball dress. She had made it just in time. She dashed behind a pillar and whipped out the banner from beneath her petticoats, yanked one free and then the other. Quickly she seized the moment, did what she'd set out to do. She'd intended to wait until the end of the ball, to linger until the crowds dispersed, but with the banners released she grasped her opportunity while everyone else was in the ballroom. She had just completed the deed when her parents appeared, full of concern after seeing her leave the ballroom. Steering them away from the evidence of her activity, she pleaded a sudden fever, with her hand to her forehead. They called for the carriage instantly and took her home. She didn't see Adam Beaufort again.

She released another sigh. He was the only person she had ever told about how strongly she believed in the suffrage cause. Had he been mocking her? As she replayed the conversation in her mind she decided not. She could only hope he'd keep his word and not betray her secret.

He'd trusted her with a secret, too. The lines of care on his face she'd noticed when they first met; she hadn't mistaken those. She wondered what he might look like without the burdens he carried.

Their honest conversation had seemed to bring them closer together than the waltz. When she'd finally fallen asleep that night she had dreamed about him again. In the garden of that unidentifiable house, he called up to her at the window. She leaned out, almost tumbling from the window as she tried to hear what he said, but she couldn't make it out.

When she awoke she'd puzzled over it. She recalled how he whispered in her ear, 'I hope you dance as well as you climb.' His deep voice had sent quivers through her. When she got out of bed she'd washed her face with cold water from the pitcher, instead of hot.

Even now, the next morning, in the sunshine of the park, thinking about him made her pulse flicker at her wrist under her riding glove. The night before as she lay in bed, she'd found herself lifting her fingertip to her mouth, remembering the look he gave her as he lowered his mouth so close to hers. Had he meant to kiss her? Was that blackness in the midnight of his eyes…desire?

If she were going to daydream about such matters, which of course she was not, he was the kind of man she would daydream about. But she had other matters to think about rather than waltzing with Adam Beaufort, no matter how extraordinarily wonderful it had been. Yet if she were scrupulously truthful, as she always tried to be, she had to admit her attraction to him. He was, after all, one of the most eligible bachelors in London, or so her thrilled mama had enlightened her on the way home in the carriage.

'He's related to the royal family!' her mama had gasped.

Whether Adam Beaufort was eligible or not,

there was no point in daydreaming. She'd made her decision.

She took the reins from the groom.

He tipped his cap.

She halted next to the girl she had spotted the night before in the ballroom who sometimes chatted to her.

With a clip of her whip she moved her horse away from Violet's.

Violet lifted her chin. It hadn't been pleasant to be snubbed at the ball, nor was it pleasant to be snubbed now, and she wasn't sure why. It seemed a more blatant cut than pretending not to see a waving hand from across the room. If Adam Beaufort hadn't asked her the night before, she would have sat out every dance. It made her even sorrier that she had missed being whirled into another waltz. The way he danced with her would remain in her memory, but that was all.

The Cause was more important.

Deeds, not words. She must stay true to her purpose. Yet her heart gave another strange flinch as she turned her mare towards the park gates.

'Mama?' Violet pushed open the drawing-room door. 'Where are you? There's no one in the dining room. What's happened to luncheon? I'm famished after riding. Will you allow me to come to the table before I change out of my riding habit?'

Her mother lay on the *chaise longue*. Her arm, clad in a ruffled sleeve, was flung over her face. She didn't reply.

'Mama?' Violet stepped into the room. Her father was also in the drawing room, to her surprise. He faced the fireplace, his back to her. He wasn't often home during the day. 'Why, hello, Papa. Have you come home for luncheon? We'll have to wake Mama. I think she's asleep.'

'I'm not asleep, Violet,' her mother said in a strangled voice. 'I've had a visit from some of the society ladies who invited us to the ball.'

'Oh, how lovely, Mama.' Violet cared little for such things, but she knew how much store her mother set by them and it mattered to her father, too, with his business ambitions. To have such ladies call on them was a step up the social ladder. Not that Violet had any inclination to climb it.

'No.' Her mother sat up. Her face was pale, except for two bright red patches on her cheeks. 'It wasn't lovely. It was dreadful!'

She burst into tears.

'Mama!' Violet rushed to her side. 'Don't cry so, please. What happened? What did they say to you?'

Her mother seized a lace-trimmed handkerchief. 'They said… She said…'

'You must have some idea, Violet.' Her father spoke from his place by the fireplace. He didn't turn around.

She shook her head. 'No, Papa, I don't. How dare they upset Mama so? What did they say?'

Her thoughts flew immediately to Adam Beaufort. Had there been gossip about them because she'd lingered on the balcony with him and then raced out of the ballroom? That near kiss…had someone seen them together?

Nerves fluttered in her stomach. 'What is it?'

'Someone draped a suffragette banner across a marble bust of Queen Victoria,' her mother whispered, muffled by the handkerchief. 'And the Prince Consort, too, God rest his soul.'

Violet tried to keep a straight face. It had been such a perfect opportunity.

Two legs. Two banners. Two marble busts. They'd been perched on plinths halfway up the wall, each set back in a gilt-scrolled niche. The banners had ballooned up and landed. Queen Victoria's banner around her marble shoulders, like a shawl. Quite fitting for a monarch. Prince Albert's on his head, falling over one eye, giving him a rakish look. She hadn't been able to reach to fix it.

'The ladies told me all about it.' Her mother wrung her hands together. 'At the end of the ball, when everyone came out into the hall, there they were, bold as brass. I don't know whether to laugh or cry.'

Laugh, Mama, Violet wanted to say. How she wished her mother shared her views about women's suffrage, but her mother was content with her status as a wife and mother. She didn't want to vote—she'd declared that on more than one occasion. Politics was the business of men and she had no interest in it. No, her mama would never understand.

Her father finally turned around from the fireplace. He appeared smaller than usual, almost deflated. It was because he wasn't smiling. His jolly demeanour usually filled the room.

'We know they were your banners, Violet.'

His tone shocked her. The usual warmth was quite gone.

'I don't intend to deny it, Papa,' she said quietly. 'They were my suffrage banners. I made them and I draped them across Queen Victoria and Prince Albert, too.'

'Queen Victoria. Prince Albert,' her mama echoed the names, reminding Violet of a parrot they kept for a while, when the birds had been fashionable. It had driven her papa quite cocky, he'd declared.

It wasn't the moment to remind her parents of the parrot.

'The parents of our King.' Her father shook his head. 'King Edward the Seventh.'

She nodded. She'd have draped a banner around a marble bust of King Edward, too, but there hadn't been one, and in any case, she'd only had two banners.

'Queen Victoria and Prince Albert are in their graves,' her mama choked. 'It's unseemly. Disrespectful.'

'Oh! I didn't think of it that way,' Violet said, horrified.

'Why did you do it?' her father asked, still in that empty voice.

Violet lifted her chin. 'I'm a suffragette, Papa.'

'A suffragette!' came her mama's echo.

'Votes for women, eh?' asked her papa.

With a gulp, she nodded.

Her father wiped his sleeve across his eyes. 'So it's all been for nothing.'

'Papa,' Violet whispered. Her throat constricted. It was suddenly hard to breathe.

He sank into the leather club chair by the fireplace. He appeared bewildered. 'All we've done for you. All I've worked for. And you're not grateful.'

Violet knelt beside him, seized his hand. 'I am grateful, Papa. You've given me everything that anyone could ever dream of.'

'They why did you do it?'

'Surely you understand,' she pleaded. 'I'm like you. You're a self-made man. Didn't you long to be considered an equal, to make your way into the world? Look what you've achieved, the business you built. You started from nothing. Please listen to me. I just want the same opportunity as you, to contribute to the world.'

He shook his head. 'It's different for a man.'

'A woman's place is in the home,' her mother said tremulously from the *chaise longue.*

'I want more,' Violet said simply.

Her father stared as if he hardly knew her.

'I've never had cause to criticise you. I've always been proud of you, so proud.' He took a deep breath. 'But this. You've gone too far. You've become selfish, Violet.'

She fell back on her heels. Tears smarted in her eyes. 'It's not selfish to want to be part of the world. To vote. To become educated. To work. Why, there are even women working in factories now.'

'No daughter of mine will ever set foot in a factory! That's not why I worked day and night.'

He shook his head. 'Your place is in the home. Your mama is right.'

'The world is changing,' Violet said. 'There are new ideas. Not just votes for women, but opportunities for work, for education—'

Her father held up his hand. 'Stop. I don't want to hear such talk.'

'A suffragette. How could you, Violet? We'll be shunned in society.' Her mother dabbed at her eyes. 'The ladies made that quite clear this morning.'

'Oh, Mama, we were shunned already,' Violet replied wearily. It was made patent at the ball in their lack of welcome, except for Adam Beaufort, swirling her into his arms.

If they were no longer invited into London society, she'd definitely never see him again.

Her heart sank.

'We're ruined!' exclaimed her mother.

'Surely it's not that dreadful.' But it explained the outright snub from the girl at her riding lesson, Violet recalled uncomfortably.

Had she gone too far?

Her father breathed heavily. 'I suppose we ought to leave London, before we're run out.'

From the *chaise longue* came a muffled sob.

'Leave London! Surely that isn't necessary,' Violet cried, aghast. What had she done?

'Just when Violet had danced with a Beaufort,' her mama mourned. 'I never thought I'd see such a thing. Oh!'

If they left London...

'We won't be run out of London,' Violet protested. 'What does it matter what a few society people think?'

'The Coombes are a respectable family,' her father said. 'We always took pride in that, more than anything else. You've taken our good name away.'

Full of remorse, Violet gripped her fingers together. 'I'll apologise to the ladies who invited us to the ball.'

'Aye, you ought to do that. But the damage is done.'

'Ruined,' her mother repeated in a choked voice. 'Ruined.'

Her father put his head in his hands.

Violet reached out to him. 'Papa, please listen. Would it be so terrible to go back to Manchester? We were happier there, not trying to fit in with London society. I could learn to help you in the business, make your load lighter.' Anything, she thought, her heart like a sinking stone, to make him smile again.

'No, Violet. I told you. Your place isn't in the factory.'

'But, Papa…'

'No!'

Violet jumped. Her father had never raised his voice at her before. Not once, in all her life.

He stood up, his elbows akimbo. 'Men and women aren't the same. If you'd been a son…' His voice trailed off. 'We pinned our hopes on you making a fine match. But now…'

'Ruined,' her mother chimed in from the chaise.

Violet's throat choked. The lace jabot at her neck suddenly felt too tight. She tugged it loose. Never before had her father revealed such sentiments. But she'd suspected them all along, in her heart. It drove her to her daring acts, just as Adam Beaufort had guessed, at the ball.

'I'm sorry, Papa. I'm sorry, Mama. I'll do anything to set it right.'

'It's too late,' her mama sobbed. 'Nothing can be done.'

A discreet knock came at the drawing room door. The butler entered.

'What is it?' her father asked. Having servants still made him nervous, Violet knew. At the chocolate factory her papa was the man in charge, but she often suspected both he and her mama's preference would be to have only family at home, as it had been in the beginning.

'Forgive the interruption, sir. But a gentleman has called and I thought you'd like to know.'

He held out a silver tray. On it was a small white card, edged with black.

Her father took the card. 'Adam Beaufort, Esquire,' he read aloud.

'What?' Her mama sat bolt upright.

Violet's pulse skipped a beat.

'What does he want?' her father asked.

'He didn't say, sir,' replied the butler. 'But he's in the hall. I took the liberty.'

On the *chaise* her mother frantically began to tidy her hair. She seized a small looking glass and dabbed at her tear-stained face with her handkerchief. 'Tell him to come in.'

'Do you know what he wants?' her father asked Violet.

In bewilderment she shook her head. 'No.'

She brushed back her own hair from her forehead. Wisps had escaped while on horseback and she was still in her blue-velvet riding habit.

The drawing room door opened.

Adam Beaufort took a step back as he entered the Coombes's drawing room.

He'd never seen a room like it. Every inch of the vast room was decorated. Gilt-edged paintings of pink-cheeked children and pretty country maids jostled for space on the flock-papered walls. China ornaments, again with a bucolic theme, took up every table top, apart from those crammed with silver trinkets, lamps and ferns in jardinières. The furniture was red-brown mahogany, the soft furnishings skirted, trimmed and flounced so that the room had a peculiar cushioned effect.

On a velvet *chaise longue* sat Violet's mother, whom he'd last seen attired in canary-yellow satin. She now wore a pink gown with many ruffles that didn't manage to obscure the dazzling diamonds around her neck, wrists and fingers. He winced at the thought of what some society ladies would say at the sight of such diamonds worn before evening.

By the fire, Violet's father stood robustly, belly thrust out in a loud, checked waistcoat. Yet the pair lacked the happiness that had been so apparent on their faces while dancing the night before.

Adam frowned.

'Mr Coombes.' He addressed the man by the fireplace, with a slight inclination of his head. 'Forgive my intrusion. I'm Adam Beaufort. How do you do?'

Reginald Coombes offered his hand. His handshake was firm. 'I saw you dancing with my daughter last night. Most obliging of you.'

'Indeed it was, Mr Beaufort,' said Mrs Coombes faintly.

Adam bowed to her before turning to Violet,

who stood silent, a still figure in sapphire-blue velvet by the fire. He couldn't help notice how it sculpted her curvaceous figure. But her face was white and strained.

'It was my pleasure,' Adam said smoothly. 'It's unfortunate I didn't have the opportunity for a second dance with Miss Coombes.'

He sent her a brief smile.

There was the faintest movement around her lips in return, but that was all.

Adam's frown deepened. He felt oddly responsible for the whole fiasco. If he'd pulled the banners down in time...

'Mr Coombes.' He addressed Violet's father. 'I've come about the incident at the ball last night.'

'You know about that?' Mrs Coombes squeaked.

'Most of London knows about it,' Adam said bluntly. 'It didn't help that you sewed your monogram on the banner,' he added to Violet.

'Your monogram?' Reginald Coombes looked from one to the other.

Wordlessly Violet reached into a sewing basket and drew out a banner. It unfurled like a streamer in purple, green and white. She passed it to her father.

He stared at the tiny bloom embroidered in the corner, his fist clenched.

'So that's what happened to all the purple silk,' Violet's mother said in wonderment.

'How many banners are there?' Violet's father demanded.

'Half a dozen.' Her throat was bare, white and swan-like as she swallowed. 'Perhaps more.'

Her father hurled the banner into the fire.

'Papa!' Violet's cry tore through Adam's skin.

'That's the last one you'll ever make,' Reginald Coombes said fiercely. 'Do you understand, Violet? This has got to stop.'

She made no answer. Her fingertips lifted to that pale throat, her gaze staying on the silk as it curled and burned. The scorched scent of it filled Adam's nostrils.

'Will you give up this cause, as you call it?' her father demanded.

'I can't,' she whispered.

'Can't?' her father repeated, incredulous. His bright blue eyes were out on stalks.

'I won't hang any more banners.' Violet lifted her chin. 'But I can't give up the Cause. It's in me. It's what I believe. I don't know if I can change that.'

Adam studied her. Her head was high, her hands clenched. He had to admire her. There was no question of her convictions. He guessed her parents knew nothing of the extent of her activities. They'd have been appalled to have seen her climbing his balcony, teetering on the edge. At least he'd stopped her from such dangerous endeavours.

Reginald Coombes's chin thrust out, just the same as his daughter's. Adam wondered if he realised how alike they were. 'I forbid this nonsense. Do you hear?'

His daughter's eyes flashed vivid blue. 'Being a suffragette isn't nonsense.'

'The shame of it. It's a scandal,' her mother cried.

'It's not a scandal,' Violet scoffed, but her voice wavered.

'Forgive me, Miss Coombes, I'm afraid it is.' Adam intervened. He had no choice but to break it to her. 'The scandal is all over London. I did my best to halt it, but I didn't succeed. Doubtless it's being discussed in every polite drawing room from Mayfair to Kensington. I understand it has reached the palace, though not yet the ears of the King.'

Violet's mother released a muffled shriek. She appeared about to faint.

'Where are your smelling salts, Adeline?' her husband demanded.

'The silver box,' she puffed, using her handkerchief as a fan.

Violet's father scrabbled among the multitude of silver boxes and china ornaments on the mahogany table and administered the salts. Once again Adam felt moved by the couple's devotion to each other. It was rarer than they probably knew. And they loved their daughter, too. It was obvious, in spite of the current situation.

'Everyone is overreacting. It's ridiculous for there to be such an outcry,' Violet said, low, but her voice was shaky. 'It was a protest. A deed for the Cause. Not a crime.'

Adam shrugged. 'Perhaps it is ridiculous. None the less, there are many people who are very upset by it.'

He glanced towards Violet's mother. The woman quietened, but she remained pale, clutching her husband's hand. Her distress was real, unmistakable. Violet, too, looked even paler than before, as if she were about to faint herself, though he suspected she was made of sterner stuff than her mother.

Adam shifted nearer to Violet by the fire.

'You must know the King has a deep respect for his departed parents,' he muttered in an undertone. 'Your action may be considered more than disrespectful. It's an insult, almost sacrilegious, in some court circles.'

She bit her lip. 'I didn't think of that. It wasn't meant as an insult. Is it truly that bad?'

'Yes, it is,' Adam said quietly. His honour demanded he tell her the truth.

Her father stood up. He moved like a beaten man. 'That's it, then. We'll have to go back to Manchester.'

Violet's mother let out a sob. 'Such a disgrace.'

Her daughter moved towards her as if to comfort her and then drew back. Her fingers were clenched together.

Reginald Coombes turned to Adam.

'Thank you for coming to tell us,' he said heavily. 'I regret you've seen us like this, in such a sorry state. Perhaps you'll come and visit us in the north should you ever be in our part of the country. We won't be in London again I don't expect.'

'I trust that won't be the case.'

'We won't be able to show our faces here,' Mrs Coombes wept.

'Not necessarily,' Adam said slowly. His half-formed plan began to fully take shape in his head.

He glanced at Violet. She was breathing in gasps she tried to suppress, making her velvet bodice heave.

'I came today with a plan,' he said.

Beside him Violet stiffened.

'A plan, eh?' her father asked. 'What's that?'

Adam bowed. 'With your permission, I've come to propose to your daughter.'

Chapter Four

> *'Hard is my doom and thine: thou knowest it all.'*
>
> —Alfred, Lord Tennyson: *'Love and Duty'*
>
> (1842)

Violet's mouth fell open as she stared at Adam Beaufort. 'You've come to propose to me?'

He turned on his heel and this time bowed directly towards her. There was the merest upturning of the corners of his mouth. 'Indeed.'

'Marriage?' she gasped. Was that really what he meant? Had her ears deceived her? They had only met once. Well, twice, if she counted tumbling off the balcony into his arms and that meeting couldn't be considered a formal introduction. And now he was suggesting they wed? Surely it could not be so.

The upturning of Adam Beaufort's mouth grew more pronounced. A dent appeared in his left cheek, then vanished as he spoke. 'I can think of no other proposal I would make, Miss Coombes.'

'Marriage!' her mother and father repeated at

the same time, her mother breathless, and her father's voice a stunned bellow.

'Upon my soul!' added Mr Coombes.

'I realise this is unusual,' Adam said. 'And quite sudden. I believe that is the phrase, in such circumstances. But the circumstances are unusual, to say the least.'

'They certainly are.' Violet found her voice was as breathless as her mama's. She put her hand to her bodice. Her heart fluttered like a bird in a cage.

'Marriage to a Beaufort!' Mrs Coombes reached for her fan. 'Oh, my…'

Mr Coombes clutched his chest. He staggered and reached for the side table to right himself, sending a tin of Floral Creams flying.

'Papa!' Violet rushed to help him. 'You must sit down.'

Mrs Coombes hurried to her husband's side. 'Reginald!'

'I'm all right,' he insisted, leaning heavily on the table, his breath coming in puffs.

Violet steered him to the wing chair by the fireplace. Her papa sank on to it, half-raised himself up, then sank back again. His normally florid cheeks turned a sickly colour, sweat beaded his forehead.

'Are you quite well, sir?' Adam Beaufort asked, concerned.

Mrs Coombes wrung her handkerchief in distress. 'It's his heart.'

Panting heavily, Mr Coombes waved away their alarm. 'I get the odd turn. Nothing to worry about.'

'Shall I call for a doctor?' Adam asked.

'No need, no need.' Mr Coombes puffed. 'I've seen all the best quacks. There's nothing they can do.'

Violet moved swiftly to the drinks tray. 'Stay still, Papa. I'll pour you a glass of water.'

'Give it a bit of colour, won't you? For medicinal purposes.'

'You know you ought not to drink spirits when you've had a turn.'

'I'll be all the better for a spot of whisky.'

She shook her head and added the merest drop of whisky to the water glass. There was no point in agitating him further. The doctors had been clear—the best medicine for him was peace and quiet.

Violet's hand tightened on the whisky bottle. Clearly the morning's events had upset him greatly.

It was all her fault.

Adam Beaufort frowned. 'Are you sure you don't wish me to fetch medical help?'

'I'll be right as rain in a moment,' Mr Coombes assured him, his voice already stronger. 'I always am. Where's that drink, Violet?'

'Here you are, Papa.' Violet gave her father the weak whisky and water and propped a cushion behind him.

Mr Coombes took a sip. 'Ah, that's it.'

Violet turned to her mother, who was still wringing her hands. She looked about to cry.

'Sit down, Mama,' Violet said gently.

Mrs Coombes picked up her fan. 'Oh, dear. Oh, Reginald.'

'I'm quite well, Adeline,' Mr Coombes said stoutly. 'Do as Violet says.'

Violet tucked her mother beneath a silk shawl. Going back to her papa, she took his wrist, counted and waited. His pulse was faster than usual, but it wasn't as bad as some of his turns had been in the past, as far as she could make out.

She straightened her back and glanced at Adam Beaufort. His expression was inscrutable. He was a man who controlled his emotions. He'd moved out of her way as she helped her mother and father. Now he stood by the fireplace, a tall but surprisingly comforting presence.

He stayed calm in a crisis. That was it. She'd

witnessed it before, when he'd caught her under his balcony. She liked that about him.

'Would you care for a whisky?' she asked him.

In an unhurried movement, he took out a pocket watch. 'It's rather early in the day for spirits.'

'But in the circumstances…' Violet prompted.

His mouth cornered into a smile. 'Indeed.'

She poured a large measure into the cut-crystal glass. 'Water?'

He inclined his dark head.

'Don't drown it as you did mine, Violet,' said Mr Coombes from the wing chair.

'You ought not to be having whisky at all, Papa,' she retorted, pleased that he appeared to be rallying. But her hand shook as she poured some water into Adam Beaufort's glass, spilling it on to the drinks tray. Her papa had been so angry. He'd never said such things to her before.

She blotted the spilt water. Crossing the room, she gave Adam Beaufort his glass of whisky.

His fingers grazed hers as he took it. They were warm and dry. 'Thank you.'

His touch seemed to stay on her skin, steadying her as she returned to the tray and poured herself a generous finger of whisky. She threw it back, straight, letting the fire scorch the back of her throat, only to find Adam Beaufort surveying her over the rim of his glass.

The heavy crystal clanked as she replaced it on the silver tray. Young ladies were not supposed to drink spirits, let alone before luncheon. Yet another rule for women that did not apply to men. How it irked her.

Heading over to her father's chair, she took away his empty glass. The colour had returned to his cheeks, she noted with relief. He always recovered quickly from his turns, as he called them, but she was sure they were becoming more frequent.

'How are you feeling now, Papa?' she asked.

He patted her hand. His anger seemed to have abated. 'No harm done.'

'Would you like some more water?'

'Not unless you are going to give it a bit more colour this time.'

'Certainly not,' she retorted.

Mr Coombes gave a slight guffaw and clambered to his feet. He puffed out his chest, but stayed upright.

'Won't you rest a little longer, Reginald?' Mrs Coombes pleaded from the sofa.

'I'm quite well now, Adeline. No need to fret.' Mr Coombes took one step forward, one step back across the carpet, as if testing his strength.

Violet and her mama exchanged worried

glances. Her papa loathed a fuss to be made about his health, but his turns terrified all of them.

A pang of pain clutched deep in her own chest. For her parents' sake, she had to stop the scandal.

'Now then.' Her papa's voice lacked its usual ring as he stopped on the carpet and studied Adam Beaufort. 'Let's get down to business. Are you serious in proposing marriage to my daughter?'

Adam drained his whisky glass. 'Quite so, sir.'

Mr Coombes tucked his hands into the lapels of his checked waistcoat. His elbows jutted out. 'You think a marriage announcement could halt this suffragette business. Is that it?'

'I believe it would stop the scandalmongers if attention was diverted towards an engagement,' Adam replied. 'The Beaufort name will halt adverse gossip. We're an old family. Well connected.'

'At court!' Mrs Coombes put in from the sofa, still fanning herself rapidly. 'To royalty!'

Adam smiled at Violet's mother, not appearing to mind her mentioning it. 'There are a few overlapping branches in the family tree.'

He turned back to Mr Coombes. 'If we act in time, I hope we can ensure your commercial dealings are not adversely affected.'

'Do you believe the reputation of my company

might be damaged by this stunt of Violet's?' Mr Coombes demanded.

'Surely not!' Violet put in.

'I'm afraid so, Miss Coombes.' Adam spoke quietly, but his tone was firm.

Mr Coombes looked suddenly deflated. 'I agree. Customers can take such things very badly.'

'My being a suffragette won't stop people eating Coombes Chocolates,' Violet said, incredulous.

'You have insulted the Crown. Fortunes have been lost for less.' Adam gave her a direct look that reminded her of their discussion the night before. He knew about such matters, she recalled with a sinking heart.

'What of the Royal Warrant?' From the sofa her mother's voice was hushed.

Her father shook his head. 'No chance of a Royal Warrant now. No chance at all.'

Violet clutched her corset. The painful pang in her chest moved to squeeze her stomach, as if she'd eaten too many sweets at the factory. She'd done so once, as a small girl.

The Royal Warrant. *Chocolate Manufacturers to the King.* It had been her father's abiding goal in life for as long as she could remember. Now the scandal she'd created could dash his dream.

How had it come to this? She struggled for breath. She'd never meant to insult the royal family, never once imagined that her passion for the Cause could risk what her father had worked so hard to build. Yet she couldn't regret her deed. It was the suffragette motto after all. Perhaps she'd gone too far with the banners at the ball, but she would never give up her beliefs.

'What do you think needs to be done?' Mr Coombes was asking Adam Beaufort.

'Make a formal announcement as soon as possible,' he replied. 'Notify *The Times*.'

Mr Coombes tucked his hand in his waistcoat pocket and pulled out his spotted handkerchief. 'What you're proposing might work. It just might work.'

'But why would you do this for us, Mr Beaufort?' Mrs Coombes asked, bewildered, from her seat on the sofa. Her fan still fluttered at a rapid rate, like wings of a startled bird.

Violet met Adam's eye. He raised an eyebrow.

An unspoken communication passed between them.

She held his gaze. In return, his was steadfast. To her surprise, she felt reassured. She had experienced the same security when they'd danced at the ball, after he'd rescued her from being a wallflower. He'd caught her safely when she'd fallen from the balcony, too.

'Mama. Papa.' Violet took a deep breath. 'I'd like to speak to Mr Beaufort, alone.'

'What?' Elbows out, Mr Coombes gazed from one to the other. 'Surely a marriage proposal is a matter for your father to consider.'

Violet lifted her chin. 'I refuse to be discussed like cattle in the market place. No matter how unusual the circumstances.'

The dent appeared in Adam Beaufort's cheek, as if he were trying not to chuckle.

Mr Coombes wiped his forehead with his hand-kerchief. He was still breathing heavily, Violet noticed with alarm, but his eyes were alert. Beneath his handkerchief he appeared to be summing Mr Beaufort up in his shrewd gaze, the way Violet had seen him assess potential buyers for the chocolate factory. She could almost hear his brain whirring, as fast as her own. Finally he tucked the handkerchief away.

'Very well, Violet. We'll leave you to consider this.' Wheezing slightly, he reached for her hands. 'I'm sorry I spoke to you so harshly earlier. I didn't mean what I said.'

'We were all upset.'

'You mustn't feel any pressure,' her father said now. 'Whatever happens, it will be your decision.

We would never force you into anything. I hope you know that.'

Violet's throat choked. 'Thank you, Papa.'

He gave her hands another squeeze before letting them go, but she could still see the worry in his eyes. Worse than that. There was a despondency she'd never witnessed in him before. In spite of his health concerns, he was always so cheerful.

Her stomach lurched. She'd hurt the people she loved most in the world.

'Come along, Adeline.' Mr Coombes held out his hand to his wife.

'Ought Violet be left without a chaperon?' Mrs Coombes asked doubtfully, as she got up from the sofa with a rustle of taffeta.

'We've strayed beyond all kinds of proprieties this morning, Mama, in the space of a quarter of an hour,' Violet replied.

This time she heard Adam Beaufort's chuckle escape.

Her papa steered her mother towards the door. It closed behind them.

Silence fell, but it wasn't an uncomfortable silence. She picked up the tin of Floral Creams that still lay on the Turkish carpet. Her father had knocked them off the table when he had his turn.

She clasped the tin to her bodice.

They always kept Coombes Chocolates in the drawing room. There were tins of Floral Creams in every bedroom, too. It was a point of pride for her family.

She looked down at the lid, with its swirled font and bouquet of flowers. Now it might never be adorned with the royal warrant they all wanted so much. Her papa had even left room for it in the design, believing that aiming high was the best method for success.

'Opportunities fall in the way of everyone who is resolved to take advantage of them.' Her papa often quoted that. She'd been raised on the philosophy of Samuel Smiles, the author of her father's favourite book, *Self-Help.* There was a handsome leather-bound copy of the book in pride of place at the factory office. It had been given to her papa by his employees one Christmas, after their annual party. Over two thousand people, men and women, worked at the Coombes factory. Violet knew each and every one of them. They all relied on their wages, for the well-being of their homes and families.

Now it was all at risk. The factory. Her papa's health. Her mama's happiness. The cost of being a suffragette had proved far greater than she had ever imagined.

She stared at the tin of chocolates. Its outline blurred before her eyes.

'Opportunities fall in the way of everyone who is resolved to take advantage of them,' she reminded herself.

The scent of cocoa and flowers wafted up as she opened the lid and held it out towards Adam Beaufort. 'Would you like a chocolate fondant?'

He appeared startled, then smiled. 'Perhaps later. I'm afraid my nanny drummed into me that sweets before luncheon were the road to ruin.'

Violet smiled back, the threat of tears retreating. He had a knack of lightening the mood of a situation.

She popped a violet cream into her mouth. The familiar taste, with its dark, almost spicy chocolate, the sugar-coated violet petal on top and the contrasting smoothness of the sweet fondant inside, gave her a surge of vigour.

Replacing the tin on the table, she ran her finger over the embossed picture of roses, violets, lavender and pansies. Her mother had confided once that they had planned a whole nursery full of children, the girls to be named after the flowers that had made their fortune and the first boy, her mother had said, would be named Reginald, after her papa. Those other children had never come. Violet hadn't felt lonely on her own, so she'd not missed sisters and brothers. She'd never known that her father felt the loss of a son so keenly. Not until today.

Her papa didn't have the heir he wanted. Instead, he had a daughter who had brought disrepute to the family name.

A pain stabbed at her heart.

She glanced at Adam Beaufort. His back half-turned, he stared out the window, seeming to sense she needed time to collect her thoughts. The noon sunshine coming in from between the velvet curtains outlined his profile. His jaw was strong, but there was no cruelty in it. Perhaps she ought to feel intimidated being alone with him, one of the most eligible men in London society, but she didn't. She never dreamed she'd find herself in the drawing room discussing marriage with him. She wondered if she ought to pinch herself to check she was awake.

The cherub clock chimed. Yes, she was awake. Adam Beaufort was standing by the window in real life, not in a dream, staring out into that peculiar soft London sunshine that made the streets and buildings shine like marigolds. In spite of their lack of welcome by society, in some ways Violet had enjoyed being in the capital. She'd walked to Parliament Square and listened to Big Ben while gazing at the Houses of Parliament, dreaming of laws that might be changed inside its hallowed walls.

Votes for Women! Now her papa had forbidden her to be a suffragette, all that must be stopped. She couldn't defy him now. She had already caused enough distress.

Yet the thought of giving up the Cause…

Violet moved towards to Adam Beaufort. 'Shall we have some plain speaking?'

He turned to face her. There was no doubting his smile this time. His teeth gleamed white. 'Do you speak any other way, Miss Coombes?'

'I prefer it,' she admitted. 'I would very much like to hear more of your plan.'

His grin widened. 'It isn't a plan I've refined yet, as you may have realised. I haven't been following you in the dark of night, plotting to catch you from balconies. And it's not the reason I asked you to dance at the ball.'

'Oh.' Violet felt more pleased than she expected at his saying so. The sense of being safe with him returned.

'It was an idea that came to me when I heard of your trouble. A moment of inspiration. Or perhaps it is an ill-conceived notion, something we ought to forget I ever mentioned.'

'Oh, no,' Violet said quickly. 'I'd very much like to explore your suggestion.'

Adam Beaufort inclined his head. 'Certainly.'

Violet took some air from deep in her chest, as far as her corset would allow. The breathlessness she'd experienced when he first proposed had returned, but she forced her voice to firmness. 'Would you propose marriage to me if I didn't have a fortune?'

Chapter Five

'If this were thus, if this, indeed, were all...'
—Alfred, Lord Tennyson: *'Love and Duty'*
(1842)

'You wish to know if I want to marry you for your money.'

Violet lifted her chin. 'Yes.'

The sun gleamed through the window as Adam Beaufort made a low whistle. 'That certainly is plain speaking, Miss Coombes.'

'I don't mean to be rude,' Violet said quickly. She had no wish to offend him.

'Not at all. Since you prefer plain speaking, let me be completely frank with you.' He gave Violet a wry smile. 'If you didn't have a fortune, it would rather defeat the purpose of my proposal.'

Violet bit her lip. 'Of course.'

How odd, she thought to herself. Part of her minded his admitting it. She pushed the sensation away. Of course her fortune was her attraction to him.

His smile disappeared as he spoke again. The youthfulness she'd noted earlier vanished. 'If you will allow me to explain, there's more you need to know. At the ball, we each spoke of our fathers. I told you then that my father, in contrast to yours, was not a hard-working man.'

Violet nodded. The philosophy of self-help was not embraced by everyone with the same enthusiasm as Reginald Coombes.

'That's an understatement,' Adam went on. 'My family, as you know, have a manor house in Kent. It requires a great deal of upkeep. For the past few years, I have watched it begin to disintegrate before my eyes.'

He moved away from her, his fists clenched. 'I knew my father was letting the manor run down. The house itself, and the surrounding properties, where we have tenants who rely on us. Since my father's death, I've discovered that isn't the worst of it. The manor, and our house in London, have been mortgaged many times over. It isn't merely that my father was not a good householder, Miss Coombes. He has lost all our family's money and, worse, accrued debts of amounts that I can barely perceive. We are beyond being financially embarrassed. The Beaufort family is ruined.'

Violet gasped in shock. 'How is that possible?'

'Gambling.' Adam said curtly. 'The night I saw you on the balcony, I had been at a private meeting at my father's club. The scene of the crime, so to speak.'

'I thought you considered me the criminal that night,' Violet commented with a smile, trying to lighten the moment. He looked so desperately burdened. Her heart gave a squeeze of sympathy.

'Your actions were beyond the law, certainly. You were on private property. My property, if I can still call it that, considering the size of the mortgage on it. But I don't consider you a criminal. You're standing up for your beliefs.' He smiled briefly. 'Or climbing up for them, I should say.'

Violet chuckled, then grew serious. 'So that night at the club…'

'The night I encountered you on the balcony, I'd found out the extent of the damage. It was all quite civilised, over dinner and port. But that didn't disguise the gravity of the situation. The gambling notes came out, with my father's signature scrawled on them. He lost vast sums night after night at the card table. I was angry that it had been allowed to continue. But a gentleman's word is his bond and my father had given his word that he was good for the money. On one of the gambling notes, he'd written "Beauley Manor."' A muscle moved in his cheek as he gritted his teeth. 'Offered up as a gambling marker. Our family home.'

'How dreadful for you.' She couldn't imagine discovering that her father had kept such secrets. It must have seemed as if Adam Beaufort hadn't known his father at all. But that was how she had felt earlier, she recalled with a sting. Her father had apologised for being so harsh, yet nothing could take away Violet's awful realisation that, all along, he'd wished she were a boy.

Adam gave a slight shrug. 'I'll admit, it was a most unpleasant experience. But Beauley Manor is my responsibility now, as are my mother and sisters. I had to do the honourable thing and face the truth about our family finances. It's my duty.'

'That's how I feel about the Cause,' said Violet. It wasn't a fancy, or a whim that she could take or leave. It was her duty, too.

'Then you understand,' he said. 'After some long discussions at the club I managed to convince my father's creditors not to press the matter immediately. But I have very little time.'

'So that's why…'

'I proposed to you.' He exhaled. 'We are both facing scandal, it seems. Perhaps because we're in the same predicament is why I jumped to a solution. That we make a marriage of convenience.'

A marriage of convenience. She'd heard the phrase, but had never expected it to apply to her.

'I trust I do not sound like an opportunist,' he added.

'*"Opportunities fall in the way of everyone who is resolved to take advantage of them,"*' she quoted.

'Samuel Smiles,' he said.

'You've read *Self-Help*?' she asked, astonished.

'Of course.' He chuckled, rather grimly. 'The Beaufort family currently need all the help they can get.'

Violet took a breath. 'You love your family.'

'Indeed.'

She did, too.

'I can see the opportunity in your proposal,' she said slowly, as her mind ticked. 'For the good of both our families. But there is a difficulty.'

Adam Beaufort raised an eyebrow.

Violet hesitated. She'd never told anyone about her secret decision. Yet, oddly enough, she trusted him.

'I have made a pledge not to marry,' she said at last.

Adam drew back. 'Never?'

Violet shook her head. 'It's not a pledge for life. I don't intend to join a nunnery. I simply don't wish to marry yet.'

'Is there a particular reason you intend to wait?'
She bit her lip.

'As I assured you at the ball, I can keep a secret,' he said.

'It's for the Cause,' she replied at last. 'I wish to devote myself to it, entirely.'

Amazement was etched on his face. 'The Cause means that much to you?'

'It does.'

Adam whistled. 'That's quite a sacrifice.'

'It is a sacrifice I'm willing to make.' With resolve, she lifted her chin. 'When I first heard about the Cause, I knew it was my calling to become a suffragette. Whatever needs to be done, I will do. I intend to dedicate myself to it until women have the vote.'

'And when women have suffrage…'

She nodded crisply. 'Only then will I consider marriage.'

He shook his head. 'Women getting the vote could take years.'

'Surely not years,' Violet protested. 'We will win our argument soon, I'm sure of it. Parliament will soon see the error of their ways in denying half the population of England the opportunity to contribute to our government. It cannot be more than a few years away.'

He raised an eyebrow. 'I'm not so sure.'

She shrugged. 'In any case, it is my decision. However many years it takes, for as long as women cannot vote, I will be no man's wife.'

'When did you make this decision?' he asked.

'When I became a suffragette. Three years ago.'

'Do your parents know?'

'No. I don't mean to deceive them. When the suffragettes win the day, I will marry—I mean, I hope I will—and my parents will be none the wiser.'

He stepped closer. 'Keeping such a secret must have been difficult.'

She was amazed by his insight. It had been lonely to know that she could not seek a partner in life, or tell the reason why.

'It has been difficult. And I've not spoken of this matter to anyone before.'

He inclined his head. 'I'm honoured by your trust, Miss Coombes.'

'I wish to concentrate my energies.' She was eager now to explain her reasoning. Growing up, she'd watched her mama unquestioningly devote herself to her husband and home. She loved her mother, but she didn't want the same life. 'Once women have a home and a family, they are not free to follow their own causes. They are under the rule of their husband.'

He frowned. 'Not all husbands wish to rule their wives.'

Violet pressed her lips together. 'A man owns his wife. I am determined that no man shall own me. The law, as it stands, gives a man dominion over a woman.'

The forked lines between his eyebrows deepened. 'Marriage for women does not have to mean servitude.'

'It may not,' Violet agreed. Her parents had a happy marriage, after all. 'Please do not mistake me. In marriage, there are bonds of love that bind a woman. When she becomes a wife and mother, her family becomes her greatest concern. I have no objection to that, when it comes.'

'Unless it comes too soon,' he said.

'Exactly,' she answered in relief. He'd grasped her meaning. 'I'm not opposed to the institution of marriage. But I am certainly not looking for a husband. Not until women have the suffrage we deserve.'

'Yet here you are in London, for the Season. There is a general view that during the Season a young woman is…'

Violet grimaced. 'Husband hunting?'

He smiled, deepening the dent in his cheek. 'Something like that.'

'It's my parents' wish to move higher in society. There is the Royal Warrant my papa hopes for. It takes connections that we can only get in London. I'm here for my parents, not for myself. I am older than most debutantes, but this is the first year our family have had the right invitations.'

And now she had risked it all, she thought with remorse. A whiff of scandal and it would all disappear, and along with it her parents' hopes and dreams.

'You must have had suitors,' he commented.

'Only a few.' Her lack of serious suitors was no cause for alarm to her, in the circumstances. In Manchester, the boys she'd grown up with were now too shy to approach her, thinking themselves no longer cut of her cloth. More moneyed London society hadn't offered any alternatives.

Except for Adam Beaufort.

From the corner of her eye she studied him. She felt entirely at ease with him. He lacked the snobbery that she'd encountered so keenly at the ball. The way those Dowagers had laughed at her mama. It still made her fume.

'Thus far I have managed to avert any serious interest,' she said.

'I'm surprised.'

'Because of my fortune?' she asked candidly. 'My devotion to the Cause tends to be off-putting.

Most gentlemen prefer women weak and help-less.'

He raised a brow. 'Do they indeed?'

For a moment their eyes met.

Violet dropped her gaze first. 'In any case, my situation has now changed. As you know, my father has forbidden me to continue as a suffragette and I can't risk agitating him.'

'Of course,' Adam said swiftly. 'I understand.'

'You saw the problems with his health. My opportunity to support the Cause, limited as it was, has diminished considerably.'

Votes for women! So boldly her handmade banner had declared it. All that would be gone now, she thought, with another of those painful pangs. If she and her parents went back to Manchester, she would certainly be constrained from her deeds as a suffragette. She couldn't risk her papa's health worsening. What was it he had said? 'No more of this suffragette nonsense!' Those words hurt Violet as much as him wanting a son rather than a daughter. Being a suffragette wasn't nonsense. It was about honour and justice.

It was about duty.

Adam put his hands together in a steeple. 'Perhaps, Miss Coombes, my marriage offer may be convenient to you after all.'

'How can marrying you be convenient?' Violet blushed. 'I'm sorry. I sound impolite again.'

Adam's grin flashed. 'I'm becoming accustomed to your frankness. Please. Do go on.'

'I can see the benefits of the scheme for you,' she mused, 'in that your family's current financial embarrassment would be remedied. But what do you offer me? I don't mean your status in society. I know some people care for such things, but I don't. I hope I haven't offended you by saying so,' she added hurriedly.

'Not at all.'

'There is simply no attraction for me in going to society functions, or being addressed in a certain way, or being bobbed to by all and sundry. I would find it quite irksome.'

He made a sound, somewhere between a chuckle and a cough.

'I can't deny that not having to face a scandal would be most welcome.' Violet sighed. Her protest had gone so badly. The way she'd hurt her parents…it hurt her, too. 'But surely the scandal will pass. I can live it down. There will be other scandals to take its place.'

'The Beaufort scandal, for a start,' he said grimly.

'Oh, I didn't mean your scandal,' Violet said.

'Although it's not fair to think of it as your scandal. It isn't your fault. Not in the slightest.'

He bowed. 'It is my duty to fix it.'

'It's my duty to do what I can to fix what I have done, too.'

'We both want to do our duty. Yet as you say, if it is to be a marriage of convenience, it must be convenient to us both. Hmm.' Adam rubbed his hand along his chin. He was clean shaven. His skin was quite tanned against the crisp white of his collar, as if he spent a lot of time out of doors. 'It does appear that the advantages of the match are mine more than yours. So much for an illustrious name. It's all we have left and even that's about to be dragged through the mud.'

So was the name Coombes. Not only her reputation, but the reputation of the family business was at stake.

'Do you have anything else to bring to this… marriage of convenience?' she queried, tentative. 'If it's not offensive to put it that way.'

'You wanted plain speaking.' He rubbed his chin again. 'I'm afraid the family jewels went long ago and what is left of them adorn my mother.'

'I'd never want your mother's jewels,' Violet said quickly. 'In any case…'

'Let me guess. You don't care for them.'

'Not much,' she confessed.

'Horses? At Beauley Manor we still have a reasonable stable. It's not what it was, but we've kept some of the best horses.'

Violet thought of her riding lesson that morning. 'I already ride a thoroughbred.'

'Of course you do. Travel? I've been on a Grand Tour. I could accompany you to Europe. Show you Rome, Venice, Paris.'

'I've been to Paris.' Violet felt apologetic. 'And we have a house in Venice. On the canal.'

He creased his brow in concentration. 'Presenting you with a bouquet of flowers or tempting you with sweets, I suppose, is out of the question for the Coombes Chocolates heiress.'

'I like flowers, but…'

'You have a garden full of them.'

'Fields,' she admitted. 'To make flavouring for the chocolate fillings.'

'Fields of flowers. Factories of sweets.' Unexpectedly, he grinned. 'This is more difficult than I expected. And you already have a fortune. Hmm.'

He snapped his fingers. 'I have it.'

She widened her eyes. 'You do?'

'Indeed. There's only one thing I can offer you.'

'What's that?'

He moved closer to where she stood by the

fireplace. His eyes gleamed. 'Freedom, Miss Coombes.'

Freedom.

She tasted the word on her lips, as if it were a new flavour of floral cream.

She'd never experienced true freedom. She tried to find it as best as she could, in her parents' home, but there were strictures. It was why she'd become a suffragette. Most of the rules that governed her daily life seemed to be based upon the fact that she was a woman whose place was in the home. She rarely had time to support the Cause as she wished. She found a few moments here and there, but any freedom had to be snatched, hidden, like the banners in her embroidery box.

'Freedom.' This time she spoke the word aloud.

Adam leaned in. The gleam in his eyes deepened. 'That's what you really want, isn't it? To be a free woman. It's why you're a suffragette.'

He understood, she realised, amazed. For a moment, her throat choked. 'Yes. It is.'

He bowed. 'Let your freedom be my part of the bargain, Miss Coombes. If you marry me, you can support the Cause in whatever way you choose.'

'You'd support my vocation as a suffragette?' She couldn't believe it. So many men loathed the suffragette movement. She had to be sure. 'Is that what you mean? You'd allow me openly to follow my beliefs. You wouldn't try to stop me, in any way.'

'I vow it. If you marry me, I will not constrain you.' He inclined his head. 'Until women get the vote, you will be free to follow your own desires.'

At his last word Violet moved closer. 'And what do you desire?'

Adam took a step back. Behind him the fire irons hit the marble hearth with a clatter. He picked up the iron poker before it rolled away and prodded it back into a bucket of coal.

Violet Coombes's blue eyes were frank and wide.

He noticed again how pretty she was. Her riding attire suited her better than the ball gown she'd been wearing the night before. The riding habit was blue velvet, not black broadcloth as his sisters wore. A deep midnight blue that made her eyes like the brightest forget-me-nots. Her curves were shapely and the creaminess of her skin was emphasised by the loosened lace jabot at her throat.

'A marriage of convenience is all very well,' she said crisply, 'but I need to know more before we agree to terms. I have no intention of being a sacrificial lamb.'

'The terms...' he clarified.

'I presume you will want an heir.'

Adam exhaled sharply. He'd been clenching his jaw along with his fists, he realised, as he rolled his fingers from their tight ball. It had been harder than he'd predicted to be so honest about his family's predicament. Yet it hadn't been difficult to confide in her. That wide, honest gaze of hers had encouraged him. It was extraordinary. He felt better for having shared his concern with her, to not be alone with it.

Now their conversation had turned into one of the most awkward he'd ever had and, in the course of trying to save the family fortune, he'd had a few.

He decided to match her frankness. 'My offspring are not a matter to which I've given much thought. I've been too intent on ensuring there is something to inherit. But if I were to think about it, yes, I would want children. A son.'

She winced. For a moment her lip trembled, then she firmed it. Two pink spots appeared on her cheeks. 'A son is what all men want.'

The quickly hidden hurt with which she spoke surprised him. She tried to disguise it, but he heard it in her voice.

He wanted to ask her what was wrong, but he couldn't pry.

'Beauley Manor will go to a male heir,' he said evenly. 'That's the law.'

'Many laws need changing.'

'Certainly. But as it stands, the Beaufort name will continue under the male line.'

'So would a male heir be part of the bargain? Would I need to provide you with a son? Or would eleven daughters be found wanting?'

Adam frowned. Her words held an almost bitter note. He was a good judge of character. Chocolate could be bitter, he supposed, but it didn't match the sweetness of Violet Coombes.

In any case, the conversation had become even more damned awkward.

He gave a slight bow. 'Perhaps my marriage proposal was a bad idea. It was a spur-of-the-moment notion. Forgive me, Miss Coombes, if I have upset you. I'll take no more of your time.'

'Wait!' Violet put out her hand. 'It is I who must ask you to forgive me. Today's events have been very upsetting.'

She sat on the sofa, patted amid the cushions. 'Please.'

For a moment Adam towered over her. Then his long legs folded as he took a seat on the other end of the sofa. There was very little room for them both to sit amid the tufted pillows her mother adored so much. His thigh almost grazed hers.

Austere, he met her gaze. 'Miss Coombes. I have no plan to trick or entrap you. My intentions are to see if we can help each other.'

'A husband has rights,' she said quietly. 'That is the law, too.'

Outrage flashed in his eyes. 'Do you think I would take my rights by force? I'm a gentleman.'

'That word means little to many men.'

He squared his shoulders. 'To me, it means a great deal.'

Violet studied Adam Beaufort. She had offended him. She hadn't meant to.

There was only one thing for it.

She leaned in and kissed him.

Chapter Six

'Or seem to lift a burden from thy heart
And leave thee freer....'
　—Alfred, Lord Tennyson: *'Love and Duty'*
(1842)

Violet sought Adam's mouth with hers.

He pulled back, but only for a moment.

His mouth was hard as she pressed against it with her lips. There was a slight tingling sensation. Again he moved to pull away. In reply she pressed more intently, running the tip of her tongue between the firm edges of his lips, as though seeking access. As if she had spoken a secret password between them, his mouth opened over hers.

Violet gasped. Under the sudden searching pressure of his mouth, her lips parted. Now there was more than tingling. She fell back against the cushions as he explored her mouth with his tongue. Her eyes fanned closed as her hands reached for more of him, catching the rough edge of his hair at the base of his neck, her body pressed into the cushions. Still seeking her with the heat of his mouth, Adam wrapped his arms around her, as her lips yielded to him.

His hands moved upwards, running his fingers through the tendrils of her hair, to cup her chin in his hands, as if drinking her in. Cushions fell to the carpet as she slid beneath him on the sofa, pulling him closer. Whirling sensations built in her body, as if they were waltzing once again on the ballroom floor. Thought vanished. Only his mouth, his tongue, his breath, only that mattered now.

Deeper. His tongue dived into her, tasting her, searching her, seeking her. His body on hers was hard. More cushions tumbled as she sought to explore him in the same way, matching the pressure of his tongue.

There was no resistance between them now. Her fingers found the strong edge of his jaw, the same way he had cupped hers, drawing his mouth, his body, on to her.

With a muttered expletive he wrenched himself away.

There was no sound, only the ticking of the cherub clock and his breathing, as ragged as her own.

With her elbows Violet raised herself on the sofa. Adam's back was to her as he rested his head in his hands.

Her bodice heaved as she struggled to sit upright. What had she done?

Adam raised his head. 'You taste like violets.' He sounded stunned.

'What? Oh. The chocolates.' Violet glanced at the tin of Floral Creams, taking the opportunity to catch her breath. Her heart raced.

She had never expected a kiss to be like that. Not that she had any experience. It was her first kiss.

She peeped at Adam. It could not be his first kiss. Surely he had been—skilled. He'd kissed her in the same way he waltzed. Strong, secure, practised.

The whirling, dancing sensation returned to her body, quivering through her core, trembling down, even into her legs. She wondered if she would be able to stand.

He had not got to his feet, either. He was still seated on the edge of the sofa, amid the tumble of cushions, his body bent away from her.

'I suppose you think me forward,' she said at last.

Young ladies were not supposed to kiss gentlemen. Yet another rule that only applied to the female sex. Another rule by which she refused to abide.

He twisted his head towards her and smiled, unexpectedly. The dent darted in his cheek. 'You've surprised me upon every occasion we have met, Miss Coombes. But this, may I say, is the most pleasant surprise so far.'

Violet blushed. For a moment she thought he was going to kiss her again. She leaned towards him before her brain had time to function.

He shifted. 'Forgive me. I don't quite understand. Earlier you implied that you didn't wish to…' he paused as if trying to find the right words, '…marry.'

'That is correct.'

'So why—?'

'Did I kiss you?'

The dent darted again. 'Indeed.'

'I'm a modern woman,' she said earnestly. 'Or I hope to be.'

He cleared his throat. 'Ah. Of course.'

'Women will win the vote, and soon,' Violet explained. 'It will bring all kinds of release.'

'Hmm.'

'I've studied the subject of marital relations,' she confided. 'In medical journals. I have no wish to be ignorant.'

'I see.'

'I'm aware of what happens in marriage, between a man and a woman.' She bit her lip. 'I cannot abide hypocrisy. I would prefer to say what I mean. Do you think we might be—well matched?'

'I believe so, Miss Coombes. I believe so.' His grin flashed again. 'Forgive me. There are no words for these circumstances. I am at a loss for them.'

'Deeds, not words,' Violet said.

'I'm sorry?'

'It's the suffragette motto.' Violet reached for the tin of Floral Creams. 'Might you care for a chocolate after all?'

'That would be most welcome.'

She proffered the tin. He took a violet cream, she noticed.

'We're discussing marriage.' She selected a rose cream this time for herself. 'Not a commercial arrangement. I have no wish to find ourselves repugnant to each other.'

He finished his chocolate fondant in a single bite. 'There's no danger of that, Miss Coombes.'

'Would you like another?' She held out the selection.

He shook his head. 'I think one is enough, for today at least.'

Violet let the rose fondant melt in her mouth. She could still taste his kiss on her tongue, along with the chocolate's sweetness.

She swallowed. 'Will you be able to...wait?'

She floundered over the question. She had managed to be forthright in their discourse so far and had surprised even herself by kissing him. But to discuss male needs...

'I possess the required self-control, Miss Coombes, if that's what you're asking,' Adam drawled. 'You need have no fear.'

'I hope it will not be too many years before the momentous occasion occurs.'

'The momentous occasion...'

She stared at him in astonishment. 'When women get the vote.'

'The vote.' He shook his head. 'Quite right.'

'I cannot say when the date will be. But when it does arrive, we can begin married life.'

He crossed one long leg over the other. 'It's a sound plan.'

'You'd be happy with this arrangement?'

'We both share the desire to put duty first.' His mouth tightened. 'I am not averse to waiting, for reasons of my own. Having witnessed the chaos of my parents' marriage, caused by my father's habits, I'd prefer a straightforward, workable approach to married life.'

'I see.' She waited to see if he would say any more, but he did not.

'I, too, would like children one day,' she said, after a moment. 'But not...'

'Not yet,' he concluded. 'You've been very clear, Miss Coombes. It's been most enlightening. I promise you, I understand your meaning completely. Until women win the vote, we can be—friends.'

'Friends,' she echoed him now, like her parents' parrot.

His eyes glinted in amusement. 'It's possible for a man and a woman to be friends, I believe.'

In relief she released the air trapped in her corset.

'When the time does come for children, I'd prefer a girl,' she confided.

'Perhaps we might settle upon one of each.'

Violet's own cheeks flamed hot again. 'That sounds most satisfactory.'

The cherub clock chimed.

Violet jumped.

He glanced at the clock. 'I have no wish to pressure you, but time is of the essence if we wish to avert a scandal.'

She nodded briskly. He was right. There was no time to waste. 'If we make an agreement between us, what shall we tell our families?'

'Your parents already know of my proposal. There would be no difficulty there.'

'That's true.' They would be relieved. The distress she'd caused—now she would be able to put it right. Seeing her papa have one of his turns had shaken her. She didn't want them to suffer.

And perhaps, she thought with sudden dismay, it might be a relief to her, too. She would always love them, but she could no longer live easily under her parents' roof. Not any more. Not knowing that she was considered second-rate. Her papa loved her, but his views had made her even more determined to support the Cause. Perhaps one day, having a daughter would be considered as valuable as having a son. She would do her part to make that happen, if she could.

'What of your family?' she queried of Adam. 'I wouldn't want you to feel a need to be deceitful.'

'I only have my mother to consider and my two sisters. Jane and Arabella. I will simply inform them we have decided to wed, that it is a sudden but happy decision.'

'Will they enquire further?'

'If they do, I will make the necessity of our match clear to them. Otherwise, our private arrangements can be kept quiet. All we shall say to our families, and to other friends and acquaintances, is that we both want the match and we hope they will be pleased for us.'

'I have no wish to lie,' Violet said.

'You won't need to. It's no business of anyone else. No one needs to know it is a marriage of convenience except ourselves.' He creased his forehead. 'An announcement in *The Times* will suffice. The less we say, the better. That's the way to end any scandal. And the sooner we set a wedding date, all the better, if you're agreeable.'

'My mama will want to organise my wedding dress and trousseau.' Violet cast a doubtful look around the drawing room, with its frills and furbelows. Perhaps having less time would prove an advantage. She adored her mama and would defend her frills against anyone, but, truth be told, their dress sense differed greatly.

He ran his hand through his hair. 'Shall we set the date for one month's time?'

'Would that satisfy your creditors? If it's not indelicate to ask.' She hoped she wasn't sounding rude again.

'You must believe me when I say I admire your frankness. To be equally frank, it's somewhat of a relief to be able to discuss the matter with you. There are rather a lot of them. Debts, I mean. But I believe one month would be satisfactory.'

'My settlement could be made earlier,' Violet offered.

'I'm sure it won't be required.' He glanced again at the cherub clock. 'This really has been an extraordinary morning, or should I say afternoon. Is there anything else you wish us to consider before we embark upon our engagement? Because once we make an announcement…'

'There'll be no turning back.' Violet lifted her chin. 'I must be certain. When you say you would give me freedom, Mr Beaufort…'

'My name is Adam. If we're betrothed, I don't think we can expect each other to continue with our formal titles. No more Mr Beaufort.'

'And no more Miss Coombes.' That would be true in more ways than one, she realised with shock. 'You must call me Violet.'

His gaze lingered on her lips. 'That won't be hard to remember.'

She took a deep breath. 'I must prepare you… Adam. I will throw myself entirely into the Cause. I wish to attend rallies, and meetings, and marches, and give speeches. It's been a secret dream of mine ever since I heard Mrs Emmeline Pankhurst give one. She founded the suffragettes, you know. She was so rousing. Deeds, not words. It changed my whole view of a woman's life, of a woman. To be able to convince others of the validity of the Cause, to show how worthy women are of a right to speak, to take part in our country's future, means everything to me.'

The admiration in his eyes was sincere. 'You've already convinced me.'

'It's been such a frustration, having to keep my views secret.'

'Under your petticoat, so to speak,' he drawled.

Violet burst out laughing. 'Exactly.'

She became serious. 'There are not many men who would support their wives in this matter.'

'Our marriage will be different. It will be more convenient.' He got to his feet to tower beside her. He was so tall. He leaned towards her, his gaze on her mouth. For a moment she thought he meant to kiss her again as he moved closer.

His breath swept her lips. 'I swear it you, Violet Coombes. You will have your freedom.'

Silence fell between them, as quiet as a church.

He held out his hand. 'Shall we shake hands on it?'

'Is that what they do in the gentlemen's clubs?' She sought to lighten the moment. There was an extraordinary atmosphere between them, almost sacred.

'Indeed.' He grinned with chagrin. 'Not that every gentleman's handshake is honour-bound. But mine is, I assure you.'

Her skin tingled. She believed him.

'Do we have an agreement?'

'We do.' Violet held out her hand in return. 'I didn't expect making a marriage of convenience to be so civil.'

He took it in his. His grip was warm, encasing hers. 'We haven't made our marriage yet.'

His touch, skin to skin, so soon after their kiss, made her quiver inside. One day it would be a real marriage, not a sham, regardless of whether or not it began as a marriage of convenience. This man would be her husband in word and, one day, in deed.

Adam glanced up at the balcony of his family's London town house.

He wondered if he would ever be able to look at it again without thinking of Violet Coombes. In his mind's eye he could still see her shape as she clung to the edge, attempting to hang her banner in the dim moonlight. Then the feel of her as she fell into his arms, the softness, combined with the strong will that he was beginning to recognise more and more. It was in her movements, in her voice, in her courageous approach to life.

It was in her lips.

Adam groaned aloud.

That kiss. She'd stunned him with it. He'd found himself unable to pull away from her, even though his gentlemanly reaction had been to do so. He'd kissed women before, but the kiss he'd shared with Violet had been different.

She was extraordinary.

Their conversation had been extraordinary.

It had been, without doubt, a most extraordinary kiss.

After leaving the Coombes' home, still astounded by the morning's events, he'd gone straight to *The Times* office and had managed, through some miracle of fate and timing, to get the announcement into the next day's paper.

He stopped short on the pavement. His proposal had seemed a sensible solution to both their problems. Yet an unexpected dimension had emerged between them. That kiss, for a start. He hadn't expected it from her, nor had he expected his own response.

It was not what he sought, or anticipated. The idea to propose marriage had come to him instinctively, but upon reflection, a marriage of convenience would suit him very well. After witnessing the emotional scenes that had been such a feature of his parents' marriage, especially following his father's drinking and gambling bouts, he sought an unemotional and straightforward life. He was guided by principle, by duty. It was surely a better, higher course.

The fact that their marriage would begin as a platonic one, and remain in name only for some time, was a further convenience. It would enable him to ensure unnecessary emotions were not stoked up. Violet Coombes understood duty as well as he did. He would make certain, from now on, that their marriage was civil and friendly, but no more than that. Emotional entanglements and, God forbid, emotional scenes must be avoided at all costs.

Adam firmed his jaw. They'd been honest with each other. There had been no pretence, no playing at courtship. Simply two people, treating each other as equals, looking for a way to solve their predicaments.

He took the marble steps two at a time and threw open the front door.

'Adam?' A querulous voice came from the drawing room to his left.

He lifted off his top hat and left it on the stand in the hall.

In the drawing room his mama was seated by the fire, even though the day was warm. She'd become frailer, of late.

Jane gave him a wink. She was seated by the window, looking out into the street. Next to her was Arabella, her hands occupied with a book. She was always buried in a book, but her education had been patchy, mostly at home. Perhaps Arabella would have enjoyed going away to school, or to Oxford, as he had done.

Adam lifted the corner of his mouth. Violet Coombes had begun to convert him already.

'You're terribly late,' his mama reproved. 'Where have you been?'

'Making an announcement at *The Times*,' he said.

'An announcement! What can you mean, Adam? Not more bad news, I hope,' said his mother faintly. 'I simply can't take any more.'

It had taken a toll on his mother, all the anxiety, no matter how much Adam had tried to protect her.

'On the contrary,' he reassured her rapidly. 'I have good news.'

Arabella looked up slightly from her book.

'Oh, I do like good news. What is it?' Jane asked eagerly.

He took the advertisement copy from his coat pocket and read aloud.

'"*The engagement is announced between Adam, eldest son of the late Mr Edmund Beaufort, Esquire, and Mrs Beaufort of Beauley Manor, Kent, and Violet, only daughter of Mr and Mrs Reginald Coombes of Manchester.*"'

Violet hurried into her bedroom and closed the door. Leaning against it, she took a deep breath. Then another.

She stripped off the coat of her velvet riding habit, her fingers fumbling at the buttons, and hurried to the jug and basin. Leaning over, she lifted the jug and splashed cold water on her face.

When she glanced into the looking glass above, she saw her cheeks were hot and pink. Her lips, too, were pinker than usual, where his mouth had pressed against hers. The swirling sensation came over her again as she remembered the searching hardness of his kiss.

She reached once more for the pitcher of cold water. Both the pitcher and bowl were decorated in a blue and white pattern. At the bottom of the bowl was a landscape of a lake. A small sailboat floated on the painted lake. She stared at it.

The boat seemed to be setting sail across the water.

So was she.

She must avert the scandal that threatened her family. She had to seize the opportunity to make amends.

Violet ran a fingertip over her lips. So many emotions swirled inside her. Relief. Trepidation. And the sensation of his kiss, still on her lips.

She could only hope she had made the right decision.

In one month, she would marry Adam Beaufort.

Chapter Seven

'So let me think 'tis well for thee and me...'
—Alfred, Lord Tennyson: *'Love and Duty'*
(1842)

'Violet. Are you sure?'

Violet smiled at her mama, peeping around the bedroom door. 'I'm quite sure, Mama. There's no need for more flowers in my bouquet.'

Mrs Coombes entered the bedroom, bringing a waft of rose scent in her wake. 'There have been so many things to think of and I do want everything to be perfect for you.'

Almost tripping over the long train of her dress, Violet hurried from where she had been seated in front of the dressing table over to her mother and kissed her cheek. 'Everything is perfect. No daughter could ask for more. Thank you so much for all you have done.'

Her mama brushed away a tear. 'I've been preparing for this day since you first arrived in the world. This is the most important day of your life. If only we'd had more time for all the wedding arrangements.'

Violet looked in the mirror at her white-satin gown. The long train, flounced with lace, could be looped at the side and later removed, so the dress could continue to be worn. Some women used their wedding dresses as court dresses for at least a year, the seamstress had told her. The sleeves were puffed and ruched with ribbons, as were the low décolletage and ruffled bodice. Down the centre of the bodice were pearl buttons, with more at the back to hold the dress securely in place. The silk sash was embroidered with pearls and tiny violets with green leaves that she had sewed herself. She'd given up embroidering her banners, but she'd managed to have the colours of the suffragettes—purple for loyalty and dignity, white for purity and green for hope—represented in her gown. One of the editors of her favourite women's magazine, *Votes for Women*, had devised the colour scheme and now it was everywhere. She was proud to wear the colours. Even if she hadn't promised her father not to make any more protests, there had in any case been no opportunity to continue any other work for suffrage before the wedding, with the countless fittings for her bridal gown and trousseau, and the seemingly endless wedding preparations. Nor had she wanted to upset her parents, who were still sensitive to any scandal that might be caused if Violet continued her passion for the Cause.

Not for long. She smiled inwardly. As a married woman, she wouldn't have to hide her passion for women's suffrage any longer. She could stand up for her beliefs. She could attend meetings and rallies. She would speak out for what she believed in, at last.

As soon as she married Adam Beaufort.

Her stomach lurched.

Adam. That's what she called him now and, most of the time, she thought of him by that name, too. But they'd only seen each other at a few social occasions, parties and entertainments, before her parents had rushed her back to Manchester to prepare for the wedding. As Adam had predicted, the scandal over her banners had been averted by the announcement of her engagement. Even so, her papa had deemed it wise to leave London. The banns had been read in both their parish churches and no objection had been raised to their match, even if, as Violet suspected, more than a few eyebrows had been raised in society circles.

Mrs Coombes smoothed out the veil that lay on the bed. It was so enormous it formed a lacy coverlet that almost completely swathed the eiderdown beneath. Next to it lay a lace shawl and a pair of satin gloves that glistened like vanilla ice cream. The left glove had a removable left ring finger, so that a wedding ring could be placed upon it.

Violet rubbed her bare finger. Adam had presented her with no engagement ring, but she hadn't expected it, she told herself quickly. Theirs was to be a marriage of convenience, after all.

'If only we'd had more time for all the arrangements,' her mother continued to mourn.

'I never wanted a big, fashionable wedding,' Violet replied. 'It's better this way.'

The morning wedding at St George's Church in Hanover Square would be followed by a luncheon reception at one of the smartest hotels in London. The Beaufort connections had smoothed the way for the wedding to be held at such a fashionable church, to her parents' delight, and her papa had offered to put on an enormous affair afterwards. Fortunately, there hadn't been time for the guest list to grow too big. The thought had made Violet shudder. She had no desire to be a society spectacle.

'Marry in May, rue the day,' Mrs Coombes recited worriedly.

'Oh, Mama.' Violet suppressed a surge of apprehension with a laugh. 'That's just an old superstition.'

'You could have been a June bride, with lovely roses, if only you had waited a few more weeks.'

'The violets are still out in May and I couldn't get married without violets,' she told her mama, with a hug.

She'd wanted to wear violets in her hair, too, in a simple crown, but her father had bought her a diamond tiara and presented it to her with such pride that of course she couldn't refuse to wear it.

Moving back to the dressing table, she dabbed some Parma violet cologne behind her ears. The scent of it reminded her of Adam.

'You taste like violets,' he'd said, after she kissed him.

She touched her lips. It had become a habit with her. They still seemed to tingle.

That one kiss had been the only intimacy between them, apart from when he'd held her in his arms and swept her around the ballroom in that wonderful waltz. How long ago that night at the ball seemed. They'd barely been alone together again.

'*Oh, dear.*'

Violet turned to her mama. She was gazing into the mirror, tugging at the puffed sleeves of her pale pink silk and lace gown. The sleeves were heavily ruched and ribboned in the latest style.

Violet smiled. 'You couldn't look finer, Mama,

if we'd had a year to prepare for my wedding, rather than a month.'

Mrs Coombes moved her hand to the diamond necklace that encircled her throat. 'Oh, Violet, do you truly think so? I know there was all that trouble with those banners and your father was very upset, more upset than I have ever seen him, and then he had one of his terrible turns, but we are so proud of you. I do so want you to be proud of us.'

Violet's eyes welled. 'I'm proud of you both, Mama.'

'I'm rather afraid of the Beauforts,' Mrs Coombes confessed. 'They are practically royalty.'

'Why, there's no need to be afraid of them,' Violet said staunchly. She had met her future family in-laws for tea and cucumber sandwiches, before the Coombes had gone back to Manchester. The Beaufort women were somewhat daunting, but Violet had refused to be intimidated. Mrs Beaufort was very grand, but it was clear she loved her son. Adam's elder sister, Arabella, had been rather standoffish, but his younger sister, Jane, seemed lively and great fun.

Mrs Coombes tugged at her puffed sleeves again. 'I wonder what Mrs Beaufort will wear to the wedding. Will she wear black, even to a wedding, as she is recently a widow? Is it a year since her husband died? Is the family still in mourning?

Ought I to be wearing pink? Oh, dear, I didn't think of that. Oh, dear!'

Violet laughed. 'The Beauforts must take the Coombes as we are. For better or worse.'

Mr Coombes popped his head around the door. 'Might I come in?'

'Of course, Papa.'

Smartly dressed in a dark frock coat that strained around his belly, her papa embraced her before reaching for his checked handkerchief. He blotted his eyes. 'Well, now. Well.'

Mrs Coombes beamed. 'Doesn't Violet look beautiful?'

'The most beautiful bride in England.'

Violet hugged him. It gave her joy to see him happy and well again. He'd not had another turn for a month, ever since she'd told them she would marry Adam Beaufort.

'Do be careful of your wedding dress!' exclaimed Mrs Coombes.

'My dress will survive. Thank you, Papa.'

'It's true,' he said stoutly. 'The most beautiful bride and the best daughter.' Her father pulled back and looked at her. 'Now. This is the last time I'll ask you. Are you sure you want to go ahead with this marriage?'

Violet took a deep breath. She had gone over her decision countless times, tossing and turning on her pillow before she went to sleep. Always, the answer was the same.

'I'm sure.'

'Very well,' said Mr Coombes. 'Let's show London society how it's done!'

Violet gave him another hug. She loved him so much, but she couldn't deny there was a new constraint between them, ever since the matter of the banners. He'd apologised again for what he'd said, but they couldn't be unsaid, those words. He had wanted a boy. He'd have preferred a son to follow him into the business. No matter how much Violet tried, she would never be who he truly wanted her to be.

She sighed inwardly. It had grown harder, not easier, to live with that truth. It was a relief to have said goodbye to their big house in Manchester. Violet had never imagined she would feel that way about her childhood home.

'Violet.' Her mama popped back again after her parents had left the room. 'This note came for you. A nice young lady dropped it in earlier, but she wouldn't stay, or tell me her name.'

Perplexed, Violet took the envelope. It was a pale lilac colour.

'There's something else.' Her mother hesitated.

'What is it, Mama?'

'There are matters between a married man

and a woman that I feel I ought to mention.' Mrs Coombes turned as pink as her dress. 'Certain matters, regarding your wedding night.'

Violet patted her hand. 'It's quite all right, Mama. I'm going into this marriage with my eyes open.'

'You are?'

'I am,' Violet said firmly. How astounded her mama would be if she learned of their marriage agreement.

After her mother left the room, Violet picked up the lilac envelope and slit it open with a nail file. Inside was a single sheet of paper, again in the same shade. Curious, she began to read.

Comradess!
Greetings! We understand you are one of the valiant who support Women's Suffrage. We send you this invitation to join our special group of suffragettes committed to the noble Cause and to changing the wicked laws that constrain women from freedom in this land.

Our group is made up of a membership committed to militant action. Our campaigns are dangerous, but vital. We will do all that can be done to win the vote, with no regard for any penalty, in the name of womankind.

No longer will we be angels in the house. We will be devils in the street.

The membership of our group is strictly top secret. Although we know your name, we will not disclose it to any other member of the group and nor will you learn ours. We correspond only by mail, giving instructions for our next action.

We warn you, some of these actions are against the laws of England. But we consider no law is law to us if we, as women, cannot vote for our lawmakers.

Reveal the contents of this letter to no one. If you wish to join our comrade sisterhood reply to this letter at the address below. All you need to do is state that your vote is YES.

If you join, you will hear from us soon. If you do not, you will never hear from us again.

Votes for Women!

A Piccadilly address was printed at the bottom of the sheet of paper.

Violet sank on to the stool of her dressing table. Her bridal reflection stared back at her.

From today, she would be a married woman. A *free* woman.

Under their terms, Adam had agreed she could

pursue her passion for the Cause. They hadn't discussed militant action, it was true, but they had shaken hands on their agreement.

Violet bit her lip. Their agreement meant that, at last, she would be able to be open about her suffragette activities. It had been such a relief. No more hiding.

What did the letter say? She scanned it again.

Some of these actions are against the laws of England.

If she joined, she would be honour-bound not to reveal such law-breaking actions. It could risk the group's safety. She understood that. Not all her suffragette activities would need to be kept secret, of course, only those connected with the militant membership. Yet she would be forced to begin her marriage to Adam with a deception.

Perturbed, Violet went to the window and stared out into the plane trees that lined the square. She loathed the idea of having to lie to Adam. He had been honest with her and she had been frank with him. Being otherwise went against her nature. She prized plain speaking, she had told him so. But how could she turn down such an opportunity to further the Cause?

Violet returned to the dressing table, her satin train swishing over the carpet. Ignoring her pang of disquiet, she retrieved a fountain pen. Her blue-leather writing case had been packed in the large trunks that had already been sent to Beauley Manor, but there was still some writing paper in a dressing-table drawer, with her name and address embossed on it.

Violet R. Coombes

She ran her hand over the print. It was the last time she would use her maiden name. It was fitting that she should use it now, for this special purpose.

Quickly, she wrote her reply and signed her name with a flourish, before sealing the envelope. She would take her reply and the lilac letter with her to the church. She couldn't risk it being found.

Reaching into the dressing-table drawer again, she pulled out another item she had sewed.

Lifting her skirt, she stood and slipped it on.

'Yes,' she said aloud, to her reflection. 'Yes.'

Violet tightened her sash.

Adam drummed his fingers on the chimney piece.

He'd been waiting for what seemed like hours for his mother and sisters to be ready to go to the church. They weren't far from St George's and they were planning to walk, but even so, he wanted to allow plenty of time. Brides might be able to be late to a wedding service, but not bridegrooms.

His bride. Miss Violet Coombes.

Perhaps she, too, had awoken early on this, their wedding day. He wondered whether she had woken happy, or with a sense of dread. Might she be experiencing cold feet?

He paced the drawing room, looked down on his own highly polished boots. *Damnation.* Was it his imagination, or were his own toes cold?

He chuckled, then sobered.

Their practical, platonic approach to marriage meant that their wedding day would be different from those of other brides and grooms. It was fortunate that Violet didn't seem the kind of young woman to indulge in romantic dreams. She was a suffragette, after all. She knew their terms.

Thus far, their arrangement had gone well. He'd upheld his side of the bargain. He'd attended a number of social events with Violet and stood coolly at her side, daring any challenge. There'd been ripples of adverse comment, of course, but he knew that no one would dare cut him, or make a snide remark in his presence. The Beaufort family name hadn't been wrecked by his father's behaviour and his own reputation stood for something. Many men would have walked

away from debts incurred by their fathers, but
that wasn't something Adam could ever do. In his
life he upheld honour. Even in his schooldays he'd
been known for it. But stopping the scandal for
Violet had been a close-run thing. He'd needed
to have a few quiet words with his club and court
connections and only just in time.

His mother and Arabella had protested about
the Beauforts having to mix with the Coombes,
but they hadn't protested long when he'd explained the financial embarrassment they would
face was far worse than any imagined social embarrassment.

For himself, he liked the Coombes family more
and more. They were a breath of fresh air. Hopefully his mother and Arabella would appreciate
that soon. His mother might be too old to change,
but he suspected Arabella might like Violet, if
she got to know her.

The financial settlement her father had made
astounded him. He'd known the Coombes were
prosperous, but the dowry Violet brought with
her would settle all the Beaufort debts twice over.
He'd experienced relief in knowing that his family was saved from ruin, but it rankled. He'd never
wanted to have been left by his father in such a
compromised position.

So much for old money. It was Violet who

had grown up with the best money could buy. The Coombes's money could purchase the best homes, clothing and furnishings, but in some circles there were those who believed it could never buy class, just as some people thought women should never be able to vote. Perhaps there would come a day when class didn't matter any more, when being a woman or a man didn't matter either, when there was freedom for people to simply be themselves. He hoped so. That was what Violet wanted, too, as a suffragette. How easily she might have become spoilt, with all the money available to her. She could have sat on a *chaise longue* all day, eating chocolates. Leisured, languid, like some of the women he knew. Instead, she fought for women's rights. He had to admire her for it.

He put his hand in the pocket of his silk waistcoat, as he'd done already a number of times that morning. He'd chosen a dark claret colour, paired with his black morning coat. Inside the pocket was the gold ring he'd discovered among the estate jewellery, to slip on her finger in front of the altar. Their initials, A and V, and the wedding date had been engraved inside the rim when he'd had it sized, guessing what might fit her. She was as tall as his sister Jane, but not as tall as Arabella, so he'd made the ring size smaller.

He'd made sure that courtesy was done, although he'd not been able to buy her a decent engagement ring. That lack rankled with his gentlemanly pride, too, marriage of convenience or not. Using Violet's own dowry to buy her a ring was, of course, tasteless and out of the question.

He rolled the gold band inside his palm before tucking it away again. No one knew the Beauforts had been so close to financial ruin. His creditors at the club, where debts were kept hush hush, had been all too obliging to allow time for him to pay his father's debts when they learned of his upcoming nuptials and, with his careful management of the situation, both he and Violet managed to avert their respective scandals. He was glad, not only for the Beauforts, but also for the Coombes. Reginald Coombes had appeared devastated to the point of ill health at the thought of scandal tainting his business, and no wonder. The man had amassed a fortune, not only in the form of Coombes Chocolates, but also in property, rail and shipping. The Coombes had the golden touch.

'Adam.' Jane, dressed in her finest, though well-darned, frock, slipped her arm through her brother's. 'I've been watching you for the past few minutes. You've been pacing up and down so I thought you'd wear out the carpet and it's quite worn enough.'

Adam looked down at the once-fine Persian rug. It was threadbare in places.

'Is this what bridegrooms do?' Jane squeezed his arm. 'I thought it was the bride who ought to be nervous.'

Many brides would be nervous about their wedding night, Adam reflected, but it would not be an anxiety for Violet Coombes. He'd arranged for them go to Beauley Manor for their wedding night, away from prying eyes. He had no wish for them to keep up a farce of besotted newlyweds.

He shook his head in semi-disbelief. Their whole agreement was extraordinary, bordering upon the absurd. Yet he knew they both had a similar commitment to duty.

Duty would serve them both better in marriage than any romantic notions. Yet, damnation, if the aroma of violets hadn't tantalised him ever since he'd tasted it on her lips.

As he'd done so many times in the last month, Adam pushed away his body's recall of that violet-scented kiss.

He seized his top hat. 'Let's get to the church on time.'

Violet peered through her lace veil. Beyond it, the graceful spired outline of St George's appeared misty, as if she were in a dream.

The footman opened the carriage door. Smiling gratefully at him, she placed one satin shoe, then the other, on to the carriage box.

Her father waved the footman away. 'Take my hand, Violet.'

Violet stepped into the square and adjusted her train on its loop. A gust of wind caught at her veil.

'Easy does it,' said her papa. He handed her the bouquet of lilies and violets before, beaming, he tucked her arm in his.

Violet looked up the church steps. The heavy wooden doors were open. With each step higher, her trepidation grew.

Her breathing became fast and shallow. What was she doing?

In the safety of her bedroom, she had been so certain of her course. Now, it seemed inconceivable. She was marrying Adam Beaufort, a man she hardly knew. Surely making a marriage of convenience was madness.

At the church door, she stopped and let the train of her dress fall to the ground. Inside, the full length of the marbled aisle lay in front of her, with people crammed on either side, into every pew. Her breath came even faster.

At the far end of the aisle stood Adam. As she

watched, he turned, waiting for her. He was too far away. She couldn't see his face.

Unexpectedly, she yearned to push back her veil, to be able to see him.

The organ music started up, making her jump. She had to step forward.

Loyalty and dignity. Purity. Hope.

Violet marched up the aisle.

Chapter Eight

'Wilt thou have this Woman to thy wedded Wife, to live together after God's ordinance in the holy estate of Matrimony? Wilt thou love her, comfort her, honour and keep her in sickness and in health and, forsaking all other, keep thee only unto her, as long as ye both shall live?'

Broad-shouldered in his frock coat, Adam knelt beside Violet at the altar. She peeped up at him from beneath her veil. His dark head was bowed, his profile stern. Beneath the line of his chin was a perfectly tied cravat, emphasising the set of his jaw.

His voice came strong and steady. 'I will.'

Next, the priest addressed Violet. When her turn came to answer, she took a breath, so deep it sent the veil in a waft of air. After her bold walk down the aisle, her nerves and trepidation had returned as the marriage ceremony began.

There could be no turning back now. In spite of

her quaking limbs, she forced her voice to come out as firmly as Adam's. 'I will.'

Mr Coombes then hurried forward, beaming, to give Violet's hand to the priest, who placed it in Adam's.

Adam's long fingers curled arounds hers. As it had been when they shook hands on their marriage of convenience, only one month before, his grip was warm and strong, strangely reassuring.

In his deep clear voice he repeated the words.

'I, Adam Edward Charles, take thee, Violet Regina, to my wedded Wife...'

Adam Edward Charles. That was her bridegroom's full name. She hadn't known. It struck her again how little she knew about the man who stood beside her.

They loosened hands, then Violet took his.

'I, Violet Regina...' She repeated the familiar phrases after him. It was strange how she seemed to know the words, how easily they came to her.

Adam released her hand. From the pocket of his waistcoat he took a gold ring and laid it on the prayer book. The priest returned it to him. As he reached for her left hand he gave a perplexed frown at the sight of the satin glove. Rapidly she freed her ring finger, tugging away the removable satin section of the glove, and saw his start of surprise. The dent appeared in his cheek. Her finger looked so bare, waggling there alone. She felt tempted to laugh, her tension gone completely.

We will be friends she told herself. *That's what we agreed. I don't need to be afraid.*

He slipped the ring on her finger.

Finally, they stood together, man and wife.

His fingers brushed her cheek as he lifted the white veil.

Violet stared up at him. Instinctively, she took a step forward and lifted her face to his. The filmy veil in his hands, he, too, leaned towards her, so close, their lips almost met.

Then, with a start, Adam backed away.

'Adam tells us you're a suffragette.'

Jane, Adam's younger sister, smiled eagerly at Violet.

Violet lifted her glass of champagne. 'I am.'

Raising the glass to her lips, she drank. She needed refreshment after the wedding service. In spite of her near giggle over her glove, it had been more solemn than she had anticipated, with Adam kneeling beside her.

She glanced down at her ring finger. It was no longer bare. On it was the smooth gold ring that had a look of antiquity about it, even though it fitted her perfectly. A wedding ring meant their marriage of convenience must be taken seriously.

They had promised themselves to each other, before God. She was still unsettled by how much the ceremony had affected her. It had been a bigger commitment than she'd anticipated, one that resonated to the depths of her being, in the same way as when they'd shaken hands on the terms. Promises were promises. Vows were vows.

Violet creased her forehead. When Adam lifted the veil she'd worn throughout the service, they had almost kissed. His lips had nearly brushed hers, then he'd stepped away. It was customary, though not always followed, for the groom to kiss the bride at that moment in a wedding ceremony, but no one else had noticed what had happened, she was sure. She'd been amazed at how instinctive it had been to seek to seal their vows with a kiss. Of course, they intended to keep their marriage on a friendly basis, but she couldn't help wondering what it would have been like. Would it have been brief, a mere formality, or more like the kiss they had already shared?

It came again, the recollection of his lips on hers, when they had set their terms. She took another quick sip of the bubbly champagne.

'I want to know everything about the suffragettes,' Jane said, to her surprise.

Violet spluttered her champagne. 'You do?'

'They're marvellous!' said Jane. 'Why would women not want to vote?'

'I want to vote for my government,' Violet said seriously. To make a difference in their homes, in their communities, in their country, women had to have a voice.

We will do all that can be done to win the vote... No longer will we be angels in the house. We will be devils in the street.

The phrases from the letter she'd received before she set off for the church came back to her. In the pretty bridal reticule that matched her dress was her signed reply, along with the letter. It seemed to burn through the satin pouch.

Adam's elder sister, Arabella, joined them.

Violet smiled at her. Arabella inclined her head haughtily, but did not smile in response.

'So you're a suffragette, not a suffragist,' Jane said to Violet. 'I believe there is a difference.'

Violet nodded. 'The suffragists have been making polite argument for the vote for fifty years. They're led by Millicent Fawcett, who advises patience and convincing men that we are worthy of the vote. I admire Mrs Fawcett, but if we go by her methods, we suffragettes believe we'll be waiting for eternity.'

'And the suffragettes...'

'That's what the press call the group founded by Mrs Emmeline Pankhurst and her daughters Christabel and Sylvia,' Violet explained. 'The Pankhursts formed the Women's Social and Political Union. They considered Mrs Fawcett's progress too slow.'

Jane's eyes were on stalks. 'Have you met any of the Pankhursts?'

Violet shook her head. 'I've heard them speak. They are fine leaders for the Cause. Mrs Pankhurst and her daughters are the most inspiring women. They have such resolve, such determination, that on this issue women must be seen and heard. Deeds, not words.'

'That's the suffragette motto, isn't it?'

Violet nodded. It was one she was prepared to live by.

Taking another sip of champagne, she glanced around the reception hall. She spotted her mama, looking terrified, conversing with Mrs Beaufort, grand in grey silk and pearls. Adam had been standing beside them, but she couldn't see him now.

It suddenly struck her. She, too, was Mrs Beaufort. Mrs Adam Beaufort, for women's first names were not generally used. Precedence in address went to the men, like the vote.

One day, she said to herself.

'We saw a suffrage play once,' said Jane. 'It was called *Votes for Women!* It was all about the Cause.'

'Oh, I did want to see that play,' said Violet. It hadn't reached Manchester, to her disappointment.

'It was marvellous,' Jane told her. 'Do you remember, Arabella?'

Arabella pursed her lips. 'Vaguely.'

'The suffragettes have been undertaking all kinds of daring deeds here in London,' Jane said, agog. 'Holding rallies and going on marches. I read about suffragettes who throw eggs at Members of Parliament and chain themselves to railings, and smash glass windows.'

'They're breaking the law,' said Arabella coldly.

Violet lifted her chin. 'Militant means are necessary.'

'Would you be jailed for the Cause, Violet?' Jane asked breathlessly.

Hanging her banners was against propriety, certainly, and climbing Adam's balcony had been dangerous enough. And now...

She twisted the handle of her reticule. 'If you believe in the Cause, as I do, then you must be prepared to go to any lengths.'

Arabella sniffed. 'It sounds foolhardy to me.'

'Doesn't it bother you, Arabella?' Violet asked passionately. 'That we have no rights? What are your views on the Cause?'

'I am not opposed to suffrage, but there are methods that seem much more respectable.'

Violet lifted her chin higher. 'The time for being respectable has passed.'

'So you'd put yourself in danger.' Jane sounded awed.

'We suffragettes won't wait any longer. The vote won't be given to us—we must seize it ourselves. Increase the pressure. Be more active, more visible. We must rally to the Cause in a bold new manner.'

Unexpectedly, Jane hugged her. 'Oh, Violet, Adam is the best brother in the world and I'm so glad you're our new sister.'

Arabella looked down her nose.

Champagne glass in hand, Violet hugged Jane back. How lovely it would be, if they became good friends. She was an only child and, though she'd never felt lonely, she would value Jane's sisterhood.

Sisterhood.

Smiling and nodding to the guests, Violet made her way out of the ballroom into the hotel lobby and looked towards the front door of the hotel.

She needed some space and air. A moment to think, to breathe.

Then, from the satin pouch, she pulled out the lilac letter.

Among the fountains, Adam strolled the hotel garden. The hotel the Coombes had chosen for the wedding reception was magnificent, a pure white building that reminded him of Violet's wedding dress. No expense had been spared, although it was a small wedding, by society standards. Only one hundred guests, but the reception room had become constricting. He'd had to get away.

He liked London and knew it well, of course, but at moments like this he longed for Beauley. He preferred the space of the Kent countryside. The manor wasn't far from London, but it was far enough away to feel the freshness of the country air, to see the broad fields, the open sky.

He breathed in and frowned. The London air held its own scent of carriages and coal, but that wasn't it. He could smell violets. He could pick out the fragrance easily now, as if he'd become sensitised to the scent.

Sure enough, following his nose he found a tiny clump of them in a corner of the garden, hidden in the undergrowth, as if shy. Yet their fragrance was lingering, powerful. He stroked a purple petal with his finger.

Walking on, he passed a pond, spotted a wrought-iron seat. He slumped on to it and rested his top hat in his hands.

The wedding ceremony had been more demanding than he had anticipated. When the organ struck up, he'd watched Violet coming down the aisle, frosted in a pure white veil. Her step was firm, her head high. In spite of her purposeful stride, he'd sensed her nerves during the ceremony. He'd sought to steady her with his presence and, after a while, she'd calmed.

The threat to his own equilibrium had come later, when he'd lifted her veil.

He'd never dreamed that one simple act would be so provocative. At that moment, it was as if he'd never seen her before.

She was now his wife.

His wife.

He'd lifted the filmy veil over her hair, revealing its rich chestnut tones, piled up in loose curls. Encountered those blue eyes, so wide and frank. Seen the steady chin and the pink bow of a mouth he'd avoided thinking about for the past month, reminding him of that stupendous kiss.

Then she'd smiled.

That smile.

Open.

Alive.

Free.

He'd almost kissed her then, his new bride, lured by that intoxicating violet scent that wafted around her like the filmy veil. Just in time he remembered his prudent plan not to do so. Their marriage had to be maintained on a platonic footing. It was best to start as they meant to go on. But his own reaction, that surge of desire, had been impossible to ignore.

He'd known it at that instant.

He had feelings for her. Dangerous feelings that he must resist. Feelings that weren't part of their terms of agreement. The kind of feelings that meant a gentleman should not enter into a marriage of convenience.

Damnation.

'Cheer up, old chap.' A voice came from behind a rhododendron bush. 'You've only just got married.'

Adam looked up to see Mr Coombes approaching, puffing an enormous cigar.

Mr Coombes chuckled. 'Marriage takes a fellow by surprise.'

That was one way of putting it, Adam thought drily.

'Cigar?'

Mr Coombes plopped on to the bench beside Adam with an audible groan. His belly protruded, imperilling his waistcoat buttons.

'No, thank you,' Adam replied. 'I don't smoke.'

'I'm not supposed to.' Mr Coombes winked. 'Bad for my heart.'

'How is your health now?' Adam had been concerned for the man.

'Fully recovered. No more turns. But the ladies worry. That's why I'm hiding out here, out of sight of Mrs Coombes.'

Mr Coombes inhaled, coughed and blew out a puff of smoke. 'Fear not. I know I'm now your father-in-law, but I'm not going to give you any marital advice.'

Adam's shoulders relaxed. Even though he'd grown in respect for Reginald Coombes and his considerable business prowess, he didn't want any personal advice. He'd done without it all his life. His father had never proffered any, nor been capable of it. And Adam's marital situation was unique, to say the least.

'Best thing there is, marriage,' said Mr Coombes.

Adam jerked back his head. 'A man doesn't hear that view very often.'

Certainly not at his club, where many men hid from their wives on a daily basis. Or at home, growing up. His parents had demonstrated how

marriage could deteriorate into bitterness and ac-
rimony, with continual arguments over money.
He'd done his best to protect his sisters. Jane had
escaped the worst of it, being younger and still in
the nursery, but Arabella, like himself, had unfortunately witnessed many distressing scenes. His
father's drunken anger, his mother's storms and
tears. All he knew was that, in marriage, emotions could run out of control. He would ensure
that in his own they did not.

Mr Coombes gazed into the distance, took another puff of his cigar. 'Look after her, won't
you?'

'I'm sure Violet would say she can look after
herself.' Adam recalled his first sighting of her
on his balcony. She'd been fearless.

'She would at that,' Mr Coombes agreed, with
a chuckle, as he tapped the end of his cigar on
the edge of the cast-iron seat. 'She's no shrinking violet.'

Adam smiled. He had to admit his instinct to
rescue her had come into play at first. But she
had made it clear she didn't need rescuing. Her
negotiations in their marriage of convenience had
been endearing, as well as intelligent and remark-
ably businesslike. She was so like her father with
his honest stare. She'd clearly inherited his skills
as a businessman. Coombes Chocolates was an

empire, not as vast as King Edward's, but one that required astute management all the same. It was a shame Violet couldn't follow him into the business. She had the ability.

Adam stood, and put on his top hat. 'If you will excuse me, I must find Violet.'

Mr Coombes waved his cigar. 'Of course.'

Adam strode away. He knew what he had to do. He had to be with her, alone.

Inside, the hotel ballroom with its vast ceiling picked out in swirls of gilt seemed even more crowded. The chamber orchestra played on valiantly in spite of the noise. Yet after a few minutes pushing through the gabbling crowd of people, some seated at tables, some standing, all swilling champagne, and many of whom he barely recognised, he still hadn't found her.

No bridal veil. No white dress was to be seen.

'Have you seen Violet?' he asked Jane, after another hunt.

Jane shook her head, surprised. 'I spoke to her earlier. She was telling me all about the suffragettes.'

Adam returned to the hotel garden.

Past the fountains. Down the path through the flower beds. Past the pond. The only sign of life was a curl of cigar smoke from behind the rhododendrons and an audible cough.

Through the French doors, back inside the ball-room. At a corner table he could hear his mama still holding forth in conversation with Mrs Coombes, who looked rather pale.

He searched on, with increasing urgency.

Jane rushed up. 'Have you found her?'

Adam shook his head.

Up the stairs, two at a time, to the landing and hotel chambers. Downstairs, through the lobby, outside, down the steps, the heels of his boots crunching on to the curved gravel drive.

At the doors of the hotel Adam came to a halt.

There could be no doubt.

Violet had vanished.

Chapter Nine

'Gave utterance by the yearning of an eye...'
—Alfred, Lord Tennyson: *'Love and Duty'*
(1842)

'Have you seen the bride?'

The hotel doorman, resplendent in a royal-blue jacket with gold epaulettes on his shoulders, looked at Adam with startled expression and shook his head. 'I've only just come on duty, sir.'

'Thank you.' Adam spun on his heel and headed back into the hotel lobby. The huge chandelier sent light dancing over the marble floor, but he didn't stop to admire it.

'Sir!' the doorman called.

Adam rushed back to the front of the hotel.

The doorman pointed. 'I've not seen any other brides today. Is that yours?'

'Indeed,' Adam said through gritted teeth.

A slender, firm-footed figure, dressed in white, hurried towards the hotel. There was no mistaking her. Her veil was gone and she wore a white-satin wrap, thrown loosely over her head and shoulders. The train of her wedding dress had disappeared. Just another detachable part of her attire, it seemed. He recalled how she had whisked away the finger of her satin glove to allow him to slip on the wedding ring. He'd heard her suppressed giggle. He'd wanted to laugh himself.

He didn't feel like laughing now.

Relief at the sight of her safe and well flooded his veins, combined with a blast of anger.

'Where have you been?' he demanded, when she reached the columns that flanked the front steps.

She looked up at him with her candid blue eyes. They flickered with surprise, followed by caution. She removed the wrap from her hair, let it fall to her shoulders. 'I needed some air. And... I had some business to attend to.'

He drew her behind one of the stone columns, away from the doorman. 'What in damnation do you mean by that? What kind of business could you possibly have today?'

She bit her lip. 'Suffragette business.'

Adam took a step back. 'On our wedding day?'

She hesitated, then nodded.

He ran his hand through his hair, pushed it back from his forehead. He'd long lost his top hat, searching for her. 'You left the reception. Without telling me.'

Again, a nod. Nothing more.

'Where did you go?' he asked, infuriated. Somehow he managed to keep his voice low. Her behaviour was outrageous.

She set her lips together. 'I can't say.'

He gazed at her in disbelief.

'I didn't go far,' she reassured him. 'It wasn't on purpose, but it took longer than I expected. I'm very sorry. I hoped no one would notice I was gone.'

He raised an eyebrow. 'You didn't think your bridegroom would notice?'

Her mouth twitched. 'I've never had a bridegroom before.'

The humour of the situation finally found him. He felt the corners of his own mouth lift.

'It's quite disconcerting,' he said drily, 'to have misplaced one's wife so soon after the ceremony.'

The twitch of her mouth became a tentative smile. 'I'm sorry.'

'Please don't disappear like that again.'

She seemed to debate with herself, then the pink bow of her mouth set again in a firm line. 'I can't make any promises.'

He jerked his head back. She reminded him again of Reginald Coombes, her self-made millionaire father. They were made of the same stuff.

She lifted her chin, in what was becoming a

familiar gesture. 'I warned you. Being a suffragette means everything to me.'

Adam exhaled. He'd never anticipated this from
her. Even on suffragette business, as she called
it, he couldn't allow her to simply set off on her
own.

Adam glanced around. The doorman was making a patent effort not to appear to listen. He
would have to pursue the matter another time.
He would let it go, for now.

'Why were you looking for me?' Violet asked.

'I want to take you to Beauley Manor,' he said.

Adam glanced at Violet from the opposite seat
of the carriage. 'We're almost home.'

Home.

From beneath the brim of her hat, Violet stared
out of the open carriage window. They had been
on the same woodland road for many miles. Min-
gling with the woods was a patchwork of fields
and hedgerows, and winding lanes that led to
houses, orchards and hop farms.

Such a lane would soon lead to Beauley Manor.
She wondered what it would be like. It was old,
she knew that, since Adan had told her it dated
from Tudor times. Beyond that she knew nothing of his home.

His home and now hers.

The evening sky was clear of clouds and the lowering sun still shone, but the evening air had begun to chill. She took a gulp of air. The country air was so much fresher than in London and in Manchester, too.

Violet pulled her satin coat tighter. It had the same pearl buttons and embroidered violets as her wedding gown. The long, lacy train of her wedding dress had been removed before the wedding reception. Now the dress formed an underskirt of the cutaway coat, designed for her going-away ensemble. It could be worn indoors or out. Beside her was the satin wrap she'd hidden herself under as she'd hurried to and from the hotel.

They had travelled almost silently together, all the way from London. To her dismay, tension had developed between them at the hotel, when she got back from posting her letter and refused to tell him where she had been. It was a tension she regretted.

In the hotel suite her father had provided, she'd rapidly removed her long veil and seized her satin wrap. She'd first intended only to take some air, but the idea had come to her that she might as well deliver her reply to the militant group, before she lost her nerve. She hadn't wanted to ask anyone else to post it, for the sake of secrecy, and she hadn't had a stamp, or thought to ask for one at the hotel. Presuming the Piccadilly address on the letter to be quite close by, she'd seized the chance and hastened there by foot. Once again, her lack of knowledge of London's streets had landed her in trouble. It had taken her far longer than she had expected.

She'd slid her reply into the brass letterbox of the anonymous-looking terraced building, then raced back full of anxiety, only to find Adam waiting for her between the marble columns of the hotel, glowering.

How she loathed not being able to reveal where she had been, to have a deception come between them on their wedding day. It seemed wrong and not how she wanted to start their life together. But she had joined the top-secret suffragette group now. There was no turning back.

She peeped at Adam. Hatless, still attired in his frock coat and cravat, the breeze from the open window blew a lock of dark hair across his profile. It shielded his expression as he stared out of the window, but she suspected his thoughts weren't on the passing view.

His flash of anger when she'd disappeared from the wedding reception had passed quickly, but it had alarmed her all the same. It didn't bode well. He knew there was something she was keeping from him. And at the church, he hadn't kissed her. Again the unsettling recollection popped into her mind.

Pushing it away, she, too, forced her eyes to stay on the view outside the carriage, not on the man seated across from her, his knee only inches from hers.

The oak woods they passed through were wild and beautiful. The trees were dense enough to be a forest, more than woodland. Among the trees she'd recognised the wings and calls of kestrels, wrens and swallows. Butterflies darted among the early bluebells and wood anemones. She thought she even glimpsed a badger, too.

'Not far now,' Adam said. 'The road to the manor can be marshy. But we've been lucky today.'

'The weather's been marvellous,' Violet replied.

Help, she thought. We're discussing the weather. Their new tension seemed like a dark cloud over them. But the day had remained sunny, for May. The bright sky beckoned them onwards, towards the setting sun. She took off her hat and lifted her face towards it.

They turned down a lane, past a gurgling water mill, and into a small, pretty village. Thatched cottages lined the road, some stone, some half-timbered. In the square was a stone church, a public house, a bakery and a dairy, and a village green where a few boys were playing cricket.

'The village of Beauley officially lies in the manor grounds,' Adam told her. 'Or rather, it used to. The cottages are still tied to the manor, but much of the land around the village has been sold off.'

'Recently?' she asked.

He gave a rueful smile. 'In my father's lifetime, yes, if that's what you're asking. But perhaps it is for the best. Perhaps it isn't right to own a village. The social reformists would certainly think so.'

'The Cadbury family have built a village and they are social reformists,' Violet said, eagerly, relieved to find a safe but interesting topic they could discuss. She wanted to return to their former ease. 'Perhaps you've heard of the place. It is called Bournville. It not only provides excellent conditions for their workers, but low-cost homes, too. It has three hundred houses, each with their own garden, for the growing of fruit and vegetables.'

He raised an eyebrow. 'So you're not only a suffragette, but also a social reformer.'

'If I could have my way, I would like Coombes Chocolates to provide more pleasant conditions for our factory workers.' It was something she'd long wanted to discuss further with her father, if she had been able to follow him into the Coombes Chocolates business. 'At Bournville they provide such marvellous facilities. There are kitchens for hot meals, a school for the workers' children and a nurse to visit the sick. The factory is surrounded by parks and recreation grounds. It's known as a factory in a garden.'

'A factory in a garden,' Adam mused. 'Kent is known as the Garden of England.'

'I can see why. It's beautiful.' She glanced out the carriage window again. The village of Beauley couldn't be more charming. A few of the villagers waved as they went past, recognising the carriage. 'I hope you don't mind me discussing matters of business.'

'Not at all.'

'Some men do.'

'I can't say I'm a social reformist,' Adam said slowly, 'but I am certainly interested in such things. I, too, would like to make village life at Beauley as conducive to happiness as possible for those who live here.'

'I'm of the belief that employers have significant social obligations,' Violet said. 'I suppose it is the same for landowners.'

'Not all landowners. But that's the case for me now, at Beauley. Up at the manor we have significant duties to our tenants and workers. The question is whether we can meet them. I certainly intend to.' A muscle flared around his mouth, then his jaw firmed. 'Perhaps we can take a tour of the Cadbury's Bournville factory one day. Together.'

'Really?'

His glance was direct. 'It's your money that will help make village life better for the people of Beauley. Do you think I won't allow you to have a say?'

Violet breathed out. She'd been holding her breath the whole journey, judging by the way the whalebones of her corset rubbed painfully against her ribs. His reaction when she returned to the hotel had alarmed her. But his controlled anger appeared to have passed.

'I'd like to do that,' she replied with equal directness. 'Very much.'

'Then we shall travel together,' he said.

The carriage turned another corner.

'Here we are,' Adam said.

Violet threw open the carriage window.

Adam pulled wide the gates. He always opened the heavy iron gates himself, rather than having the coach driver struggle to hold the horses at the same time. They were rusty now and creaked as if they yawned. Once upon a time there had been a gatekeeper at Beauley Manor, but those days were long gone. Only a crumbling shell of the gatehouse remained.

He waved at the coach driver to pass through the stone gateway. As the wheels crunched into the drive, he saw Violet's enthralled face as she gazed out of the open carriage window. Her chestnut hair was blowing in the wind, curling around her face, her cheeks pink and her blue eyes wide. She looked like a royal visitor. A princess. In a way she was. A chocolate princess. Yet her matter-of-fact manner, her concern for others, her social reformism and her passion for women's suffrage—they made her someone real, not confectionery.

He heaved the gate wider. Her disappearance at the wedding reception and her refusal to tell him where she had been rankled with him all the way on the long drive home. Only now, as he reached Beauley, did he feel the tension in his body dissipate, as it always did when he came home.

The carriage stopped. At a run he reached it, grabbed the handle and leapt inside. With a rap on the inside roof of the carriage, they were off again. The horses were slower now, as if relieved to be home, too.

The drive narrowed. There were woods on either side of the manor, still owned by the Beaufort family. They had been stocked with deer once, but they too were long gone.

Yet his heart lifted at the sight of Beauley.

He watched Violet's face, struck by how important it was to him that she like it, too. Normally, he would have his eyes fixed ahead, but this time he found himself transfixed by Violet as she encountered his home for the first time.

Another twist in the drive.

The pink bow of her mouth opened as she gasped. Her mouth had been the subject of his ruminations as he'd fallen asleep the night before, he recalled. Her mouth and the taste of violet creams.

He opened the carriage window and let the cool air blow. As he watched the manor appear to rise up before them, as it always did, as if surrounded by water or mist. The ancient bricked building of mellow stone was a red so faded it was now the colour of a rose, its two square towers crenelated with battlements had stones missing in places, but still it lost none of the effect, although it had never been a true fortress. Arrow slips crisscrossed the towers.

The carriage rolled on towards the circular drive. The lower windows were arched, giving it the impression of a church. At the centre, above the massive door, the front of the house was white, striped with timber beams in the Tudor style that had become prevalent in Shakespeare's day, but the studded, wooden doors were that of a small fortress.

He drew his head inside the carriage. Violet was silent, staring, as if spellbound.

'Beauley Manor was designed upon a fort, but it has never been a real one,' he told her. No battles had ever been fought at Beauley Manor, unless you counted those waged in the hall between his mother and father, after one of his father's drinking and gambling bouts. 'The Tudor Beauforts went in for effect. It even had a moat.'

She peered closer. 'I can't see a moat.'

He grinned ruefully. 'There's no moat any more, but I can show you the damp foundations it left behind in the cellars.' It wasn't even possible to store wine there without it being ruined, but with his father's habits, his mother had always called that a blessing in disguise.

She looked at him over her shoulder. 'Could the manor ever have a moat again?'

'I suppose so,' he said. 'But it would cost—'

'A fortune?' she put in, with a smile.

She'd made him laugh. The last of the tension dissipated between them, like the mist around Beauley.

She returned her gaze to the manor. 'The effect

is magnificent. I admire the taste of the Tudor Beauforts.'

'Would you like the history lesson?'

'Yes, please.'

'The manor was built by Sir Thomas Beaufort. At the time of its design, fashions were changing and he planned to build an entire Tudor house in the new style inside the fortress walls. It was aimed to impress their visitors, especially royal visitors.'

'Have there been many royal visitors?'

'A few, over the centuries. In any case, that's why there are remnants of both styles. It's rare for such fortress aspects to remain. They are certainly what I like best. I played up on the battlements with my bow and arrow as a boy.'

One of each. A boy and a girl.

The memory came into his head. That's what they'd shaken hands upon, when they'd agreed to their marriage of convenience. But they wouldn't have children, not yet.

He cleared this throat. 'The original Beauforts who built the manor changed the spelling of their name, to make it sound more French. It was the fashion of the day.'

Violet smiled. 'My mama would approve of that.'

'They were an ambitious family, Sir Thomas

most of all. Or perhaps it was his wife with the ambitions. She was known for her striving at court.'

'It must be extraordinary, to be able to trace your family back to Tudor times,' she said. 'I'm not sure the Coombes family can.'

'We all had ancestors in Tudor times, whether we can trace our families or not. Otherwise neither of us would be here.'

She burst out laughing. 'I never thought of it like that.'

'I'm sure we'd both turn up the same number of scoundrels,' he drawled.

He pointed out of the carriage window at the pale red sunset. 'I'm glad you're seeing Beauley now. The manor is at its best at this time of day.'

The horses sauntered on, the gravel crunching beneath their hooves as they came closer to the manor. Closer, its proportions were even lovelier, full of grace.

Violet raised her hand to shade her eyes. 'It's as if there is still a moat. I can imagine it so clearly.'

A muscle moved in his jaw. She saw his home as he did. 'It does seem that way, to me.'

She turned to him, with her eager expression. 'Now I understand.'

Adam raised an eyebrow.

'Why, it's alive.' She pointed to the manor. 'It's

the same as the trees, and the plants and the flowers. It's a living thing.'

She clasped her hands together. The gold ring glinted on her finger. 'I didn't realise it before. We're alike.'

Adam leaned forward. 'In what way?'

'Beauley Manor,' Violet said. 'It's your Cause.'

Violet took Adam's hand as he helped her down from the carriage. 'Welcome home.'

Home. The word tingled through her at the touch of his hand. It had caused another of those unexpected sensations that travelled through to her core. It was as if her entire body was on alert.

'Thank you.' Moving away from the carriage, she took a steadying breath and looked about eagerly. She'd been amazed by what she'd seen as they'd driven towards the Manor. She had been expecting grandeur, not beauty and serenity, and up close, it was even more dazzling.

'It's beautiful,' she breathed.

He crooked a smile. 'That's what it means. Beauley. A beautiful piece of land.'

How perfect he looked at Beauley Manor, she thought. Even more lines seemed to have disappeared from his face.

She peered about. She ought to be wearing her

hat, but the sun was setting fast behind the manor and she didn't want to waste a minute.

'Would you like to come indoors?' he asked. 'Do you need refreshment after the journey?'

She shook her head. 'The light has almost gone. Can we take a walk in the grounds first?'

He looked down at the tips of her satin shoes, visible beneath her skirt. 'Some ladies would want to mind their shoes.'

Her shoes had already scurried across Piccadilly, but she wouldn't remind him of that. 'A short walk,' she pleaded.

He gave a slight bow. 'As you wish.'

As they turned towards the lawn, a bark came from behind them. Violet spun around to see an orange-and-white dog racing towards her.

Adam's voice rang out. 'Beau!'

Violet laughed as she pulled off her glove to ruffle the dog's fur. 'Hello!'

She looked up to meet Adam's eyes, dark blue and unfathomable as he watched her. He still wore his long dark coat with his bow tie loosened around his neck, his hair whipped back by the wind from his high forehead.

'What name did you call the dog?' she asked, breathlessly.

'Beau.' He shrugged. 'Hardly original, I know, since our name and house are based on the same word, as I've just told you. But our dogs have always been called Beau.'

'Is he a spaniel?'

'He's a Brittany. They're a kind of spaniel. They're bird dogs. Good for hunting.'

Half-kneeling beside her, he ran his hand through Beau's fur. 'He's a bit old now. Past his best as a gun dog, aren't you, boy, but still good company.'

'He's lovely.'

Beau barked.

Adam surveyed her quizzically, yet his mouth had curved. 'Beau doesn't take immediately to many people. What a puzzle you are, Miss Coombes. I mean, Mrs Beaufort.'

'It's strange that women change their names upon marriage, but men don't, is it not?' Violet made conversation as they set off, with Beau at their heels. The tingling sensation in her body, caused by his closeness, continued as they began to walk the grounds.

'I must confess I have never given it much consideration,' he said. 'But now you mention it, I suppose the custom is strange.'

'There are many customs that I'm sure we are used to that would seem strange if we came upon them elsewhere,' she said.

'Certainly.'

Violet bit her lip. She was talking too much. She rarely did so, unless she was nervous. She regretted that the exchange at the hotel had come between them. Yet there was more to it than that. Surely he was less forthcoming than before. His reserve, his detachment, seemed more pronounced.

They followed the path as it led around the long lawn to garden beds bursting with bright flowers: jonquils, daffodils and the first of the bluebells. A squirrel darted among the trees.

She lifted her face to the last of the sun's rays. It was companionable, walking without having to make conversation, and their former ease began to return. He was taller than she, longer legged in his trousers, but she kept up with him, even in her skirts.

'We hold a garden party for the village here in the grounds every summer,' Adam told her as they returned to the front of the Manor. 'It's a big event for everyone in the village and in the area, especially the children.'

'I can imagine children playing on the lawn,' she said, before recalling their discussion a month ago about having children. She felt herself flush.

Whether he also recalled it she couldn't be sure. He indicated the huge, wooden front doors. 'Are you ready to see inside?'

A thrill of excitement ran through her. There was something magical about the old fortress. She nodded.

Adam clicked his fingers. Beau, who had been bounding around nearby as if he were a puppy instead of an old dog, went instantly to his side.

Violet followed him to the doors studded with iron. She half-expected a butler to open them at their approach, but Adam turned the iron handle himself.

'Do you have many staff here?' she asked curiously. He'd opened the gates, too, she'd noted from the carriage.

'There are a couple of servants. Old retainers mainly, in the kitchen and garden. Most of the staff are in London at the moment, so we're on our own tonight,' he replied, over his shoulder.

Inside, the hall was square and dimly lit. A suit of armour stood in one corner, and some deer antlers adorned the walls.

He seized a candelabra and lit the stub of a candle. 'I'm afraid the decor hasn't changed much over the centuries.'

'It's charming.' The atmosphere held her in thrall the minute she stepped over the threshold. She half-expected to see a ghostly welcome committee of previous Beauforts, so thick was the aura of history.

The suit of armour creaked noisily, as if someone were inside it.

She jumped back, unable to suppress a louder noise that was half-squeal, half-giggle.

Adam chuckled. The younger look on his face returned.

'Are there ghosts here at Beauley?' she managed to ask.

'Ah. There may be a few on the staff.' He knocked on the helmet of the armour. 'But I think they're in London tonight, too.'

Violet's giggle turned into a full-blown laugh.

He grinned. 'If your nerves will hold and you'd care to explore further, we go upstairs first. There's a solar. It's my favourite room. An old-style Tudor room that has been retained.'

'I've never heard of a solar,' she said, fascinated.

He indicated the stairs. 'After you.'

Aware of him behind her, she ascended the wooden staircase, scuffed in places, up to a small gallery on the landing with glass windows in the bold colours. A red-tiled passageway lay in front. She stopped and looked at the glass. It featured a crest, a stag gazing straight at her, on a red-and-blue background.

'The Beaufort coat of arms,' Adam said. 'The solar is the next door to your left.'

Violet pushed open the chiselled wooden door with interest. The solar was a large room, lined with faded tapestries on the painted walls. Many of the tapestries were moth-eaten with holes. At the arched windows were wide cushioned ledges for seats. The cushions, again, were faded and worn, so thin they barely looked comfortable, but they were scrupulously clean. At one end of the room was a hooded fireplace, with wooden screens on each side, and more of the threadbare cushioned seats, plus some scratched leather club chairs and an old sofa.

He indicated the wooden screens. 'Those screens used to hide the beds. In Tudor times.'

'Do you mean this is our bedroom?' she asked, astonished.

'Not any more. It's a sitting room by day, designed to catch the warmth of the sun. But in times past, the whole family would have slept in here. Now there are bedrooms further along the passageway. They were built later.'

She gazed around in fascination.

Adam stepped back from the doorway. 'Come downstairs again and I'll show you the great hall.'

She followed his broad back down the stairs.

'Oh…' She sighed when they entered the huge room. 'It's wonderful.'

She stepped into the hall to see more clearly.

On a side wall a large fireplace lay beneath a stone arch so big several people could have sat inside it. The walls were part-stone, part-plaster in a pale shade of primrose that blended with the red-brown tiles on the floor. At the other end of the hall a long, polished table stood on a low wooden dais.

'I feel as if I'm in the tale of Arthur and his knights,' she confessed. How easily she could imagine the vast room ringing with laughter and talk, food and wine laid out on long tables. 'There must have been many a feast in this room.'

'There have been many, over the years.' Adam glanced at his pocket watch. 'I can't promise you a feast, but we can have supper here in the hall or in the solar, as you like.' He looked at her directly. 'There's something I need to discuss with you.'

Unexpectedly Violet's heart thumped. 'What's that?'

'Kissing the bride,' said Adam.

Chapter Ten

'The lights of sunset and of sunrise mix'd
In that brief night; the summer night...'
—Alfred, Lord Tennyson: *'Love and Duty'*
(1842)

Violet's voice came out a little higher than usual. 'I believe it is the custom for the groom to kiss the bride.'

Stood in front of the altar, they had almost done so. Was he annoyed with her, for the way she had lifted her lips to his? She'd sought his kiss at that moment, she could not deny it. Her face flushed.

Adam exhaled. 'I believe it is.'

He roamed away from her, towards the long oak table that stood at the far end of the hall.

Perhaps this matter would be better discussed over dinner,' he said at last 'It has been a long day. You must be tired and hungry.'

'I'm not particularly hungry.' Nor was she especially tired. A nervous energy coursed through her veins.

'All the same,' he said evenly, 'I'd prefer not to have this conversation on an empty stomach. I asked for some food to be left for us. I'll go and see to it.

He left the hall. To distract herself from their forthcoming conversation, and from the heat still warming her cheeks, she gazed again around the hall. It was beautiful. Even its age and shabbiness couldn't disguise that. The evening sun that came through the diamond-shaped window panes lit the room in a golden glow, even though no fire or lamps were lit. But it would be draughty, she guessed, in the cold of winter.

As she drew closer, she saw that the old oak table was highly polished. So, too, were the tall silver candlesticks upon it, with white wax candles in them, unlit. In spite of the obvious age of the Manor, there was not a sense of neglect. Adam had said there were not many staff, but they evidently worked hard. She wondered how much of that was to do with Adam's obvious love for his home. From the way he had leapt down to open the gate for the coach driver, he was clearly thoughtful towards his staff and they doubtless respected him in turn.

Behind the table hung a faded tapestry, depicting a hunt. It showed a similar stag to the stained window upstairs. Moving closer, she examined it. She was deeply interested in women's handiwork. Why, the stitching was exquisite, but it needed repair, in places. She ran a gentle finger over it. A cloud of dust emanated at her lightest touch.

'That tapestry is believed to have been hand-worked by a Beaufort.'

Adam's voice came from behind her.

She swung around.

He lifted the silver tray he carried. 'Gatekeeper and now butler.'

She smiled. She liked the side of Adam Beaufort she was seeing at Beauley Manor, but her stomach remained tight with nerves.

He propped the tray on the table. 'I hope you won't be averse to some champagne and sandwiches.'

Violet looked down at the tray of food. They weren't the kind of sandwiches she expected to be served. Instead of thin, delicate quarters without a crust, thick slabs of bread encased orange slices of salmon and green curls of cress.

'In Manchester we call sandwiches like those doorstops,' she said, before she could stop herself.

He looked perplexed.

'Sandwiches that are so big you can keep doors open with them,' she explained, wishing she had held her tongue.

To her relief he laughed. 'These ones might even keep the Beauley doors open. Forgive my handiwork. The cook has gone to London. Unfortunately my instructions have not been followed with regard to our meal, in the excitement of the wedding, no doubt.'

He moved around the table to stand beside her. He seemed to carry the scent of the woods around Beauley Manor on his skin.

'May I?' He indicated towards the light satin coat she still wore. 'Since I am playing butler.'

He'd removed his dark frock coat and his neck-tie, too, leaving only the wine-coloured waist-coat and a pristine, cuffed white shirt, revealing his strong throat. She'd not seen that part of his body before. She tried not to stare. 'Thank you.'

He shifted behind her, his presence even more acute. With suddenly fumbling fingers she undid the pearl buttons at her bodice that held the coat together and shrugged it off. Without touching her, he stretched his arms around to lift it from her shoulders. Only his warm fingers brushed hers as her he took it away.

He laid it over one of the carved chairs and pulled out another for her.

She sank on to the chair with a sense of relief as he lit first one, then another of the tall white candles.

He shook the match to blow it out. 'Parts of Beauley are still to be converted to electricity.'

Violet hid her surprise at the information. By

the tightening of his jaw made evident in the flickering candlelight, she suspected it was another expense his father had spent at the gaming tables instead.

A cork popped. Adam poured the champagne into round, flat glasses and passed her one. 'What shall we toast on our wedding night? Perhaps you would care to make it.'

Violet raised her glass.

'To women's suffrage,' she said firmly.

'Indeed.' He, too, raised his glass, the dent playing in his cheek. 'And to Beauley Manor. Let us toast our respective causes.'

He touched his glass to hers. As he did so, their fingers brushed again.

Violet took a gulp of champagne.

Silently he passed her the plate of sandwiches. Both the bread and the salmon was fresh. It tasted delicious.

'I was hungrier than I thought,' she said between mouthfuls.

'I thought you may be.' He, too, finished one sandwich and then another.

'Would you care for another glass of champagne?' he asked.

Violet shook her head. She couldn't wait any longer. Plain speaking was always best. 'At the church. At the end of the wedding ceremony…'

Adam laid his champagne glass on the table. 'Did you want me to kiss you?'

Her face flushed again.

'I hadn't considered it beforehand.' Yet she had almost kissed him, she had to admit to herself. It had seemed so natural.

'I wanted to kiss you,' he said slowly. 'That's why I didn't.'

The wooden legs of his chair scraped across the tiled floor as he pushed it back. Going to the window he pulled the curtains across the glass, leaving the room in darkness, except at the table, where the pool of candlelight reflected the silver candlesticks in the polished top.

Violet stared at the stag on the tapestry. In the flickering light it seemed almost to move as fast as her beating pulse.

He returned to his seat. With only the candle-light now to see by, his expression was more difficult to discern. 'I have no dispute with our marriage of convenience. The terms suit us both well. But it might be prudent if we discuss further the practicalities of keeping our physical contact to a minimum.'

Violet gulped. 'Oh.'

He reached for his glass. 'We must avoid… entanglements.'

She drew a breath. 'Entanglements…?'

He drank again, more deeply. 'It seems insensitive to discuss the subject on our wedding day.'

'We agreed to plain speaking,' she said quickly.

'Indeed.' He paused. 'Perhaps it will make it easier if I explain more fully why our current arrangement will suit me.'

Violet nodded. She wanted to know more about him, very much. Beauley and its owner were beginning to fascinate her.

His eyes darkened. 'I grew up in this house, as you know. But there are certain aspects of life at Beauley I wish to leave behind. My parents had a volatile marriage, exacerbated by my father's drinking and gambling. There were constant quarrels, angry arguments, that took place right here in this hall. I have no wish to witness such scenes in my life ever again.'

He spoke with detached control, but Violet could sense the profound sense of unhappiness reined in by his dispassionate words. Suddenly, she could picture him as a young boy, listening to his parents rage at each other.

'It must have been terrible for you,' she said with compassion.

He shrugged. 'It was a difficult environment for a child, certainly. There was constant tension, with the threat of unpleasant scenes, or worse.

That's why it is so important to me that we be honest and open with each other.'

Her stomach lurched. She wished she'd been able to be more honest with him at the hotel, about delivering the letter. But she'd had no choice.

'For years, the whole of Beauley Manor has been in chaos,' he went on. 'It is something I abhor. My goal now is to bring security and stability to the family, to the estate.' He slid aside the candle to look directly into her eyes. 'There's another matter to consider that we have not discussed. We have no idea how long we might have to wait until women get the vote. We must have a way out.'

'What do you mean by that?' she gasped. Her racing pulse seemed to thud to a halt.

He reached for his glass. 'If our circumstances change, we need to be able to release each other with the minimum of unhappiness.'

Violet stared at him in shock. 'You've considered how we would release each other from our marriage?'

'In theory,' he said, after a draught of champagne. 'Of course. It is certainly not my intention to do so. I made a vow today and I intend to honour it.'

'So do I,' she replied honestly.

'Even so. We do not know what the future holds. We both entered this arrangement with our eyes open, but we must be aware of the possible dangers.'

Violet looked down at her plate. One of her doorstop sandwiches was still unfinished. She pushed the plate away. Her appetite had disappeared. 'It seems I have been somewhat naïve,' she said after a moment.

He set down his glass, his fingers firm around the stem. 'We're in uncharted territory. Marriages of convenience don't come with a handbook.'

She bit her lip. 'I suppose I ought not to have kissed you, when you made your proposal.'

'On the contrary,' he drawled, 'I'm very glad you did.' His unexpected smile took the tension from their conversation as he toyed with his champagne glass. 'You were right to assess our, ah, compatibility. But as we do not know how long our terms of agreement must last, it's important we consider all the eventualities. It would be irresponsible not to do so.'

Violet reached for her own glass of champagne and finished it in a gulp. She wished now she had accepted his offer of a second glassful. 'The day will come when women can vote. Soon. I'm sure of it.'

He shrugged. 'We can't predict anything. Until

then, we must take no risks. I will respect the terms of our agreement, in word and deed. Entirely.'

'That sounds very sensible,' she said.

Adam nodded. 'It seems a logical way to move forward. It's for the best.'

Violet held out her glass. 'I think I would like some more champagne, after all.'

Violet slipped the tin of Floral Creams under the lace-edged pillow. She always kept some chocolate fondants in her bedroom, in case of hunger pangs in the night. Not always under her pillowcase, it was true, but tonight, she wanted to have them close by. She felt oddly in need of some familiar reassurance and she didn't fancy having to find her way to the cellar kitchens of Beauley Manor.

She smoothed out the pillowcase. Like the rest of the manor, the pillowcase had seen better days, but it was beautifully laundered. The feathers were flattened and the lace was full of holes, but the linen, the pillowcases and the sheets were of good quality, the kind that would last.

A massive, carved four-poster bed, curtained with faded red-and-gold brocade, dominated the room. An unlit stone fireplace, browed with a chimney piece that appeared to be a single tree trunk, faced the bed.

At one end of the room were a chest of drawers, pitcher and basin, and two massive wardrobes that still would never fit all the garments in her trunks.

She snapped open the brass catches of one of her leather trunks and threw back the lid, rummaging to find her nightgown and peignoir. The rest of her matching luggage, two even larger trunks and four suitcases emblazoned with her new initials, V.R.B., were beside it. Their brass and leather gleamed. In spite of the size of the room, they took up a sizeable portion of the wooden floor.

She held up the nightgown before laying it on the bed. The sheer fabric was so light it could balloon into the air, as Violet had demonstrated at one of her trousseau fittings, to her mama's protestations. It was made of the finest lawn, so diaphanous her shape could be made out beneath, but not enough to be too revealing if she did not wish to be so. Embroidered white on white, it had fashionable half-sleeves and tied with a ribbon under the bust. The peignoir that covered it was longer and looser, wrapping over the sheer bodice.

They were made to be seen by a bridegroom

on a wedding night, but they would not be seen by hers.

Violet glanced towards the oak double doors adjacent to the window.

Beyond those doors, in the connecting room, was Adam. It was extraordinary how strongly she could sense his presence, even through the heavy wooden doors. Or perhaps she was being fanciful.

His side of the room, which she had seen only briefly, was of a similar size to hers, with another large bed, though without the wooden posters. It was sparsely furnished with heavy oak furniture. She realised a stone fireplace set into the same wall as the connecting doors also served his side of the room.

She wondered what he was doing. Was he, too, staring at the closed doors?

She dragged her attention away from the doors and moved to look out of the window. Their bedroom was at the back of the manor and she could see little now, in the darkness. The garden at the rear had not been fully tamed, Adam had told her, when he showed her the bedrooms and explained how their rooms connected. There was a river, too, and a wooded path that led to the marshes beyond, he'd said, before leaving her alone for the night. From the other side of the door, the key had turned in the lock. It was for her sense of privacy, she was sure, but it made her feel surprisingly alone and, to her consternation, a little frightened.

She lifted her chin. There was nothing to fear in the manor. It had been a long day and now she was in a strange environment. That was all. With a sigh she pulled closed the curtains. The fabric was ancient, possibly hand-stitched. She examined it more closely. As downstairs, the work was magnificent, but somewhat worse for wear.

Slipping off her satin shoes, thankfully undamaged by their run through London, she trod the wooden floor on her silk-stockinged feet.

Opposite the four-poster bed was a dressing table. It was clearly a woman's piece of furniture and it struck an unusual note in the room. It was far more modern than the rest of the heavy oak fixtures. Made of a light, golden wood, its curves were highly polished. In front of it was a round pink-velvet stool.

Violet stood in front of the mirror, she untied her silk sash and let it fly, like a banner. It floated to the floor in a silk ribbon of white, purple and green. The embroidered violets lay as if in fallen snow.

'Did you want me to kiss you?'

Adam's words rang in her head.

'I wanted to kiss you. That's why I didn't.'

Rapidly, she unbuttoned the pearls that held her sleeves closed at the elbow. It was difficult to undo the buttons at the back and front without help.

She glanced towards the connecting door.

No entanglements.

She was surprised at the complexity of emotions his comments at dinner had raised in her. She'd married him knowing that their relationship would be platonic, to begin with at least. Of course, it was sensible to avoid further physical contact. Yet she could not deny her attraction to him. It had begun at the ball, with that heavenly waltz, though she'd managed to quash it. And then, that kiss…

Her fingers faltered on her bodice. That kiss had awoken sensations that she hadn't anticipated, sensations that seemed to pull her closer to him, even as common sense pushed her away.

She must not allow her attraction to her husband to become a distraction. Through their marriage she had gained her freedom. It was fortunate that the terms of their agreement suited them both so well. As Adam had said, it mustn't be put at risk.

Finally, she managed to release all the pearl buttons. Removing the dress with care, she stood in her camisole and busked corset that cinched her waist into the fashionable, S-shaped hour-glass. Some called it the health corset, though Violet had always found it as uncomfortable as any other.

Next she removed her white-silk waist petticoat, letting it form a circle of lace and ruffles at her feet.

Stepping out of the pile of ruffles, she pulled out the velvet dressing-table stool. It twirled as she spun it and sat down. The seat was a trifle unsteady, but the tri-mirror reflected her from the front and both sides. Her eyes were bright, larger in her face than usual, and she could see the tension around her mouth.

She ran her finger over her lips.

'Did you want me to kiss you?'

The question came again.

She hadn't known the answer to his question when he asked it.

Be honest, she told her reflection in the mirror. She'd expected him to kiss her, stood in front of the altar, after they'd been pronounced man and wife.

'I wanted to kiss you. That's why I didn't.'

She rubbed her fingers on her scalp. Her head hinted at an ache. Too much champagne.

With the release of a few hairpins she loosened her hair. It tumbled to her shoulders. She reached instinctively for her hairbrush, but it wasn't on the glass table top. It must be in her trunk.

Kneeling in front of it, she delved inside. No hairbrush. With a groan at its weight, she pulled out one of the other, larger trunks and threw back the lid.

With an enormous crash, the trunk vanished in a cloud of dust.

Violet shrieked.

Adam heard Violet cry out from the next room from where he sat at the edge of the bed. He'd shrugged off his waistcoat, unbuttoned his shirt and was now pulling off one of his boots.

At the sound of her voice he slid the boot back on and leapt to his feet.

'Damnation.' The key jammed in the lock of the connecting doors. It hadn't been used for years. His mother had taken a separate room, which she still occupied, a long distance from her husband years before.

He slammed his foot against the wood, gave the key a sharp turn and wrenched it open.

Violet, her face streaked with dust, stared up at him from across the room. She knelt near the bed, leaning over what appeared to be a huge hole in the floor.

'What the blazes!' Adam rushed to her side,

seized her by the shoulder and hauled her back from the jagged wooden edge. 'Get back!'

He tugged her to safety. Shivering with fear, she clambered to her feet.

'What happened?' he demanded. 'Are you hurt?'

Her eyes were huge in her face. 'I'm not hurt. It was extraordinary. My trunk fell through the floorboards. It was a heavy one, you see. I opened the lid and it just disappeared.'

Adam swore.

'There must be a rotten floorboard.' He peered over the edge of the hole into the abyss below. 'I can't see the trunk. It must have gone straight down to the floor below.'

'What's underneath this bedroom?' she asked.

'The hall. Hopefully the trunk hasn't caused too much damage.' He brushed off his hands as he got up. 'I'll have to go and have a look downstairs.'

He turned back to Violet. 'Are you sure you're all right…?' The question died on his lips.

'Good Lord,' Adam said.

In a single glance, he took her in from head to toe as she stood there.

Her chestnut hair was now only half-piled on her head. Loose, it fell to her bare shoulder with more wave and curl than he'd anticipated. Her ice-cream-smooth wedding dress was gone now, leaving only the ruffled lace of a camisole, edging the creamy mounds of her breasts, still lifting and falling from the shock.

His gaze travelled down. Her stiff busked corset, pushing up those full breasts, moulded her waist into a tiny column, so small he could have spanned it in his hands. Beneath the corset were a pair of lacy knickers, their ruffled edge coming to the middle of her thigh.

And below it, there was the item that had made him step back.

'What is that you're wearing?' he asked hoarsely.

'Oh! These are called knickers.' Violet indicated the frilly shorts. 'Camisole knickers. I find them so much more comfortable than long pantaloons. They're quite the fashion.'

Adam coughed. He'd never seen such a ravishing pair of drawers, if they could be called that. They were little more than lace. 'It's not the… ah…knickers.'

He pointed at what was tied inches above her knee.

Green, Purple. White. Around her perfectly formed, stockinged leg was a striped suffragette garter.

Violet looked down and laughed aloud, the wholehearted, unexpected laugh he'd begun to appreciate so much. 'I wanted to wear something to remind me of the Cause as I went down the aisle.'

He swallowed hard. Her legs were stupendous. He could hardly stop staring at them. 'Most brides wear something old, something new, something borrowed, something blue. That's the old rhyme, I believe.'

'Something green, purple and white means more to me,' she explained. 'There's a meaning to the colours. Purple for loyalty and dignity, white for purity and green for hope.'

He managed to drag his eyes away from the garter and up to her face. 'So you're a suffragette through and through.'

She laughed again. 'I suppose I am. Perhaps it reminds you of how you came to propose to me. When we danced together at the ball, I had my suffrage banners hidden under my petticoats.'

'Yes, I remember.' He hadn't dwelt on it too much, where she had hidden those silken banners. But now...

He seized a white dressing gown that lay on the bed.

'Here.' Swiftly he passed the filmy cotton to her. 'Put that on. For your safety, you'd better wait in my bedroom while I go and check the damage.'

As fast as he could, Adam left the room.

* * *

In Adam's side of the bedroom, Violet undressed.

Rapidly, she slipped off her shoes, removed the garter and unrolled her silk stockings. Making a tent of her nightdress, she removed her corset, leaving her camisole and knickers underneath. Over the nightdress, she tied the peignoir.

Her heart pounded, but she knew it wasn't merely from the shock of her trunk falling through the floorboards.

It was Adam.

His expression when he'd spotted her striped garter had been one of incredulity, then it had changed to something else, something more.

Desire.

She'd recognised it the instant he felt it.

Because at that moment, she'd felt it, too.

A strong, pulsing cord had formed between them, so strong it had almost dragged her into his arms. She'd managed to answer his questions, to laugh, all the while sensing that desire alive between them.

At his washstand, she poured water from the pitcher into the bowl and splashed it on her cheeks. Wiping the droplets away on a towel revealed that she was covered in dust. A few more splashes and the dust was gone, but not the heat in her cheeks.

It was the second time she'd needed to cool herself with water after an encounter with Adam.

To her surprise, she hadn't been embarrassed to stand in front of him in her undergarments. Her attire was no disgrace. She despised prudishness. If she had been at the swimming baths, she might have worn something similar. Yet the effect on him…

She was shuddering now, as more than the shock set in. Quickly, she returned to her bedroom, avoided the broken floor and seized the tin of violet creams from under her pillow. Back in Adam's side of the room she ate one, then another. The sweetness on her tongue restored her.

'The damage doesn't appear to be permanent.'

Violet dropped the tin on a table near the bed and spun around to see Adam coming through the connecting doors. He held a lamp in his hand.

'I've taken a look upstairs and down, as best as I can tonight,' he went on, as he laid the lamp on to a table by the fireplace. 'The damage can be contained. The trunk went straight down, as I thought. It looks worse than it is, but I think it can be fixed, and there's no destruction to the floor of the hall. That stone tile is ancient, but it took the weight.'

'I'm so sorry,' Violet said. Her trunk had damaged his home. She knew how much he cherished it.

'It's not your fault. There have been some years of neglect, I told you that. It appears to be only one floorboard that's the issue, as far as I can make out. I'll get it mended, but the manor needs a complete survey.' He shook his head. 'It was lucky you weren't hurt. I'd never have forgiven myself.'

'It's not your fault, either,' she reminded him.

'All the same, it's my responsibility. You ought not to use that side of the bedroom, to be on the safe side.' Adam ran his hand through his hair. 'You can sleep in my bed tonight.'

Violet drew in her breath. 'With you?'

He shook his head. 'I didn't mean that. I'll find somewhere else to sleep.'

Alarm rippled through her. 'But there's no one else here at the manor.' Pulling the peignoir closer, she moved towards him. 'Please don't go. Not tonight.'

His head jerked back. 'What are you saying, Violet?'

'I don't want to be alone after what's happened. I've never spent a night at Beauley Manor before.' She bit her lip. To her embarrassment, it almost quivered. She refused to let Adam see that fatigue and fright were eroding her usual courage. 'You don't need to find another room. We can both sleep here in your bed.'

A muscle worked in his cheek. 'There's little likelihood of any more furniture falling through the floor. It was just the one floorboard—at least, I hope so.'

Violet swallowed hard. 'I'd feel better if you were near. I understand what you said at dinner. But when we made our terms, you said we could be friends. And after all, no matter what happens in the future, tonight is our wedding night.'

He pushed back his hair from his forehead. 'You want us to share a bed.'

'To sleep,' she said quickly. 'I'm not suggesting… an entanglement.'

Adam gazed at her for a long moment, inscrutable.

'Very well,' he said at last. 'Only for tonight.'

Violet lay in the darkness. Beside her she could hear Adam's slow breathing. He had finally fallen asleep. She'd heard the moment. His breathing had changed, deepened. His body, some distance from hers, had become still.

It was strangely intimate. She had never slept with anyone before, let alone a man. Yet it had seemed so natural, the way they had pulled back the covers, taken one side each. He'd blown out the candle then and they lay there in silence. But not alone.

Startling her now, he rolled on to his back. She could make out the shape of his strong profile, his chin and neck, and his body beneath the covers.

She hoped she hadn't been unfair, asking for his company. It was most unlike her, but she had been perilously close to tears. She hadn't wanted to be left alone in the huge, empty manor. Not without him near.

Did you want me to kiss you?

As sleep began to take her, the answer to Adam's question floated into her consciousness. She knew the answer now. It was the same one she had given to the question in the lilac letter.

Yes.

Adam awoke. Normally, in the morning, his eyes went to the curtains, to see the daylight coming in. Now he stared at the woman who lay beside him.

Violet.

His wife.

She was still asleep. Her hair, now completely loose, was curled around her face and shoulders, like a veil. Her lashes were gold tipped, he noted, resting on her pink cheeks. Her mouth was slightly opened, her soft breathing a whisper on the pillows.

He was drawn to her, lying peacefully beside him. Her skin was soft and smooth. He'd thought her merely pretty, not beautiful, when they first met, but now he saw she had a beauty and a secret vulnerability, while her pugnacious chin gave her strength and her bow-shaped mouth its character.

His body stirred.

He redirected his attention to the window. Daylight edged the curtains. The velvet was so thin that the golden morning light formed a patchwork of light and shade on the fabric. In spite of the dilapidation, it, too, had its own beauty.

She was sleeping soundly now on a thin feather pillow, probably a far cry from the luxurious bedding she was used to. He wondered idly what her parents' home in Manchester was like. Enormous, he imagined, with every modern convenience, completely fashionable and up to date. Like her frilly knickers. And as for that garter in the suffragette colours—it had almost undone him.

He stifled a laugh that became a groan. There had been a spark of passion in her eyes that he imagined she barely knew she possessed. One night with her in his bed was all he could manage. After the disaster of the worn floorboards that had sent her trunk hurtling through the floor, he hadn't been able to leave her all alone, as she stood there in her nightgown. She'd been frightened, he'd sensed, even though she'd tried to hide it. There she was, in an unknown house, with a man who was practically a stranger, all for the sake of her parents' health and happiness, and for a Cause she believed in. As she'd stood there he'd witnessed, behind the raised chin, the same sensitive nature he'd spotted at the ball when she'd been a wallflower, before he asked her to dance. She touched him, with that combination of valour and vulnerability.

The night before, at dinner, she'd called herself naïve. She was. It was no crime. She had a natural curiosity for life. It struck him anew how limited the opportunities were for women, regardless of wealth or status.

He glanced over at her again, drew back.

Her blue eyes were open. She was awake.

They stared at each other.

'Have you slept well?' he asked eventually, as his body roared into life. With a will of iron, he clamped it down.

'Very well, thank you,' she replied.

'Good. Perhaps you would care for some breakfast in the hall. I'm afraid there aren't any staff to bring it up to you here.' If he could ever get out of the damned bed.

She raised herself on one elbow, her long hair falling over the bodice of her white nightgown. 'There's no need. It's my turn. I can serve breakfast.'

To Adam's amazement Violet jumped out of bed and retrieved a tin of chocolates.

She laughed.

'Would you care for a violet cream?'

Chapter Eleven

'Then when the first low matin-chirp hath grown
Full quire, and morning driv'n her plow of pearl
Far furrowing into light...'
—Alfred, Lord Tennyson: *'Love and Duty'*
(1842)

'Good morning, Violet.'

'Good morning, Jane.' Her younger sister-in-law gave a warm smile.

'Good morning, Violet.'

'Good morning, Arabella.' Her elder sister-in-law gave a haughty nod.

Violet stopped at her mother-in-law's empty chair at the long table in the hall.

'Mama is unwell,' Arabella answered Violet's unspoken question. 'She is having breakfast in bed.'

Breakfast in bed.

Violet took her own place at the long table and reached for some toast from the silver rack and the pot of marmalade.

Only a few weeks had passed, but it seemed an age since she and Adam had shared violet creams in bed for their breakfast after spending their wedding night together in his room. Her night in his bed hadn't been repeated. The next day, after the floor surrounding the area that had fallen through had been checked and boarded over, Adam had deemed it safe for her to return to her own bedroom. It was as safe as any other part of the first floor of Beauley, he'd said, so firmly she hadn't dared argue with him.

A full survey of the state of the manor was now underway. The entire building was being assessed, from attic to cellar, and the results would soon be known.

Meanwhile, the connecting doors between them had been shut tight.

Violet was shocked by how much she missed him. They had only shared a bed together that first night, but she now found it difficult to sleep alone. Each night, as she undressed, washed in a copper tub by the fireplace and brushed her hair in front of the mirror, she would hear him moving about in the next room before he went to bed. Each night, she would gaze at the connecting doors and wonder what he was doing. Whether the doors were locked any more, she wasn't sure. She didn't dare try the handle. Once or twice she approached the closed doors, tempted to tap, or lay her cheek against the wood. Yet so far, she hadn't given in to such temptation.

Her awareness of Adam beyond the door continued once she was in her bed. She would read a little, but she found it hard to concentrate. When she blew out the lamp and lay against the pillows, she would imagine him lying in the next room. She knew now the way he fell asleep, the way he slept, turned, rolled. On their wedding night, she'd fallen asleep beside him into a slumber so deep, so refreshing, that all sleep since had been disturbed.

What must it be like, then, to sleep in his arms?

Violet spread her toast with the orange marmalade.

In the mornings, she often didn't see him. Violet was up promptly for breakfast in the hall by nine o'clock, but Adam was often long gone, out on the estate with the workers. He worked harder than anyone else and was held in great esteem by the estate workers.

She'd caught sight of him that morning, however. She'd heard him moving about, later than usual. She'd knocked and asked if he had any letters he wanted her to post. He'd opened the door with one hand, bare-chested.

'Gatekeeper, butler and field hand,' he'd said

drily, as with the other hand he thrust a loose cotton shirt over his broad chest.

She bit into her toast.

'Violet! Would you care for coffee?' Arabella sounded exasperated.

Violet dropped her toast. 'I'm sorry?'

She hadn't meant to annoy Arabella.

Jane giggled good-naturedly. 'Are you quite well this morning, Violet?'

Arabella brandished the silver coffee pot. 'I hope you are not coming down with the same flu as Mama,' she said severely.

'Oh, no,' said Violet. 'I am quite well. Very well.'

She felt a flush rise to her cheeks. She hoped her sisters-in-law wouldn't notice.

Her relations with Jane were very good now. They had become friends. But Arabella remained a closed book.

Book was an accurate description, Violet mused. Arabella read constantly, and not merely novels, but books of law, history and philosophy. Violet liked to read, too. She would have enjoyed discussing their reading with Arabella. But Arabella remained haughty. Or perhaps she was simply reserved, as Adam sometimes was. He preferred to remain in control in his life, Violet had noticed. Only Jane was bubbly and un-inhibited.

'I do hope Mama will be better by the garden party on Saturday,' worried Jane.

Violet sipped her coffee. They had been preparing for the garden party for weeks and she was looking forward to it.

'Your mama will be sorry to miss the garden party,' Violet said to Jane. She'd formed a cordial relationship with her mother-in-law and was sorry to hear she was ill.

'She won't, greatly,' Jane confessed. 'Mama has to give a speech to open it for everyone. She doesn't like having to do so.'

'I will look in on her later,' said Arabella.

Jane passed the toast rack. 'What are you doing this morning, Violet?'

She glanced out the arched window. The sun blazed on to the lawn. It was the most glorious day. Hopefully, it would stay that way and any rain would hold off for the garden party. 'I'm planning a walk into the village. I have some letters to post.'

'Are they suffragette letters?' Jane asked eagerly.

'Some of them.'

It was a relief to no longer have to hide her dedication to the Cause—except, of course, for her membership of the lilac-letter group, as she now called them. She'd received one more letter so far, acknowledging her change of name and address, and advising her that activities were imminent.

In addition to her membership of the lilac-letter group, Violet had also joined the Women's Social and Political Union led by the famed Mrs Pankhurst. She received their pamphlets and correspondence, as well as other women's journals and magazines that supported the Cause, sometimes reading items of note aloud to Jane, who was most enthusiastic. As for Arabella, she could not tell if her elder sister-in-law had much interest in the suffragettes. When they were together in the solar, she always held a book in front of her, though sometimes, when Violet told Jane about the rallies and meetings and other exploits, she noticed that Arabella rarely turned the pages.

One suffrage task Violet had taken up with alacrity was writing letters to Members of Parliament, demanding they support the women's vote. The more letters they received, the more pressure was put upon them. She'd even written to the local Member for Beauley, a Mr Burrows, asking for his support, but she had received no reply. He was, however, going to attend the garden party. She would make a point of seeking him out and discussing the matter with him.

'I wish I could come for a walk with you,' Jane said wistfully. 'I do so enjoy hearing about the activities of the suffragettes. How wonderfully courageous you all are. But I must make Mama some peppermint tea to help with her flu.'

Violet smiled at Jane. 'It would have been lovely to walk with you. Perhaps another time.'

If she was out walking alone, perhaps she might see Adam.

Violet hung her basket over her arm as she approached the woods. It was part of her trousseau, made of straw, with artificial flowers on the side. It was made to look rustic, although it had been frightfully expensive.

The basket was pretty, but not as pretty as the flowers around Beauley Manor and they cost nothing at all. Nor did the artificial flowers on her basket have the scent that she breathed in as she entered the woods. Full of oak, willow and ash trees, wild garlic grew, with its strong scent, along with some late pale yellow primroses. A robin chirped as she passed.

She ought to have brought Beau with her, she thought to herself. The old dog loved to go for walks. She would remember, next time.

She had posted her letters in the village, including one to her mama and papa in Manchester, who both, according to her mama's last letter, missed her enormously.

Violet frowned. That letter had also revealed that her papa had been more tired than usual since the wedding. He was never tired, as far as Violet could remember. She hoped that the wedding and all the anxiety before it hadn't exhausted him. He had been so troubled by the matter of the banners at the ball. He hadn't had another of his turns, but her mama was worried, all the same.

In her return letter, Violet had asked if she needed to visit them in Manchester. Doubtless her papa, with his determination, would be well enough soon. Perhaps they might be able to come to Beauley Manor for a holiday. She would ask Adam, although her papa had never had a day off in his life, as he often boasted.

She went deeper into the woods. She'd explored every part of them, but today, she would walk down the marshy path to the river. It was beautiful there and near where Adam had mentioned he would be working.

He worked so hard. He was no leisured landowner. Instead, he took on any role that was needed to make Beauley Manor run.

It needed work; that was certain. She'd been aghast at some of the inconveniences in the old manor house. The plumbing was a far cry from what she had been used to at home in Manchester, where every convenience was ordered by her papa as soon as it was invented. He loved new inventions.

Violet stopped and leaned to smell a flower with the same name as hers. There weren't many left now, it was too late in the season. In the same way that she wondered at what Adam was doing beyond the connecting doors of their bedroom, she found it difficult not to think about him when he was out on the estate all day. She wasn't sure if he thought of her as often, or if he thought of her at all. She didn't know if that moment of desire she'd witnessed in his face on their wedding night was some kind of reflex, gone and quickly forgotten. But she hadn't forgotten it, or that connection between them. So strong, so powerful.

She was forced to admit it to herself.

Her attraction to him was growing, day by day, like the wildflowers in the wood. No matter how often she reminded herself that her feelings would pass if she ignored them, they sprang back, like the blooms at her feet.

Of course, it wasn't that she didn't have other concerns and interests herself that totally absorbed her. She did. She threw herself into whatever she was doing. That was her way. She was like her papa in that, she supposed. But all the while, as if he stood beside her, in her mind, was Adam. Always present. Always there.

How strange their relationships was, in their marriage of convenience. They were married, yet unmarried. Friends, yet strangers. Increasingly, she wanted to spend time with him to get to know him better. She didn't want to interrupt Adam's work on the estate, or to become a distraction to him, any more than she wanted him to be a distraction from her suffragette business. Yet she was struck by how much she yearned to see him and by how much she hoped he felt the same.

He'd said he was working on a wall. She would find him. Out of the woods, she headed for the river path. She had skirted the formal garden by going through the woods, but now she looked back at Beauley, glowing red in the morning sun. She had come to love the manor, and its grounds, in only the few months she had been there. She couldn't imagine returning to Manchester, or living anywhere else. How quickly the house had worked its magic on her. How quickly it had become her home.

Home. Adam had welcomed her home to Beauley, the day of their wedding. Back then the word had sounded strange. Now it felt right. From the very start, he made her feel welcome, as if she belonged.

On the sloping river bank she slipped in the marshy ground. The ground was boggy, in spite of it being summertime. Slowly, she descended the riverbank, the heels of her walking boots slipping through the grass and mud.

In the river stood Adam.

Violet stopped, transfixed.

Adam's dark head was bare, as were his feet, judging by his trousers, rolled to below the knee. His chest was bare, too, for he wore no shirt, his muscles rippling as he plunged his hand into the water, pulling up rocks, one by one. She watched as he looked at one, ran his thumb over its smoothness and tossed it, as lightly as if it was a pebble, to the pile that lay by the riverbank.

As he picked up the next stone, he turned and saw her. 'Hello.'

She managed to find her voice. 'Hello.'

'This is unexpected.'

'I hope I'm not interrupting you.'

'Unexpected,' he drawled with a smile, 'but not unwelcome.'

'What are you doing?' she asked, curious.

'I'm collecting river stones to fit the wall I'm

fixing. There's a quarry not far from here, but river stone has always been used at Beauley, too.'

He tossed the smooth stone he held on to the pile.

He grinned. 'Come in and I'll show you.'

'What?'

He laughed and indicated where the water came to his calf muscles. 'Come on in, Violet. The water's fine.'

She hesitated, looked down at her pretty, ruffled blue blouse and dark blue skirt. Then, aware of his scrutiny, she seated herself among the riverweeds at the edge of the water. With a tug she pulled off her boots, and unrolled her stockings, one after the other, sensing his gaze as each bit of silk unfurled.

Standing, she rolled up her sleeves, lifted her skirts and stepped into the water. 'Oh! It's freezing!'

'You need to get to work to warm up.'

Catching her unawares, he seized her bare hand and dived it into the water.

At the shock of the cold water and his sudden touch she almost shrieked. But he kept tight hold of her wet fingers as they delved below, guiding them around the shape of a smooth stone, helping her to dig beneath her fingers into the sand beneath to release it and then bring it up to the surface.

Plucking the stone from her cupped palm, he tossed it alongside the others. It landed with a clunk.

'Do you understand the method?' He grinned. 'It's fairly simple.'

'Yes.' Her teeth chattered as she reached down to the riverbed and, with both hands, pulled up her first stone.

'I did it!' She raised the dripping stone aloft.

Adam laughed. 'We need more than that.'

Together they began to work in companionable silence, under the warm sun. Soon they formed a rhythm. One stone, then another, hit the pile on the bank. His, then hers. The pile grew. She forgot the cold water, forgot everything, except Adam beside her.

'My papa would call this men's work.' Violet tightened her fist around a hard stone. 'I tried to help him at home and at the factory, too, but he wouldn't allow it. He…he wanted a son.'

Adam shaded his eyes as he studied her. 'There's plenty of work on this estate for both men and women, if you'll let me teach you.'

She loosened the stone in her clenched fingers. Her papa's words had weighed heavy inside her. Now, Adam's practical reply soothed her in a way no other might have.

He understood.

'I can teach you how to build a wall,' he said. 'If you can build a wall, you can build anything.'

'I'd like that.'

She turned to throw the stone on the pile. Her bare feet slid on the slippery riverbed. With a shriek she fell backwards, into the water.

Just in time, Adam pulled her upright from behind. Violet tried to find a grip with the soles of her feet. His hands glided over her hips and up to cinch her waist, spanning her corset. How neatly their bodies fit together, his lower body cupping hers from behind. Her toes slithered in the mud, she struggled to stand, but he kept hold, his fingers firm as they pressed into her waist, before he plonked her back on her feet in the calf-high water.

Splashing, he came around in front of her, his teeth gleaming. A shout of laughter burst from between his lips, then faded as their gazes met. The colour of his dark blue eyes turned to a reflection of the summer sky.

Who took the first step, she barely knew. As they moved together in the water his body pressed into hers, his hands wrenching her closer as their lips found each other. He tasted clean and water fresh, with another taste all his own that she hadn't known she hungered for, until now. She opened her mouth; her hands slid up his wet muscled back and into the damp tendrils of hair at the base of his neck. In return his hands moved, his fingers tangling in her hair and up to cradle her face.

When he'd seen her in her undergarments on their wedding night, she'd witnessed desire in his eyes. Now desire was in his lips. She tasted it. It matched hers as her body awoke, a coiled energy blasting through her core.

In her lips, on her tongue. Surely he tasted her desire, too, as with her kiss she told him. Told him of the desire she'd discovered, the secret longing she'd been keeping inside.

Nothing mattered but that kiss, just then, and what he told her with his lips. He wanted her. She wanted him, too, she told him with her searching tongue, with something deeper than desire, more real, more powerful. The powerful feel of his body almost overwhelmed her. Entwined, they fell back against the marshy bank.

Her hands ran over his broad bare chest, then to his muscled back as with a tear of buttons he opened her blouse to find her breasts, jutted over the top of her corset. She gasped as with his tongue he lifted each tender point into his mouth. Toyed, teased, as her fingers dug into his bare skin. Then with a splash he slid her up, out of the water. His kiss, river deep, found her lips again, sent her arms up to pull him deeper into her embrace. He wrenched her body closer still, keeping his lips hard on hers. Pushing her skirt up her bare legs, he slid his palm up her wet thigh.

On the outer part first. Then inside.

She tensed, but didn't pull away. He reached higher, beneath her petticoat, to find what he knew she wore beneath. To enter the ruffled edge.

He paused, as if in question.

In answer, she showed him.

She wanted him to touch her there. Body and mind told her so, as she slipped her body down the bank to thrust into his hand, sending her bare lower legs into the water's edge. Cold. Heat. At the same time. Exquisite pleasure rippled through her core, like the river around her feet as he searched the most secret part of her. He pulled her closer against him as he entered her, his fingers going deep. Instinctively she pushed her hips forward, as she threw back her head in a gasp, opening her mouth wider. His lips widened hers again, entering her mouth with his tongue at the same time his fingers pushed further still.

She tautened. His finger circled, outside, in. Darting deeper inside, bringing with it a strange new pleasure. She gasped aloud.

Her arms had gone around his neck as their kiss deepened, her mouth wide, her body now pressed against his bare chest. Hard. And below. Harder still.

She wanted to touch him, too. Sliding her hands down his chest, she reached for the buckle of his belt.

Instantly he released her. Hauling himself to his feet, Adam backed into the river, a curse beneath his breath. *'Damnation.'*

Water splashed as he sloshed out of the river, towards higher ground.

Droplets flew as he spun around. 'Forgive me. It won't happen again.'

He clambered up the bank and strode away.

Violet tore off her wet skirt. It was soaking halfway to her knees, covered in mud. Somehow, she'd found her way back to the Manor and to their bedroom, with its tightly shut connecting door. Where Adam had gone after he strode away so furiously from her in the river, sending water surging into foam around him, she didn't know.

She shivered, but with not cold. With passion. With desire. Emotions she had never considered before, that she had barely fathomed to exist.

They certainly hadn't been covered in the medical literature.

She let out a breath. Never could she have predicted how she would respond to Adam when she was in his arms. If he hadn't stopped them…

Violet lifted her chin.

She'd had time to reflect on what he had said to her, on their wedding night. It was he who'd made it so clear that all eventualities be considered, and must be prepared for. How had he put it? They needed to be able to release each other. He wanted no entanglements.

Those words had smarted, like a sting on her bare skin, but she knew he was right.

Violet shivered again.

She had never imagined she would feel like this.

Adam took the steps two at a time up to the solar. Outside the door he stopped.

Where there is a will, there is a way.

Beneath his breath he quoted Samuel Smiles. He'd taken to reading *Self-Help*, or, in its full title, *Self Help: With Illustrations of Character and Conduct*, each night before bed, in the hope of girding his own strength of character. Sleep had recently proved almost impossible. He'd manage a few hours before getting up with the birds and throwing himself into physical labour on the estate to burn off his excess energy.

By God, after that encounter in the river, he'd need to gird his character tonight.

He gripped the doorknob and flung it open. Inside he found Violet. For once, she was alone.

The evening sun made the wood panelling glisten like gold, but not as brightly as her hair as she bent over her embroidery. On her lap was spread an enormous suffrage banner, striped at the edges in purple, green and white, with what he assumed would read VOTES FOR WOMEN! embroidered at the centre. She was halfway through sewing the motto, the word 'VOTES' in bold violet, edged with gold thread.

Still sewing fast, she looked up and smiled. A cautious smile, but not without warmth, nor the humour he appreciated so much in her. But her hand was gripped rather tightly, surely more tightly than usual, around her sewing needle.

'You've missed dinner,' she said. 'It can be served downstairs for you, in the hall.'

'Not yet. I need a drink.' Two drinks, maybe three. Maybe more. Or perhaps a violet cream. He'd developed a taste for them. Morning, noon or night.

He sloshed whisky into the glass. 'Would you care for anything?'

She shook her head, sent a chestnut curl spiralling.

He sat opposite, watching her sew. Her fingers were nimble, the rhythm strangely soothing.

She finished the letter F, snipped a gold thread with her teeth. It pouted her bow-shaped mouth, reminding him of the feel of her lips beneath his. He suppressed a groan. He could have dived into the water with her that morning, clothes and all. Peeled off the soaking layers, the way she'd peeled off her stockings, until they were skin to skin.

He threw back some whisky. 'Where are Jane and Arabella?'

'They are looking after your mama.'

'Is she any better?'

'I'm not certain,' Violet said. 'I hope so. It would be a shame for her to miss the garden party.'

Adam ran his hand through his hair. The garden party was a highlight of the summer for many people in the community, especially the children. It was a huge expense, but one he never begrudged and never would.

Violet continued to stitch industriously. 'I have some other news. There's a suffragette rally, I believe, coming up in a few weeks' time in London. I plan to attend.'

'You must do as you wish.' He glanced at the large banner and grinned. 'You won't hide that under your petticoat.'

She laughed. It broke the tension.

She laid aside her sewing.

He went to her. 'Violet, about what happened today...'

She stood to face him. In the firelight her brown hair shone. 'I want to talk to you about that, too.'

He clenched his jaw. Her response to him earlier, or, rather, her initiation of further exploration, had brought him to his senses. He wouldn't make love to her in the river, though God knew he'd wanted to. *No.* He wouldn't make love to her at all. That was their agreement.

'It ought not to have happened,' he said evenly. 'It's important we stick to the terms of our agreement. I told you I could control myself and I can.'

'It wasn't only your fault,' she said quickly. 'It was mine, too.'

She moved a step closer.

The solar door flung open.

They sprang apart.

Jane rushed in. 'Oh, Adam, Violet! I have bad news.'

'Is it Mama?' Adam asked. With some kind of miracle he kept his voice offhand as he retrieved his whisky glass and sat down.

Jane nodded. 'She's much worse. She's not going to be well enough to attend the garden party. Certainly, she says she cannot give the opening speech.'

'That will be a relief to her, I dare say,' said Adam.

Jane giggled. Then she wrung her fingers together. 'Who will open the party? Will you do it, Adam?'

'There's no need for me to do it.' Adam glanced over the rim of his glass at Violet. 'We have another Mrs Beaufort on hand. Violet can open the garden party.'

'What?' Violet exclaimed.

She'd moved away, back to her sewing basket, the image of composure, but he knew better. Her cheeks, always tell-tale, were pinker than usual.

'You're perfectly capable of welcoming the people from the village and all the local dignitaries to Beauley Manor, aren't you?' Adam enquired.

Violet shook her head, sent her chestnut curls rippling. 'It ought not to be me. How about you, Jane?'

'Oh, no,' Jane laughed. 'I could never give a speech.'

'Then Arabella.'

'What about Arabella?' Her elder sister-in-law had come into the solar, behind Jane.

'Would you like to make the opening speech?' Violet asked.

'If Mama is unable to attend the garden party, then it is Violet's role to play hostess,' said Arabella.

'But this is your home, Arabella.'

Adam glanced at Violet. He'd noticed how thoughtful she was to his mother and sisters. By rights Violet ought to have the higher status. As his wife, Beauley Manor belonged to her now. Yet she was always careful not to take up any role that Arabella might think was hers.

'You must have attended many garden parties here at Beauley. You ought to give the speech,' Violet continued to address Arabella.

'Certainly not,' his sister replied crisply.

Adam glanced at Violet. 'Well?'

'Will the local Member of Parliament be there?' she asked, unexpectedly.

'Burrows?' Adam queried. He knew the man, but hadn't warmed to him. 'I expect so.'

Violet lifted her chin, the gesture he'd come to know in her as a sign she'd come to a decision.

'I'll do it,' she announced. 'I will give the speech.'

'Excellent.' Adam stood. 'Now, if you will excuse me, I'll go and find my dinner.'

They hadn't discussed what had happened in the river. But perhaps it was just as well.

Chapter Twelve

'Why took ye not your pastime? To that man
My work shall answer, since I knew the right
And did it; for a man is not as God.'
   —Alfred, Lord Tennyson: *'Love and Duty'*
                                    (1842)

'What a perfect afternoon for a garden party!' Jane pulled the drawing-room curtains wide. 'Why, the clouds have completely cleared up. Look at the sunshine!'

Violet stood by her sisters-in-law at the bay window. The garden, dappled in sunlight, did look glorious with its array of summer flowers. Roses, peonies, irises, delphiniums and foxgloves created a blaze of colour. White-wicker garden chairs and tables and seats had been placed on the lawn and at the other end she could see the cro-quet hoops had been laid out. The local regiment band had already arrived and they could hear the faint toot of a horn and a blare of a trumpet from where they were getting ready to play.

Along one side of the lawn, stalls had been set up for the ladies' bazaar, to sell handiworks to raise funds for the parish. Long tables for refreshments were ready and the kitchen staff were smoothing out the long white tablecloths, laying out plates, tea cups and tea spoons that glinted in the sun. A Punch and Judy puppet show was ready for the entertainment of the children. Later, there would be a treasure hunt and running races. By the bandstand a white tent had been put up and a small wooden podium had been set up, ready for the speeches to be made before the fête opened.

'It's like a fairy land,' Violet said. 'Or a knight's tournament.'

Adam came up behind her. She felt his presence, even before he spoke.

'There's no tournament today,' he said. 'Only cricket in the next field.'

'I suppose you'll score a captain's innings, as usual,' Arabella said with a rare, indulgent smile at her brother.

Adam shrugged. 'The gardeners have done well. I've just been out working with them.'

'Butler, cook and gardener?' Violet queried, over her shoulder.

'Indeed,' he drawled.

They looked at each other, then looked away.

'It's the new fashion to have a whole garden in one colour,' Violet said hurriedly, seeking a safe topic of conversation. 'To have an all-white garden, or some other shade.'

'Would you like that?' Adam asked her, unexpectedly.

'Perhaps,' she replied. 'There are certain colours I like very much.'

He cast an appreciative look at her dress. She'd had it made especially for the garden party. Of a light, gauzy cotton, trimmed with white lace, it was gathered at the waist with a green sash. 'You look like a violet today.'

'The shade is mauve,' she replied, flustered by the effect of his regard. 'It's very fashionable.'

'And perfect for this afternoon,' said Jane, with a quick smile at Violet.

'Mama is fond of mauve. It's a shame she is unwell,' said Arabella.

'It gives Violet a chance to open the garden party,' Adam said.

'Look, people are beginning to arrive!' exclaimed Jane.

'I'd better go outside.' Adam headed for the door.

'Are you nervous about your speech, Violet?' Arabella asked.

Violet's stomach turned over.

'Yes,' she admitted. 'I've never spoken in public before.'

'Please remember you are representing the Beaufort family,' said Arabella, haughtily.

Jane gave her a wink.

The night before, after they'd discussed the opening speech for the garden party, an idea had blazed in Violet's head and she'd beckoned Jane over to the sewing basket. They'd worked quickly and made it just in time.

Now, Adam had left the room. Violet had intended to confide in him about her plan for the afternoon, but there was no need, she decided. They hadn't exactly been avoiding each other since what had happened in the river, but they had both been keeping a safe distance.

No entanglements. Freedom. That was her goal. And this afternoon, if all went to plan, she would take a big step towards it.

Her stomach lurched.

Violet strolled across the lawn, wending between the chairs and rugs, nodding and smiling. 'Good afternoon. Good afternoon.'

'Good afternoon, madam.'

'Good day, Mrs Beaufort.'

The sun blazed down. Thank goodness she had her parasol and such a wide-brimmed hat. It was white, but to match her frock it had been trimmed with mauve ribbons.

By the podium she saw Adam standing with a small group, his dog Beau beside him. Taller than the rest, he wore a blazer over his white flannel trousers and shirt, ready for cricket. For a moment she experienced a strange sensation, as if they had been together at Beauley for many garden parties before. She shook her head as if to clear it. What a fanciful notion.

Beau leapt towards her with a bark of welcome as she approached. She gave the dog a quick pat.

As she reached Adam he gave her a slight bow that tilted his Panama straw-boater hat. His eyes gleamed as she stared at the small violet that adorned it on one side. For a moment it was as if they were the only two people in the garden, in spite of the crowd.

Violet smiled.

So did Adam. A long, slow smile.

The vicar coughed.

'There are people here this afternoon I would like you to meet.' Adam recovered smoothly. 'You know the vicar, of course.'

'We've already met at church on Sundays.' Violet shook hands.

The vicar bowed slightly. 'Good afternoon, Mrs Beaufort. A perfect afternoon for it.'

'And this is Mr Burrows, our local Member of Parliament,' Adam said.

'How do you do.' She held out her gloved hand to the portly man. He appeared hot in his dark three-piece suit.

He shook her hand. 'How do you do, madam.'

'I'm pleased to make your acquaintance.' How convenient. She had planned to make a point of seeking him out and discussing the matter of her unanswered letter. 'I have a great interest in politics.'

The man jerked back his head. 'Not a matter for the ladies, is it?'

'To the contrary,' she replied, startled. 'It is very much a matter for the ladies. An urgent matter.'

The M.P. appeared to snort.

'A lot of nonsense going on these days,' he muttered.

Violet bit back a retort. *Hold your fire*, she told herself. *Hold your fire.*

She turned to Adam. 'It must be time to open the garden party, is it not?'

He glanced at her intently, then at his pocket watch. 'Indeed. Shall we get started?'

'Indeed.'

Violet snapped her parasol shut.

On the podium, Violet adjusted her hat. Her hands were perspiring; they felt clammy in her lace gloves.

Amid applause from the crowd, Adam stepped forward beside her. 'Welcome, once again, to Beauley Manor for our summer fair. I'm delighted you are all able to be here in what has been a tradition for so many years. In the past, the garden party has been opened by my mother. Today, I'm pleased to welcome my wife, the new lady of the manor, to open the festivities.'

Adam stopped and took a breath so deep that Violet wondered if he was feeling unwell. The moment passed. He held out his hand, indicated for her to stand beside him.

Violet marched to the front of the podium. Her legs were unsteady, but she held her head high. In the crowd she could see Mr Burrows, the M.P., Arabella and also Jane, who stood towards the front, as they had arranged.

Adam gave her a smile of encouragement. It strengthened her to speak, even if he didn't know what she was going to say. Now she wished she had taken an opportunity to tell him the contents of her speech, but it was too late.

She took a breath and began.

'Ladies and gentlemen, boys and girls. Thank you so much for coming this afternoon to Beauley Manor. My husband and I are glad to welcome you here on such a glorious summer day.'

As she said the word husband, she happened to

glance at Adam. A look had come over his face, such a look as she had never seen before, a combination of pleasure and pride in her calling him by that title. It took her aback.

She cleared her throat. She supposed she had never said the word husband before and he had never heard himself described by it, but she hadn't expected his reaction. He was usually so guarded, so controlled. For a moment, she hesitated to continue her speech. But she had to. She must.

'I hope that there will be the usual merriment, fun and games today and I look forward to giving out the prizes this afternoon.' She smiled at the children who were seated on the grass in front of the podium. 'First, I would like to bring your attention to a more serious matter.'

She gave a nod to Jane, who stepped out in front and unfurled the suffragette banner in its stripes of purple, green and white. A gasp came from the crowd.

'Today, there is injustice in our land,' Violet continued. 'It is an injustice that affects every woman who is present here. It is an injustice that affects every man whose wife, mother or sister does not have the opportunity to be an equal to him. It is an injustice that affects every girl and boy whose mother does not have a fair say in shaping her children's future. This injustice is clear and simple: women cannot vote.

'Women have no voice in this land without the vote. They cannot send their representative to Parliament. They cannot call for justice. They cannot call for peace. They cannot call for equality. They cannot call for change. They cannot call for laws to be made that will ensure their homes are safe, that their families have better lives. Because they cannot vote.

'Justice must be done. It must be done now, in this new twentieth century. No longer will women be silenced. No longer will we give up our liberty.

'Join me, as we raise our banners, our arms, and our voices. Give women suffrage!'

Violet raised her right arm in a gesture of freedom. 'Votes for women!'

'Votes for women!' Jane responded fervently, lifting the banner higher. The gold-edged letters glinted in the sun.

'Votes for women!'

'Votes for women!' A few voices came from the crowd, but there was no applause.

On shaking legs Violet stepped down from the podium.

Jane's eyes were shining as she clutched the banner. 'Oh, Violet, you were marvellous!'

Violet looked up at Adam, where he stood, still on the podium. The expression on his face when she'd called him her husband, that combination of pride and pleasure, had quite vanished. A stony coldness had taken its place.

Her heart sank.

'How dare you!'

A rough hand on her arm sent her hurtling around, her ankle twisting in the soft grass.

'Mr Burrows,' she gasped through the pain.

'How dare a woman speak of such things!' The M.P.'s eyes bulged, his face was bright red. 'How dare you!'

His fingers, still clutching her arm, dug through her sleeve.

Adam leapt from the podium, sending his straw boater flying. His voice was low, yet so sharp it seemed to form a blade. 'How dare you, Burrows. Unhand my wife.'

Mr Burrows stared at Adam, then at Violet. With a coarse expletive he released his fingers from her arm as if he were a dog dropping a bone.

Adam turned to Violet. 'Are you all right?' he asked in an undertone.

She rubbed her arm and nodded.

'Beaufort!' Burrows demanded. 'You can't say you support these—suffragettes!'

'I support my wife,' Adam said through gritted teeth. 'She is mistress of Beauley Manor and any offence caused to her is an offence to me.'

Mr Burrows spluttered. 'But we're members of the same party! You know our policy for dealing with such women. They're a disgrace.'

'The disgrace is your poor manners,' Adam replied swiftly. 'I suggest you compose yourself, sir, and stop creating a spectacle.'

'It's women making speeches that's the spectacle! To use a garden party for political purposes. It's disgusting.'

Violet found her voice. 'And I suppose you have never used a social occasion for political purposes, Mr Burrows?'

The M.P.'s look of contempt took her breath away. 'I refuse to discuss politics with a woman.'

'I suppose you think women don't possess the intelligence to do so? You are quite wrong. Women have all the intelligence to participate in the government of our country.'

His fists clenched, the M.P. thrust himself towards her, his chest puffed out like an irate cockerel. 'How dare you presume to lecture me, you, you…'

Beau leapt up, barking sharply.

Adam pulled back the dog's collar. His voice

remained low, but penetrating. 'I would ask you to control yourself, Burrows. If you cannot be civil to my wife, I suggest you leave Beauley Manor. Now.'

The M.P. almost spat with rage. 'With pleasure. I wouldn't want to stay where there are such goings on. You'll regret allowing your wife to make a show of herself, Beaufort.'

One of Adam's hands was a fist, the other balled tight around Beau's collar. 'It's you who will regret it, sir, if you ever lay another finger on my wife.'

The M.P. stuck out his chest, then backed away after a glance at Adam's clenched fists. He gave Violet another glare before he stamped away.

Jane stared after him open-mouthed, the banner still in her hand. 'Well, I never. What a horrible man. You did right to stand up to him, Violet.'

Violet turned to Adam. His expression was impenetrable.

She reached out her hand towards him. 'I'm sorry. I didn't expect such a reaction.'

Ignoring her outstretched hand, Adam retrieved his Panama boater from the grass.

'Didn't you?' he asked curtly. 'I might have warned you, if you'd chosen to confide in me. We'll discuss it later.'

The violet fell from his hat.

* * *

Violet watched from the window as the last of the wicker chairs and tables were put away. The sun had gone down and the evening air had chilled. She pulled her shawl around her.

The garden party had been endless. What was supposed to have been a delightful afternoon had been marred by her awareness that Adam hadn't joined her side on any further occasion after she'd made her opening speech. He'd kept his distance, as he made the rounds of the lawn, ensuring he conversed with everyone present. He was popular, she realised, watching the women smile at him and the men eagerly shake his hand. He had an ease that drew people to him. She realised she could make out his voice among the crowd, and particularly his laugh, as he joked with some of the local boys as they tied their legs together for the three-legged race. She'd given out the prizes for the races and treasure hunt, admired the handiworks at the stalls, chatted and smiled, all the while miserably aware of Adam's avoidance of her. He'd gone to play cricket in the end and scored a captain's innings, so Jane had reported. She'd heard the shouts, but hadn't lingered too long to watch.

Yet along with her dejection her anger had grown. She had every right to speak her mind, regardless of what anyone like Mr Burrows thought. The M.P. was precisely the kind of man whom the suffragettes fought against.

But she didn't want to fight Adam.

Wearily, she made her way up to the solar. Inside was Arabella. Violet sighed. She supposed her elder sister-in-law had loathed her speech, too. Perhaps she thought Violet had discredited the Beaufort family.

'That was quite a speech.' From where she was seated by the fireplace, Arabella looked at Violet over the top of her book. 'Bravo, Violet.'

Violet stared at her sister-in-law, amazed. Arabella's usual haughty manner had quite disappeared.

'Why, thank you, Arabella. That's not what Adam thought,' she added miserably.

'Don't worry about Adam,' Arabella said. 'He's like Beau. His bark is worse than his bite.'

'Is it?' Adam raised an eyebrow as he strolled into the room.

He still wore his cricket whites and he'd caught the sun during the garden party. His face appeared slightly tanned, making his eyes more sky than midnight.

Arabella closed her book. 'Talking of Beau, I think I'll take him for an evening walk.'

Silence fell as she left the room.

Adam shut the solar door and leant against it, his long legs crossed. 'It's time we had a talk, Violet.'

All afternoon, as the garden party had dragged on, Adam had wondered what he would say to Violet. Contrasting emotions had roared around his body that he'd only been able to release out on the cricket field, as he'd thwacked the ball with the cricket bat over and over again.

Pride. Disbelief. Fury. Rage.

And an overwhelming protectiveness for his wife.

He'd said the words aloud for the first time when he'd introduced her to the crowd before she gave her opening speech. It was then he'd known that something had permanently changed inside him, something powerful.

His wife. Those two simple words, but they'd made him stop and catch his breath.

At their wedding ceremony, he'd taken his vows seriously. He'd been stunned by his feelings when he'd raised her veil. But it wasn't until she stood next to him on the podium, so beautiful to him in her white hat and purple dress, with the green sash tied around the stem of her slender waist, that he'd felt married to her.

A partner. A helpmate.

His wife.

He'd been proud to say those words. Proud of her. And when on the podium she'd called him her husband, he'd felt that same rush of pride and happiness.

It was entirely unexpected and disconcerting, to say the least.

Now, standing before him, Violet lifted her chin. He knew that movement of hers well by now, a combination of defiance and confidence.

'I agree, it is time we talked,' she said. 'Time for some plain speaking.'

'Indeed.' He indicated the sofa in front of the empty fireplace. 'Shall we sit?'

She hesitated, then moved across the room, head still high, and took a seat at one end of the sofa, allowing for distance between them.

He crossed to the drinks tray. 'Would you care for a drink?'

'No, thank you.'

He raised a brow. 'I thought you liked whisky.'

She smiled briefly. It was enough to take away the strain.

'Perhaps I will have one.'

He poured generous measures for them both. Even if it was before dinner, he needed it.

He handed her the glass, avoided her fingers.

Avoiding the sofa, too, he took his drink to one of the leather club chairs, sat and tilted it to face her.

'Did Burrows hurt you?' Just saying the man's name brought back the rage.

She shook her head. 'No. I twisted it when he pulled me, but my ankle's not injured.'

She held it out beneath her skirt. They were so fine, her ankles. Another, now-familiar emotion added to the mix as he looked at her leg in its white buttoned boot and stocking. He wondered, momentarily, if she had worn her striped garter while she gave her extraordinary speech.

He forced his mind back to the matter at hand.

'I'm relieved he didn't hurt you.' Adam took a draught of whisky. 'I'd have had him up for assault if there had been any lasting damage.'

'Many suffragettes have experienced a lot worse. They've been punched and bruised, had bottles thrown at them. I know the risks.' Violet gave another lift of her chin. 'I suppose this talk between us is about my speech.'

He nodded.

'Then please hear me out,' she said quickly, before he could speak. 'You have to understand. Being a suffragette isn't a hobby. I have to take every chance to speak out for the Cause. I told you of my desire to make speeches for suffrage. I can't miss an opportunity, especially one that presented itself as it did this afternoon. But I never meant to embarrass your family, or you.'

He raised an eyebrow. 'You didn't embarrass me. Is that what you thought? I was surprised, certainly. Taken aback. But it was a good speech. You have a talent for it.'

She widened her eyes. 'You liked it?'

'It was impressive.' No one could deny that. He'd watched the reaction of the crowd. She'd stirred them. Her voice, strong and clear, her message direct. If women like Violet continued to speak out for the Cause, women's suffrage had a chance. The annoyance of the M.P. only demonstrated what a challenge such women had become to some men.

'Then why were you so angry?' she demanded.

'I was angry at Burrows.' Angry didn't begin to describe it. To hear the M.P. insulting and then see him manhandling Violet had filled Adam with the kind of rage he'd never known existed. He'd only just managed to hold his fists to his sides to refrain showing the man quite how angry he was.

Violet shook her head. 'He's a horrible man, just as Jane said. How can you support him?'

'I don't support him personally. I support our party.'

'It's the same thing.'

'Not quite.' Adam half-drained his glass. 'I was angry with you, too, for a good reason. You ought to have told me what you were planning.'

She took a fast sip of her drink, then another. 'I didn't intend to keep it from you. I'm sorry.'

Adam threw back the last of his whisky, felt the fire go down his throat. He dropped his glass on the table, fought back the urge to seize her hands.

'This is a marriage, Violet. I haven't forgotten how you slipped away from the wedding reception. I've never pressed you about that, but I must ask you in future not to keep secrets. I didn't expect it to be the case, when we made our agreement. We don't need to keep secrets from each other.'

She bit her lower lip. 'I never thought of it that way.'

'We have to trust each other. We decided to be friends, remember? We don't want an atmosphere of deceit. This might be a marriage of convenience, but we want it to be a good marriage. Don't we?'

Slowly, she nodded, but her eyes remained troubled.

He had the impression she was holding back. There was still something she wasn't telling him. He was certain of it.

Adam exhaled. He wanted to show her, with

more than his words, what he'd discovered that afternoon. But he had to keep control.

It was damned inconvenient, the feeling that had come over him at the garden party, almost knocking him off his feet. He'd realised what it was as she gave her speech, standing there in front of everyone, undaunted. So brave. He'd had to walk away from her after the scene with Burrows, to keep control as the surge of his emotions took hold.

He'd begun to suspect it earlier, even before she spoke on the podium. In an absurd romantic gesture, the kind he never expected himself to make, he'd picked a violet, the only violet left in the grounds, the last of the season, and stuck it in his hat, merely to make her smile.

He might have embarked upon a marriage of convenience, but Adam knew he had to face an inconvenient truth.

He was entangled.

Chapter Thirteen

'And to the want, that hollow'd all the heart,
Gave utterance by the yearning of an eye...'
—Alfred, Lord Tennyson: *'Love and Duty'*
(1842)

The smell of warm crumpets wafted into the solar as Arabella lifted the silver lid.

'Time for tea, at last. I'm starved.' Jane cast aside her sewing, flopped on to the window seat and put her feet up on a cushion.

Arabella's mouth formed a disapproving line. 'You oughtn't to lie about like that, Jane. Sit up straight.'

'Oh, Mama's not here.'

Adam's mama had recovered from her influenza, but she needed more rest than usual.

'Will you pour the tea, Arabella?' Violet asked.

Arabella nodded.

They settled at the table in front of the fire. Since the garden party, the days had already become cooler, as summer hinted at autumn.

Violet carefully rolled up her own needlework. She'd taken up the project of mending the fine old tapestries in the manor. Many of them appeared to have been worked by hand, rather than on a loom, and she had some skill in embroidery. She intended to help all she could at Beauley Manor. Adam worked so hard. She wanted to do the same.

She spread a crumpet with butter. 'I had a pamphlet today. There's a new suffrage play to be put on in London. I intend to go and see it.'

Jane sat upright on the window seat. 'Oh, how marvellous! I did so enjoy *Votes for Women!* I'd like to see another of her plays.'

Violet shook her head. '*Votes for Women!* was written by Elizabeth Robins. It is soon to be published by Mr Mills and Mr Boon, I believe.' She was looking forward to its publication. Having missed seeing the play performed, she was keen to read the printed script.

'The upcoming play is called *How the Vote was Won*. Not that it has been won yet, of course. The title aims to inspire us. It is by Cicely Hamilton. I'm sure it will be excellent, too.'

'I'm sure it will,' Jane agreed. 'Might I attend the play with you?'

'Of course. I'll send for tickets.' Violet turned to Arabella. 'Would you like to come, too?'

It was unlikely Arabella would want to attend another suffrage play, having expressed some disdain for the first, but it seemed ill mannered not to invite her. Since Violet had given her speech at the garden party, a new amity had developed between them.

Arabella hesitated over the teapot. 'Perhaps I shall.'

Jane's mouth dropped open. 'You will?'

Violet closed her own mouth before it could fall open as widely as Jane's. 'That would be delightful, Arabella.'

Arabella nodded, then picked up her book.

'Suffrage dramas are being performed in private residences,' Violet said thoughtfully. 'It might be possible for us to put on a play here at Beauley Manor. We might raise funds for the Cause.'

'That would be marvellous!' Jane exclaimed again.

Violet laughed aloud. Jane's enthusiasm for the Cause was beginning to rival her own.

'I'm still to attend a suffragette rally,' Jane said.

Violet glanced at her leather writing case. Along with her other correspondence, a letter she'd received that morning had perturbed her greatly.

A lilac letter.

She wrung her fingers together. She couldn't ask Jane to accompany her to the suffrage event referred to in the letter. It would be far too dangerous.

Glancing up, she saw Arabella studying her over the top of her book. She had also been in the solar when Violet opened her lilac letter.

'Are you quite well, Violet?' Arabella asked now.

'Of course,' Violet replied with a quick smile.

She checked the little gold watch pinned to her bodice. Lately, since the garden party, Adam had taken up the habit of returning to the Manor earlier. Sometimes he even dropped in for tea. Many men considered teatime merely a pastime for the ladies, an interruption to their day, but he didn't appear to bother about such conventions.

As if she'd summoned him, the door clicked open. Adam strolled into the solar.

He smiled at Violet across the room. Her heart leapt. Her day had been so absorbing, with the unsettling letter about the Cause, but as always, she continued to think of him during the day. Her mind had been engrossed, but her body sprang into life at the sight of him. It had been that way ever since he'd held her in the river.

She hoped it would dissipate, over time, this sense of longing. It had to. But instead, it was growing more powerful. They hadn't strayed again across the line set by their marriage of convenience, but they had become closer in a way she had not anticipated after the garden party, as they both worked hard on their respective causes and the estate. They were truly becoming friends. More than friends. A partnership was forming between them, as they shared their daily lives together.

Idly, he picked up the letters that had been left for him on the silver tray. His hands fascinated her now. They were so strong, yet she knew they could be so gentle.

She watched, as if mesmerised.

With one finger, he slid open an envelope.

She bit her lip. The encounter in the river had to be forgotten between them. She had to erase the sensations he'd aroused in her, created not by words, but by touch.

The secret touch of Adam's hands.

At the letter tray, he'd moved on to a large bundle of papers. He was reading intently, a frown fierce between his eyebrows.

'You're keeping secrets,' he'd said to her, after the garden party. 'You have to trust me. We have to trust each other.'

Uneasy, Violet glanced at Adam, and again at her writing case and her own letter.

The fire in the grate flickered red, orange, yellow. The blue-and-white tiles around it, old, chipped, but holding their own, were a surprisingly good match to the array of fashionable pale blue china on Violet's dressing table, along with crystal and silver lidded pots that glistened in the firelight, as she sat, reflected in the glass.

Adam knew her routine now. It had become his most cherished hour.

Watching Violet dress for dinner.

Not that he watched her undress, of course. That would be unthinkable. He grimaced inwardly. Not to say unwise.

Yet he couldn't resist their time alone together. The habit brought him a sense of security that he'd never experienced before. Whenever he could, he came back to her at dusk, around tea-time, and always before dinner, when they had a short time alone together before going downstairs to the hall and the company of his family.

At this hour of the evening, the connecting doors were now usually open after Violet had changed her clothes, when she was adding the last touches to her toilette. When she had changed from the skirt and blouse she usually favoured for the daytime—practical, but well made—she would put on an evening dress and open the doors between them. He never opened them himself, he'd made that rule. But he made sure he was there.

At first, their connecting doors had remained

closed all day and all night. Then, one evening not long after the garden party, she'd emerged to ask him to help her clasp a necklace. She hadn't wanted to call her maid for the small task. Many women wanted their maid in constant attendance, but not Violet. He liked that about her.

'Gatekeeper, butler, field hand and lady's maid,' he'd said with a bow. 'At your service.'

He knew, from her continued similar requests, some necessary, some maybe not, that she, too, cherished the growing intimacy between them. Now he regularly clasped a diamond necklace around her slender throat, tied a sash or buttoned a difficult catch. She would help him, too, with a cravat, or to fasten his cuffs. Sometimes she would merely ask him about his day, or who was coming to dinner, or he would listen to what had passed in hers.

Tonight, out of her purview, he'd washed and was fully attired in his evening clothes. He could have gone down to dinner, or to the hall for a drink. Yet still he lingered upstairs.

Near Violet.

His wife.

She'd opened the doors already tonight. From the low chair near the connecting door, he witnessed her slow, leisurely movements. As dusk fell, many other women would draw the thick velvet curtains, but she did not. There was no chance of her being seen from outside, the garden walls were too high for that. The soft twilight coming in the window on her skin made it whiter than ever, creating shadows and curves as she lifted her arms to attend to her hair.

It had been a damned awful afternoon, but seeing her there made some of the horrors of the last few hours evaporate. Whether she was as aware of him as he was of her, he wasn't sure.

He stretched out his legs. It was all so extraordinary. He'd liked her when he'd proposed, well enough, he'd thought, to make a match of it. Surely there didn't need to be more than liking. His parents hadn't even had that, at least not by the end, when cold silence between them alternated with bitter arguments. There had always been tension, always an undercurrent. With the horrifying debts his father had been hiding he now knew why, of course. But as a young boy, he hadn't known the reasons. He'd only known that marriage looked unpleasant and damned inconvenient. A marriage of convenience was surely enough, rather than to have love turn to such bitterness.

His marriage to Violet had become more than convenience. He no longer denied it to himself. He could only suppress it.

'Adam?'

He passed over the threshold from his room into hers. From where she was seated at the dressing table, she smiled at him. She wore deep blue velvet, a favourite shade of hers, in a gown that fitted her curved form perfectly. Around her neck was a black choker with a sapphire-and-diamond jewel. Dazzlingly blue, but not as dazzling enough to take away the blue from her eyes.

She held up a diamond-and-sapphire earring. 'I'm wondering whether to wear these. I don't wish to overdress. What do you think?'

He stood behind her. 'I think you look beautiful.'

Damnation. He swore inwardly. Honour meant he could not lie to her, but paying compliments was surely ill advised.

His words hung in the air, like the scent of violets. He could smell violets now. It was the perfume she wore. It stood on the dressing table in a crystal bottle, a purple bow tied around its neck. The scent drove him to the same kind of distraction as the taste of a violet cream.

'Thank you,' she said, after a moment.

In the mirrored glass, their reflected eyes met and held.

Over her shoulder he reached for her curled hand. Her fingers opened at his touch. He took the earring as if to hold it against her ear, fought back his desire to caress the base of her ear with his lips, his tongue, his teeth. To follow with his lips the path deeper, between the crevice of her low-cut evening gown.

In the looking glass he watched her creamy skin turn to rose, as if she read his thoughts. She dropped her gaze first, fumbled for the matching jewel.

'I can put the earrings in,' she said.

He dropped the earring he held on to the glass top and backed away.

'Adam.' In her reflection, her forehead had creased as she looked at him more closely. 'What's happened?'

He sighed as he shifted away from the dressing table. 'I've had the full report on the manor.'

She spun around on the velvet stool. 'Of course. And?'

He stared down at the floorboards. It still seemed unbelievable. The floor of this very room had crashed beneath them. That had been bad enough. But now...

'Adam! What is it?'

In an instant she was beside him. She put her hand to his chest, as if testing his heartbeat. 'Tell me.'

Adam exhaled. 'Beauley Manor is sinking.'

Her hand fell as she stepped back, aghast. 'What do you mean by that?'

He clenched his jaw. 'Beauley is built on marsh-land. You saw what it means, that day at the river.'

She nodded. 'It's marshy all around. Danger-ous. It goes deep.'

'Indeed.' The marshland could be like a swamp, or quicksand, for those who didn't take care. At Beauley Manor, no care had been given for de-cades. The lack of precaution horrified him. Now, time and lack of upkeep had taken its toll. 'I told you there used to be a moat.'

'I remember.'

'The manor may as well still have a moat,' he said harshly. 'There's so much water under the building that it is slowly descending into the ground.'

She gasped. 'It can't be so!'

He gritted his teeth. He'd seen the worst of it. He'd known it was bad, but the rot and damp in certain parts of the cellar floors were horrifying. 'It's true.'

He moved away from her and stared out into the deepening darkness as the sun set.

After a painful breath he swung back to face her. Even though by law her money was now his, he had to be completely honest.

'Rebuilding Beauley Manor could sink your fortune.' His tone was blunt.

She gasped. 'All of it?'

'All of it and more. Every penny of your settlement could go into Beauley and it still may not be enough.' He hauled another breath. 'I cannot use your marriage settlement.'

'What? No! But that was our agreement,' she protested.

Adam paced the floor. 'I never imagined it was this bad.'

He'd seen the evidence that afternoon. It ripped him apart, as though he were part of the fabric of the building. In a way, he was. His family had built it, lived in it, protected it, cared for it. Until now. It wasn't of his making, but on his watch, their family home would be no more. A home like Beauley wasn't for one generation. It was for the next generation and the next. Only by preserving the past in readiness for the future could ancient homes be maintained. Certainly not by throwing it all away on a gaming table.

'It's too late,' he told Violet bluntly. 'Beauley Manor can't survive.'

Saying it aloud made it even worse. Beauley, sinking into oblivion. A rubble, a ruin. An Atlantis, beneath the mud.

She stepped in front of him. 'Adam. We have to try.'

We.

The small word stopped his pacing.

Her face as she stared up at him mirrored his concern, as though trying to take some of the burden from him. Sharing it.

Unexpectedly, his shoulders relaxed.

'If we use all our money, is there a chance we can save Beauley Manor?' she demanded.

We. That small, powerful word again. 'It's possible.'

'Then we must try,' she repeated with more firmness.

We. Again.

He shook his head. 'It's foolhardy.'

'We can't let Beauley disappear before our eyes!' she cried. 'We must save the manor.'

'No.' He bit out the word. It would be dishonourable to misuse her money, as if gambling with it. He could never do that. 'I won't risk your fortune.'

'But Beauley Manor has lasted for centuries. We must ensure it will last for centuries more.'

Adam cleared his throat. She understood what it meant, to be committed to something bigger than himself, more important. To be committed to a Cause. The manor was his cause. She'd seen that, from the start. The manor was more than a private home. It meant so much to the community, to the village, to the family.

'I wonder if there is a way,' he said slowly. 'I've been turning it over in my mind. I've developed an idea of my own that may not be so costly. We might be able to excavate, to dig down to the bedrock, and build columns, new, strong foundations.'

'That's a brilliant idea!' Violet exclaimed.

'I don't know how deep the bedrock is,' he cautioned.

'Can you find out?'

He nodded. 'There are new innovative engineers who might be able to implement my idea.'

'You're the master of Beauley, you know the manor better than anyone else. I'm sure they can make your idea work. After all,' she added with a smile, 'you told me that if you can build a wall, you can build anything.'

Adam's grin flashed. 'So I did.' Then he sobered. 'My plan will require extensive rebuilding. The manor still needs major work, from the very foundations.'

Violet lifted her chin. 'Then we will rebuild it. From the very foundations.'

Adam lifted his eyebrow. 'You seem to be speaking for us both, Violet.'

The connection between them flared into life.

'Do you think it our duty?' he asked, his voice husky.

Violet's heart tightened. 'Beauley Manor has become more than a duty to me. I've grown to love it.'

His eyes turned to midnight. 'Is that so?'

Violet swallowed hard. He'd been so honest with her. It had drawn them even closer together. She wanted to tell him what was on her mind, too, how much the thought of what she planned to do next for the suffragette Cause troubled her.

Instead, trying to keep her voice light, she said, 'There's something I must tell you, too. I have to go to London for a suffragette meeting tomorrow.'

He studied her with more perception than she would like. 'You mentioned a rally, I recall.'

She blushed. It wasn't a rally, or a meeting, but she couldn't reveal more. 'It's suffragette business.'

He looked at her quizzically. To her relief he didn't press it. 'I need to go up to London, too. We can travel together.'

'Oh—'

He raised an eyebrow. 'Is there some difficulty in my accompanying you?'

'Oh, no,' she said. 'It's just that…'

He lifted one corner of his mouth. 'Suffragette business is women only.'

'Something like that,' she said.

Now a definite smile darted at the corner of his mouth. 'I shall be at my club. Men only. Unless there is a suffragette climbing the balcony, attempting to hang a banner.'

His club. Where they'd met, or almost met. How long ago it seemed when she'd had the wrong address and ended up in his arms. 'Do you think women will ever be allowed to join such clubs?'

'Are you planning to try?' he asked with a searching look.

She tried to laugh. It came out as a kind of strangled choke. 'Of course not.'

The forked lines formed between his eyebrows.

'Women will be allowed into such clubs one day,' he said at last. 'If women get the vote, everything will change. Though it might take some time. It all depends on the vote.'

Violet nodded. Gaining the women's vote was crucial. She wouldn't, couldn't falter now, even as her longing to be even closer to Adam grew.

After he'd gone, she went to the blue-leather writing case she'd brought upstairs earlier. It had been made as part of her trousseau. She ran her fingers over the gold embossed initials. V.R.B. Violet Regina Beaufort.

She had changed her name, but not her commitment to women's suffrage. Her burning attraction to Adam was becoming more than a powerful distraction, it was a force she could barely deny. Yet she must.

Unlocking the writing case, she unfolded the letter and read it once more.

Comradess!
Hear our Call!
Valiant women who have pledged that violent protest is the only solution to gain our suffrage, it is time to act.

Bring your strength, bring your courage, bring your might. Bring tools, bring rocks, bring bricks. Hide them from view. Show your colours, but do not make contact with any other woman wearing the purple, white and green.

At the stroke of the hour, together we will take action. If they will not let us in the doors, we will break the windows.

Beneath these statements were printed a time and a date.

Beneath the time and date was printed an address that made Violet shudder.

She supported militant action, but this mission…

surely it was going too far. Yet she had pledged to it. She couldn't back out now.

Her heart sank. If only she could tell Adam. She longed to confide in him completely. To share her deepest feelings, her fears. To say everything, leaving nothing unsaid. The relationship developing between them was more than friendship, more than partnership. To deceive him now...

Violet crumpled the letter in her fist. She couldn't tell him about her new mission for the Cause. He'd told her he wanted no secrets between them, but she had made him no overt promises. She'd been careful not to, even though it had hurt. She didn't want to lie to him. It tore at her heart.

But some secrets had to be kept. Some actions had to be taken.

No matter what the cost.

Chapter Fourteen

'Will someone say, then why not ill for good?'
—Alfred, Lord Tennyson: *'Love and Duty'*
(1842)

Violet lifted her handbag and winced.

In the early hours of the morning, after lying awake until dawn, she'd hastened down to the river and collected a pile of smooth river stones. Some large, some small.

Back in her bedroom at the manor, after an anxious glance at the connecting door between her and Adam, she'd packed the stones into her brown crocodile-skin handbag, the largest one she owned, and snapped the locks shut.

On the carriage ride from Beauley to London, the bag had weighed heavily on her lap. She'd kept her fingers firmly on the handle, in case Adam offered to carry it for her as she boarded or alighted from the carriage.

She'd tried to keep her nerves hidden, though she sensed, from his quick darted glances, that he sensed something was amiss. She'd avoided his eyes, gazed out the carriage window, half-unseeing, at the trees that lined the Kent lanes. Already the leaves were beginning to fall and a frostiness was in the air. She wore an autumn-weight coat, a tweed made of wool, in shades of brown, mauve and black, plainer than she normally wore, with a white blouse and black skirt underneath, chosen for its roominess around the hem. She would never wear a hobble skirt, regardless of the fashion.

Especially today.

At the last minute, there were two other items she'd added to her attire. The first, the sash she'd embroidered herself, with violets, that she'd made for her wedding day. She wore the sash often. It went with many of her other dresses and skirts. The other item: her tricolour garter. She'd wanted to wear it to remind her of her pledge to the Cause. She'd wanted to wear it, too, she'd realised, to remind her of her marriage to Adam.

It had been hard to sit opposite him in the carriage and not blurt out her fears. A sickening sensation had been building in her stomach the closer they came to the capital. He'd made no comment, but she was sure he sensed her unease.

For some of the journey he'd been sketching out his plan to excavate and build beneath the manor. His strong hands that could lift stones so easily and build walls had a gentler touch, too, that was evident as she watched him draw. More than once he looked up to see her gazing at his long fingers as his pencil glided across the paper. She'd turned her head hastily to look at the view.

They'd passed one of the new touring cars on the road and she discovered their shared enthusiasm for the horseless vehicles. The sight of the sleek car, with its open top and tooting horn, had taken her mind off her anxiety, for a moment.

'They're the future of travel,' Adam had remarked, putting away his sketch. 'We could get from Beauley to London in half the time in a motor car.'

'My papa has a Rolls Royce,' Violet told him. 'He loves new inventions. I'm sure he'd be delighted to take you out in it, should we visit my parents in Manchester.'

That was another concern. From her mama's most recent letter, Violet knew her papa had not been in complete health. He'd had another of his turns, her mama had written, though not a serious one. It would be timely soon to make a visit.

'You wanted to visit the Cadbury chocolate factory,' Adam commented, as the carriage wheels turned. 'Perhaps we could go by motor car.'

'You'd accompany me?' she asked.

He smiled. 'If you wish.'

Why, he'd remembered what she'd told him

about her dream to make the lives of the Coombes factory workers better. 'Yes, I did. I mean, I do.'

Once in London, amid the hustle and bustle of horses, carriages, cars and people, she'd asked to be dropped off in front of Liberty department store in Great Marlborough Street.

Adam had frowned. 'I thought you were attending a suffragette meeting.'

'I have a few errands to attend to first.' Avoiding his eye, she'd leapt down on to the street before he had time to question her further, the handbag swinging wildly.

The timber-and-white Tudor-style building was a welcome sight. It was one of her favourite emporiums. It had recently begun to sell suffragette items, not only tricoloured ribbon that could be added to hats and belts, but also garments and underclothing in the suffragette shades, as well as handbags, shoes and slippers, too. She was eager to examine them, but not today.

Entering Liberty briskly by the front door, she hurried to where the new season's hats were displayed. The pretty straw boaters and wide brims of summer had been replaced by the tams and toques for the coming winter months. There were felt hats with brims, too, that could almost completely hide one's face.

Purchasing one in a drab brown shade, with a single feather, she hastened to the ladies' room and exchanged it for her fashionable black straw with a black-and-white satin bow. She'd decided during her sleepless night that some anonymity was called for. In the band of the drab hat she tucked the striped ribbon.

Purple. Green. White.

She'd bought a thin woollen shawl, too, to throw over her shoulders for when the time came.

She glanced at her pocket watch.

Soon.

Adam lifted his glass of claret and stared into its red depths. The club kept an excellent cellar, there was no doubt about it. The food, though plain, was excellent, too. It was the first time he'd returned to the place after the debts his father had accrued at the gaming tables. They'd been paid off now, thanks to Violet.

In spite of the debts that had been incurred by his father, there was no hindrance to his membership of the club, of course. That wasn't the English way. He would never be blackballed. If he'd cheated at cards—not that he would ever dream of doing so—that might have been a different matter, but financial embarrassment could be glossed over for a Beaufort. He had life membership, as his male ancestors had before him, and his male heirs would for generations to come. Yet strangely, he no longer felt as accepting of the club's rules.

It wasn't the financial embarrassment his father had caused that made him look at the club and its inhabitants with new eyes. He was ashamed to admit he'd never really considered it, but today he noticed, more than ever before, the lack of women. Was it so unconscionable to allow women into the club rooms? They'd had a female monarch in England, after all. Queen Victoria had reigned longer than any king on the throne and no one had objected on the basis of her sex. But no women could enter his club. Adam had to admit, it was starting to make him feel damned uncomfortable.

He had begun to question a great deal since Violet came into his life. It crossed his mind that he would have been delighted to have her company for luncheon, or to stay overnight at the club. It would be convenient now that the Beaufort town house had been leased. It was just around the corner, where he'd first laid eyes on her that memorable night. The town house hadn't needed to be sold any more, now the debts were paid, and the rent would bring in a welcome income. Not that the Beaufort family needed it any more, with

Violet's money, but he saw no reason to be imprudent. He'd never waste her money. He'd had enough of an example of that. The leasing arrangement had gone ahead. There were a few papers to sign, but nothing that couldn't be handled from Beauley Manor. It wasn't why he'd come to London.

Adam frowned. Violet had said she planned to attend a suffragette meeting, but her behaviour on the way to London had been puzzling. She'd been anxious on their journey, very anxious indeed. She'd gripped her handbag with whitened knuckles all the way. It was unlike her.

He'd swiftly completed his own business in London. His hand went to his waistcoat pocket. Yes, it was still there. Whether it would ever see the light of day…

'Damnation,' he muttered, as he knocked over the claret glass.

The waiter rushed over. 'We'll replace the tablecloth immediately, sir.'

Adam stood up to let him do his work. 'Apologies.'

He took in the dining room, with its white walls, hung with oils of the hunt in heavy gold frames, the ceiling picked out in gilt, the aged red-leather chairs, the gleaming silver and the glistening crystal goblets. Yet nothing was overdone. It looked more like a country home than a town house. Its shabby elegance had a curious soothing effect on the digestion, it was generally agreed. Members could lunch in groups, or alone, as he was, knowing they could converse or not be disturbed as they wished. He didn't mind lunching alone, but he would have liked the choice to invite Violet. But she wouldn't get further than the threshold before she would be stopped from entering. Politely, of course.

She would provide more interesting conversation than some of the club members. Adam hid a grin. Next to him were two white-haired gentlemen discussing the virtues of the club's potted shrimp. The shrimp was, indeed, excellent, but their conversation had been going on for quite some time.

Spotting an occupant of the adjacent table made him stiffen. He had not seen the man come in.

Edgar Burrows, M.P. Adam hadn't encountered the Member for his local area since he'd told him in no uncertain terms to leave the grounds of Beauley Manor, after the M.P. had manhandled Violet.

Remembered rage sent his fists curling. Burrows wasn't a member of his club. He must be a guest of one of the other two men on his table. One was a member Adam knew slightly and disliked. They were all huddled furtively over the white-clothed table that held more than one bottle of claret.

Burrows glanced up and caught Adam's gaze. He gave a sneer that was supposed to be a greeting, Adam guessed, but the malicious gleam in his eye took Adam aback.

Burrows licked his lips and returned to his conversation.

His senses on alert, Adam glided closer. He couldn't quite make out what the men were saying. Then he heard a word that made him lean in. *Suffragette.*

Violet crossed the road. While she'd eaten her luncheon at Liberty department store, a bouillon followed by brown-bread sandwiches and chicken timbales that she'd hardly been able to worry down, she'd studied her map. She considered that she had a good sense of direction, but London always managed to catch her out.

Along Regent Street, going past Hamleys toy shop, she murmured to herself. In other circumstances, it would have made a delightful outing. She liked to look at window displays. In Hamleys' window there was a teddy bears' picnic, but she hurried past.

Soon Piccadilly Circus came into view, packed

with carriages and quite a few of the new motor cars. A policeman was blowing his whistle and directing traffic. Quickly she crossed the street away from him.

Through to St James's Square. On to Pall Mall and there they were. The gentlemen's clubs. They lined the streets in the area, tucked in between private houses and places of business. None of the clubs had names or any other means of identification on the front of their buildings. That would be ostentatious and might lead to unwanted visitors.

Like herself.

In spite of her nerves, she chuckled. The lack of signage was the reason she'd mistaken Adam's town house for the club. Many of the buildings in the area were in a similar architectural style, so grand with their columns and arched windows. Some had the same stone balconies that had led her to end up on the Beaufort balcony that fateful night.

She hoisted her handbag. She wouldn't make that same mistake again.

With increasing urgency, she hurried on. She knew she had to find it.

Finally she stopped at the correct address. There it was, that balcony she'd never climbed, her original target for suffragette action, that bastion of male privilege, with the doors that, like the doors to the British Parliament, were closed to all women.

Violet bit her lip. Adam might be still be inside the club. He'd told her he was planning to lunch there. She checked her watch. He'd probably be gone by now.

An overwhelming longing came over her, to knock on the door, to find him. How she longed to confide in him, to tell him the heavy secrets she was forced to carry alone. Yet they were separated by those closed doors.

Doors made by injustice. Doors made by prejudice.

Doors that must be opened.

Violet lifted her chin. So much had changed since she had decided to climb the gentlemen's club balcony and hang her suffragette banner. So much had changed since she'd tumbled into Adam's arms. Her feelings for him. Feelings she wanted to share.

One thing hadn't changed.

Her dedication to the Cause.

She would never surrender.

Adam took his chance. He'd long finished his luncheon, had been toying with fruit and cheese. The potted-shrimp starter had indeed been excellent, so had the roast beef for his main course, but his attention hadn't been on the food. Within the realms of civility, he'd spent the mealtime straining to hear fragments of muttered conversation at the table where Edgar Burrows and his companions had been steadily drinking for the past hour. Fortunately, as the group of men continued to imbibe their claret, their braying voices became louder and louder.

'Dangerous nonsense.'

'Silly harpies.'

'Lock them all up.'

When Edgar Burrows left the dining room, Adam threw aside his linen napkin and sped after him. In the arched hallway of the club, he looked right and left. There was no sign of the MP in the lobby. Then Adam spotted him, a portly figure, swaying as he ascended the interior marble staircase. Edgar Burrows was almost at the landing of the next floor.

Adam took the stairs two at a time and seized the MP by the shoulder. 'What in damnation were you saying about the suffragettes?'

Edgar Burrow's eyes darted. 'Beaufort. What do you mean?'

Adam swore. 'I overheard you in the dining room. You should learn to lower your voice if you don't want every member of the club to hear you.'

Keeping hold of the MP's shoulder, he steered

him into one of the upstairs sitting rooms, done in dark green leather. It had an aspect on to the street and a wide balcony, trimmed with waist-high stone columns, each curved like a woman's corset.

It was the balcony Violet had intended to climb, all those months ago.

Adam faced Burrows. 'Let's have it. What's going on?'

'Silly harpies,' the M.P. slurred drunkenly. 'None of them deserves the vote or anything like it.'

Adam shook his head. 'I know your view on women's suffrage, Burrows. It holds no interest for me. Tell me what you were talking about downstairs.'

Burrows sneered. 'The suffragettes are about to get the lesson they deserve.'

'What kind of lesson?'

'The police had a tip-off. There's some kind of extreme militant group that's formed here in London. You must have heard the suffragettes have started smashing windows and so on. Disruption. Disobedience. Throwing bottles and stones. But this new group is even worse.'

Adam lifted his eyebrow. 'In what way?'

'This group is prepared to use more violent

means. Arson. Bombs. Attacks on members of the government. Any means at all.'

'I don't believe it,' Adam said flatly. 'The suffragettes aren't anarchists.'

'Some of them are. Today they're heading for Downing Street.'

Adam took a step back. 'Number Ten?'

The Prime Minister's residence.

'That's it. But they've got too big for their pretty little boots this time.' Burrows consulted a fat fob watch. 'This afternoon will see an end to this stupid nonsense. The police force are ready and waiting to make an example of them.'

Violet.

Adam held down his fists. 'You'll be sorry, Burrows, if I hear you've had anything to do with such a plan.'

'I know your sentiments, Beaufort.' Burrows sniggered. 'You're influenced now, aren't you, by your wealthy new wife? I keep my wife in her place. Women should go back to the kitchen or the bedroom, where they belong.'

Adam swore. 'Women want the vote. What's wrong with that?'

'Once they have it there will be no end to their demands. They'll want to be governing us next.'

'As the Member of Parliament for my area, you represent me,' said Adam, trying to restrain his temper. 'You ought to consider the mood of your voters.'

'All very well for you!' the M.P. spat. 'You don't need anyone's vote. Sitting high and mighty at Beauley Manor.'

Adam gritted his teeth. 'If I could make a difference on the women's matter, I would. That's up to Members of Parliament, in the House of Commons.'

'Then leave us to our job,' the man said unpleasantly.

'It's your job to listen to your voters,' Adam responded curtly. 'We're in the same political party. You know as well as I do, there are men who want suffrage for women.'

'They'll never get it on my guard. And after today, the suffragettes might get the message.' Burrows licked his lips. 'Oh, yes. Some little ladies will be very sorry indeed.'

'How so?' Adam demanded.

Burrows shrugged. 'None of your concern.'

Adam seized the M.P. by his necktie. 'How are they planning to stop the suffragettes?'

The man's eyes bulged. 'They've got in the mounted police. Undercover detectives, too. They'll be armed and waiting for these militant suffragettes. So will prison cells.'

Adam dropped the M.P. like a rat.

'I say, where are you going? Beaufort?'

Adam raced from the room, down the stairs and out of the club.

In St James's Park, Violet sat by the lake and caught her breath.

The park was like a lung, with its fresh greenness, in contrast to the noise of carriages, cars and pedestrians in the surrounding street. Ducks glided on the lake. Flowers danced in the breeze. Children played with hoops and kites. Other women, including a nanny with a baby carriage, were dotted around the park benches. She wondered if they, too, were biding their time.

Violet swallowed hard. She'd never experienced such agitation before, even when she made her protests, or when she gave her speech at the garden party.

Adam had been beside her, then.

She checked her watch yet again. Her legs trembled as she stood and lifted her handbag. It weighed even more heavily now.

Keeping her head down, she continued upon her way until she reached the other side of the park. Horse Guards were on parade in their red-and-white uniforms and polished black boots, their helmets glistening in the sun.

She walked past.

Big Ben chimed the quarter-hour as she entered Parliament Square.

She stopped in awe. The beauty of the Houses of Parliament took her aback. They were like churches, with their spires, towers and turrets. Sacred. Hallowed. Unexpectedly, her eyes welled with tears. Was it so wrong to want women's voices to be heard in those ancient buildings? To yearn to have a vote, a share in the government of the country she loved?

Violet ran her glove over her eyes and hurried on.

'Damnation.'

Adam muttered under his breath as he dodged a couple of bankers in their bowler hats. In spite of the warmth of the day, they held umbrellas, tightly furled.

Pelting along the crowded street, his coat flying out behind him, Adam headed for the Houses of Parliament. It was a route from the club he knew fairly well, but never had he raced there so fast.

As he ran he searched for her, glancing rapidly down streets and alleys, to the right, to the left. What had she been wearing that morning? Some kind of attractive striped hat, he recalled. He hadn't taken much notice. As usual, it had been the frank blue eyes beneath the brim of the hat that held his attention and they'd been full of fear, he realised now.

His wife was daring, brave, but she was no anarchist, he was sure of it. Her protests were of a kind to bring attention to the Cause in a sensational manner, but surely she didn't intend to cause damage or destruction. Civil disobedience was a method that the suffragettes were increasingly embracing in their desperation to have their argument heard. He knew Violet supported it. He understood it himself. But what Burrows described sounded extreme. It was the kind of militant behaviour that meant someone could get seriously hurt, or worse.

Violet.

Adam dashed across the street, narrowly avoiding an oncoming omnibus.

He had to find her, before she made a mistake that cost her what she cherished so much.

Her freedom.

Violet turned the corner. The tall, stately stone buildings on either side of the wide road loomed up, casting a shadow as she slowed to a stroll.

Second street on the right, she said to herself softly. No hurrying now. She needed to appear calm, as if she were simply out for a walk. How difficult it was, to amble along the pavement, when her body was full of nervous energy.

From beneath her low-brimmed hat she glanced about. So many men. Dressed for the city, in dark frock coats, suits, top hats and bowler hats. She hadn't anticipated how women would stand out amid the city men of business.

They were so obvious.

Too obvious.

Here and there she spotted another woman. One of them sported a purple, green and white ribbon on the lapel of her overcoat. Like Violet, she carried a large handbag. As she passed she met Violet's glance, then hurriedly looked away.

Further on, another woman, little more than a young girl, again wearing the suffragette colours, this time as a ribbon in her hair, lugged a carpet bag. Another group of women were walking further ahead.

All of them were heading in the same direction.

To Downing Street.

Violet frowned. The girl with the carpet bag was walking not too far ahead of her on the pavement. Violet could have sworn that a gentleman in a felt fedora hat and overcoat was following the girl, from some distance behind.

She glanced over her shoulder. There was another man behind her, similarly dressed in an overcoat, with a newspaper under his arm. He appeared as nondescript as Violet wanted to be. Yet he was paying her close attention. She was sure of it.

She bit her lip. Opposite, on the other side of the street, leaning against a lamppost, was a man who appeared to be doing nothing.

Except watching the entrance, two streets ahead on the left.

Her heart thudded. She walked on, holding her crocodile handbag tight against her bodice. She crossed a street. The nanny she'd spotted in St James's Park appeared from around the corner, pushing the pram. Another of the nondescript men followed behind her.

Something was wrong, Violet was certain. All her senses screamed the alert.

Still, she walked on.

Her limbs began to shake, so much so that she struggled to take the next step.

Next left, she told herself. All she needed to do was take the next left.

Head down again, she checked her watch with trembling fingers. She could hardly snap open the gold lid. Only a few minutes to go before Big Ben would strike.

So would the suffragettes.

She lifted her head.

Ahead, two women came out of the entrance of a building, their arms linked. One of them wore a hat crowned in purple, white and green.

Violet stared at the woman's hat. Instantly, the colours infused her with courage.

Loyalty and dignity. Purity. Hope. Silently, she repeated the words to herself.

Those words, those ideals, were worth fighting for.

Violet's mouth dried.

Coming the other way were a group of blue-helmeted policemen, carrying batons.

Adam raced past Big Ben and the Houses of Parliament.

The streets were far more packed than usual. As Burrows had told him, the police were out in force. He could spot the men in plain clothes, as well as those in full uniform.

Adam's breath was jagged. The pain in his chest was so sharp it winded him, almost bringing him to his knees.

He ran on, his boots slamming against the pavement as he put on speed.

At last, ahead of him he saw a figure with a familiar determined step. She wore a different hat and a shawl thrown over her shoulders, but he'd have known her anywhere.

To his horror he saw she was at the corner of Downing Street.

He surged through the crowd of people.

'Violet!'

At the sound of Adam's voice Violet spun around.

Behind her a horse reared.

Chapter Fifteen

'Then follow'd counsel, comfort and the
words
That make a man feel strong in speaking
truth...'
—Alfred, Lord Tennyson: *'Love and Duty'*
(1842)

Adam threw himself between Violet and the horse. Just in time he pulled her out of the way of the mounted police constable, at the ready with his baton.

'Adam!' Violet gasped. Her normally pink cheeks were chalky white. 'What are you doing here?'

'You're in danger, Violet.' Keeping tight hold of her arm, he pulled her around the corner from Downing Street and out of sight, into a doorway. 'The police know about your suffragette plot.'

'What?' Her heartbeat pounded.

'You must get out of here.' Adam scanned the street. 'Now.'

She shook her head in defiance. 'I must complete my mission! I have to do this.'

'Don't you understand?' His jaw clenched. 'The police are waiting for you. More mounted police are on the way. They're prepared to use any means necessary. You're walking into a trap.'

'What?' She wrenched her arm from his grip. 'Big Ben is about to strike. I must warn the other suffragettes!'

'Violet! No!'

Her crocodile-skin bag thudded to the pavement as she raced back towards Downing Street. She saw them now, the uniformed policemen, as well as the others in plain clothes, dotted among the men of business and government. The police vastly outnumbered the women. There could be no element of surprise. The suffragettes didn't have a chance.

Violet's hat took wing as she raced towards the two women with linked arms. She wasn't meant to speak to them. Those had been her instructions. She saw the surprise in their faces, then consternation, as she whispered in their ears.

Both women took off, one of them stopping to warn others. The suffragettes began to scatter like birds.

Violet sped towards the nanny with the pram. There was no baby in it, she saw in shock, as she passed on the message to the woman, who instantly abandoned the pram with its load of bricks.

The girl with the carpet bag. She, too, dropped her luggage and disappeared among the people on the pavement.

Another woman. Another. One by one, she warned them. One by one, away they flew.

Further down the street, Violet caught the arm of yet another suffragette sporting a purple, green and white rosette. 'Spread the word! Abandon the mission!'

Panting for breath, she stopped and scanned the crowd for more tricolour ribbons.

Footsteps pounded behind her.

Adam grabbed her by the hand. 'Violet! You've done enough. Run!'

Hand in hand, Adam and Violet dashed away from Downing Street. In the distance Big Ben chimed the hour. Aware of startled looks as they raced through the mass of people, she let Adam lead the way as they pelted through narrow streets she didn't recognise.

Away from the Houses of Parliament. Away from the police.

Pigeons fluttered as they raced past. They kept running. Her shawl fell to the pavement, trod on by a passing businessman. They didn't stop to pick it up.

Her hair fell from its bun on to her shoulders, tendrils blew across her eyes. She pushed them away. Her breath came faster and faster as she tried to keep up with him.

Still at a pace, Adam glanced at her over his shoulder. He must have seen she couldn't run for much longer. Instantly he slowed. Turning into a narrow street, he took another few strides and pulled her into an alleyway, into his arms.

He kissed her forehead, her cheeks, her chin, her mouth, as if checking she was there. 'I can't stand you being in danger.'

'I'm not in danger now.' Not in his arms. Ever. She knew that, with him, she was safe.

She clung to him as his mouth moved to her lips. Again that searching desire, his need to know she was safe. She reached her hands up inside his collar, to the warmth, the strength, of his neck, drawing his mouth harder on to hers. Wanting him, needing to know that he was there, too.

Their lips still joined, he drew her further into the dimness of the alley, backed her against the brick wall. She let out another gasp as he slid his hands over her hips and lifted her against him.

Their bodies melded into each other, hip to hip. All she wanted was to stay joined. To his mouth, his hands. She raised her arms against the wall as he tore her skirt higher.

Her upper back grazed the bricks as she slid deeper into his grip. His strong fingers were on her bare skin now, as his lower body thrust to find entry between her thighs. In reply she wrapped her legs around his and pulled him closer.

He stepped away from her. Her petticoats fell, covering her legs, as she shuddered against the wall.

His coat stretched across his broad back as he hauled in a jagged breath. 'Damnation, Violet.'

Adam spun back on his heel. His eyes were dark. 'I can't take you in an alleyway.'

Violet's breath heaved. 'Take me home. Now. Please.'

She loved him. It throbbed into her brain as the wheels of the carriage carried them home, side by side, her body pressed against his.

She loved him. It throbbed again, as they hastened quietly up the stairs, away from anyone else in the Manor.

In her heart, her soul, her body, she knew it, as he carried her through his bedroom, and into hers.

She loved him.

Dusk had fallen. A fire had been lit in the fireplace that connected their two rooms. It blazed, on both sides, but the curtains were open. Sunset hinted through the cloudy sky.

Silently he closed the curtains. Silently he closed the connecting door.

They had barely spoken on the journey. Now the room remained quiet, except for the sound of her breathing and his.

Near the bed she stood, waiting for him. He came to her, ran his finger up her chin to caress her lower lip, reminding her of the kiss they'd shared in London, so long ago now, before they agreed to wed. She'd been bold, kissing him first, even though butterflies had danced in her stomach then, too. She would be bold again.

She touched his finger with the tip of her tongue.

'Violet,' he groaned, with another stroke of her lips. 'Are you sure? We agreed to…'

She took a step away from him, then another, towards the four-poster bed.

She raised her chin.

'I agree to this.' Reaching behind, she untied her silk sash and let it fly, like a banner. It fell to the floor in a silk ribbon of white, purple and green.

He glanced at it, then back at her.

'I agree to this.' One sleeve, and then the other.

She undid the buttons that held the blouse closed at the elbow. Left them undone.

Lounging against the dressing table now, he watched her every move.

'I agree to this.' Slowly she began to undo the buttons at the front of the bodice of her blouse, one by one. His gaze stayed on her fingers, as if he were unbuttoning each button himself. The bodice fell open, like a flower.

Lounged now against the dressing table, he watched her every move.

Her breath even faster now, she slipped off the blouse. With a snap of the clasp at the waist, her skirt followed.

Now her breasts rose and fell as he beheld the low-cut camisole that partially revealed her. Gathered at waist and fitted with tiny buttons down the centre, it was trimmed with the finest French lace.

Still he watched.

'And I agree to this.' She reached for the top camisole button.

In a stride he was beside her. His hand closed over hers.

Together. The first button, half-hidden among the lace.

Free.

The second button, at the top of her corset.

Free.

The third button, deep between her cleavage.

Free.

Her mouth was open now. He studied it briefly, then returned his attention to the camisole buttons. The fourth button. His finger trailed down the soft skin between her half-bared breasts. The final button.

Free.

Pushing the lacy cotton aside with both hands, he revealed the pink tips of her breasts, thrust forward by her corset. Lowering his head, he lifted her breasts above the top of the corset and took one in his mouth.

Violet gasped. She reached for the carved bedpost to hold her upright as with a teasing tongue and teeth he turned one tip, and then the other, into a tingling point that drove waves of desire deep into her belly.

He lifted his head, spanned with his hands the busked corset that cinched her waist into the S-shaped hourglass. His arms corseted her now, as he undid the buttons at the back. His mouth was close to hers, so close she sensed he could feel each light breath that escaped her lips.

With a push the delicate fabric of her camisole was down her shoulders, liberating her arms before he let it also slip away. At his loosening of a tie at her waist, her white-silk waist petticoat followed, forming a circle of lace and ruffles at her feet.

His gaze travelled down.

Adam exhaled. 'You're wearing your garter.'

Adam took Violet in from head to toe in as she stood there. She had no idea how beautiful she was. Her chestnut hair lay loose on her bare shoulders. Her blouse and skirt were gone now, leaving only her corset, edging the pink-tipped breasts he had held in his mouth only moments before.

Beneath the corset were a pair of her lacy knickers, their ruffled edge coming to the middle of her thigh. And below it, her tricolour-striped suffragette garter. The garter he'd refused to let enter his mind, or his imagination, ever again, since he'd seen it, tied around her leg on their wedding night.

'Do you agree to this?'

The sapphire of her blue eyes changed to something deeper at the huskiness of his voice. He knew couldn't hold back much longer. It had been building inside him for too long.

If he undid that garter, it would be his undoing.

'I agree,' she whispered.

Her heaving breaths lifted her bare breasts, still

jutted over her corset. He unsnapped the metal hooks and eyes. Her figure was merely enhanced by the garment, not created by it. Her figure was full, her waist tiny.

The corset hit the floor, lay like a half-shell.

The sheerest of vests, finer than a veil, lace trimmed, had protected her skin from the bones of the corset. He cupped her breasts, now heavy in his hands, brushed the points with his thumb, saw her quiver, before he slipped the vest from her body, to reveal the pearl of her skin.

Now only those frilled knickers and stockings remained. Widening her legs with his hand, he rolled down each of the stockings, taking his time, and reached for the garter.

Slowly. He made it last, lingering on the softness of her thigh, watching her response, the rise and fall of her unconstrained breasts as she, too, watched him. Untying the garter, he ran it across her inner thigh and through his fingers.

She took the garter from him, with her left hand, the one that bore the wedding ring he'd given her. The ring was on her finger now. He saw the golden glint as again she clutched the bedpost, while with his own finger he reached again to thrust his hand inside the white-silk knickers, his fingers grazing the tender part that led inside. He kissed her open mouth as she gasped, exploring her mouth with his tongue at the same time he explored her with his fingers, as he'd done that first time, in the river.

He couldn't wait. Not any more. Releasing her, Adam backed away, reached for the buttons of his waistcoat.

Violet's hand covered his. 'Let me.'

Violet's body throbbed deep inside where Adam had touched her. She moved closer to him, her hand on the smooth velvet of his waistcoat. Like the linen pillowcases it was worn, but fine.

Boldness built inside her, overcame the fear of it being the first time she'd been with him, like this.

'I'm curious,' she whispered.

His mouth curved, sent the dent darting in his cheek, for a moment. It made her relax.

It made her bolder still.

He'd removed his frock coat, but not his necktie. It was loosened around his strong throat. Now she undid it, her breasts brushing against his waistcoat. With the same tantalising care as he had shown undoing the buttons of her bodice, she popped the buttons down his torso, from his chest to his belly. Her hand flickered over the top of his trousers as the last button released.

He suppressed a groan, buried it in her hair.

She stepped back, surveying her handiwork, then tugged his white shirt free. These buttons came faster, but her fingers had become faster, too, as she tore off his shirt.

He was bare chested. She'd noticed, from glimpses of him, that he didn't wear a union suit and rarely bothered with the undershirt. Yet it still surprised her, finding his bare skin and the slight dark hair of his chest. She rested her fingers over his heartbeat. The points of her breasts sharpened against his bare chest.

Her fingers hovered at the buttons of his trousers.

He reached for her before she could venture further. Lifted her and laid her on the bed. Her stomach lurched as he stood over her, between the carved posts.

His eyes were a question as he leaned in, his half-clothed body held above hers. In reply Violet reached his hand and guided it towards her lacy knickers. He slid them away.

With a flick of a button, he released his trousers. His undergarment was soon gone, too. She touched him, as he stood there, as she'd wanted to, in the river.

His hand stopped her, cuffing her wrist. 'There'll be no turning back, Violet.'

'I agree.' Her throaty voice sounded strange to her ears.

In a swift, taut movement he leaned over the bed, taking her with him, as she fell back against the sheets, his body covering hers.

Violet arched, again, as she had when he'd touched inside her. Her thighs parted wider. Through the darts of pleasure a pain ripped through her as he thrust inside.

Stronger. Deeper.

Another gasp escaped her lips, a cry, bringing Adam up to search her eyes with the same question as before.

Again, she answered. She lifted her body to meet his.

To agree.

Violet stretched. Opening her eyes, she adjusted her sight to the dimness. The fire had gone out in the grate and darkness had come. Night had fallen.

Beside her, Adam was gone.

She bit her lip. The previous day's emotions swirled inside her mind and body. The fear. The passion.

Her fingers twisted the edge of the sheet as her mind went back to the mission she'd undertaken for the lilac-letter group, the mission that had almost gone so horribly wrong. She could have ended up being arrested, not in Adam's arms. It had been terrifying, seeing the police waiting to trap the suffragettes. Thank goodness Adam had warned her in time. But it wasn't merely the mission's failure that caused her consternation as she reflected on it, still twisting the linen sheet in her hands. She pondered further. She wasn't sure she agreed with the principle of causing criminal damage to the Prime Minister's residence. She had to be honest. She'd felt uncomfortable carrying her bag of Beauley river stones.

She hadn't had a chance to discuss what had happened with Adam. In the past few hours, there had been so few words between them. He'd told her so much, with his lips, with his hands. She'd tried to do the same. But there was still so much to say.

She sat up naked in the bed. Seizing her white peignoir, she pulled it over her body.

She had to find him.

She had to tell him now, in words.

It wasn't only the estate that she had grown to love. It was the master of Beauley Manor.

Adam gazed out of the window, into the darkness, to where he knew the river lay beyond. The river where he'd held Violet in his arms.

Soon it would be dawn. Beyond the connecting door she lay asleep.

In every way she amazed him. She'd matched his every move, if not initiated it. Their first kiss, in London, had told that she had a passionate, physical curiosity. Last night, she'd proved it further. He'd been concerned, for her more than him. But he hadn't reckoned with her plain speaking. There had been no coyness. Only honesty. Her forthrightness held her in good stead, even in the bedroom. She was brave. It must have hurt her, that first time, yet she hadn't shown fear.

His fists curled around the cord of his robe.

Fear. He'd never been fully familiar with that emotion before. He'd not known it was possible to feel it with such force, on behalf of another person.

'Adam.'

He turned to find her wrapped in a silky dressing gown, her chestnut hair spilling over her shoulders. She looked so beautiful. Young. Vulnerable.

His heart clenched. Now he'd made love to her, held her in his arms, he could pretend to himself no more.

He'd fallen in love with his wife.

The moment that realisation came, another followed, fast.

He had to take control of the situation.

He had to keep her safe.

She smiled, almost shy, like a violet in the shade. 'I have something to tell you.'

'I have something to tell you, too.'

Every muscle in Adam's body tensed as the powerful, protective urge kicked in. His next words came before he even registered them in his brain. 'You must give up being a suffragette.'

Chapter Sixteen

'Of love that never found his earthly close,
What sequel? Streaming eyes and breaking
hearts?'
—Alfred, Lord Tennyson: *'Love and Duty'*
(1842)

Violet stared at Adam in horror. 'You don't want me to be a suffragette?'

His expression was cold, stern. A sternness she had never seen in him before. It made him look older, more austere, as he had when she'd first met him. Before they were married, before she came to Beauley Manor.

He nodded curtly. 'I'm resolved upon it.'

She stepped back, aghast. She'd never expected this, especially after what had happened between them. 'I don't understand.'

He pushed back his hair from his forehead. She'd run her fingers through his hair, earlier.

'It's too dangerous,' he said. 'Surely you must see that, after what happened in London.'

'I wasn't hurt,' she protested.

'Only because I saved you in time. I can't always be there to protect you, Violet.'

He moved close, so close she could feel the heat from his body, beneath his robe. 'I asked you not to keep any secrets from me.'

She bit her lip. She'd wanted to tell him before the mission. How she wished she had.

'Somehow you've got yourself involved with a group of near-anarchists,' he went on, 'Or so I'm told by Edgar Burrows.'

'Edgar Burrows would blacken the reputation of any suffragette!' exclaimed Violet.

'Is he wrong about the activities of your group?' Adam asked, evenly. 'They're militants, aren't they? Prepared to do anything.'

If they will not let us in the doors, we will break the windows.

Uncomfortably, a phrase from the latest lilac letter came back to her.

'How can you ask this of me?' She choked back her tears.

'Violet—' Adam's voice became persuasive '—you must listen to me. There are other methods. Peaceful, law-abiding methods. What the suffragettes like your group are doing is foolish.'

'What method do you suggest?' Anger began to

build inside her, hot through her veins, rising to her chest. 'What, leave it to the men, I suppose?'

He kept his voice controlled, though his eyes glittered. 'The law will change, in time.'

'The time is now! We'll wait a hundred years if we don't seize this moment.'

He shook his head. 'You've done enough for the Cause.'

'Will you tell me how to behave now?' she asked, enraged. 'How to walk? How to talk? How to dress? How to think?'

A muscle flared in his cheek, near where the dent played when he smiled. There was no smile now.

'Don't be ridiculous,' he bit out.

Tears smarted in her eyes. He'd never spoken to her in such a manner. Where had he gone, the man who only hours before had made love to her with such passion and such tenderness?

'It's not ridiculous,' she insisted. 'You promised me. We vowed to each other.'

'I didn't realise what it would mean until I saw what you were up to today. You must stop. It's a risk I can no longer let you take.'

'It's my risk, not yours!'

'You're my wife.'

'Your wife.' She threw the word back at him. 'Not your possession. You can't treat me like a child. A doll with an empty head. Is that what you want?'

'I want you safe,' he said, through gritted teeth. She sensed he was struggling to control his emotions. 'Secure.'

'My safety is my own concern,' she threw back at him.

'You have to give up your membership.' His voice had become as hard and unyielding as a police baton.

Violet lifted her chin. No matter what her own reservations about the mission, she couldn't allow him to command her. 'It's not your decision.'

His jaw hardened. 'I'll prevent you from taking part in these militant activities, if I have to.'

'What?' She staggered backward, as if his words were blows. Then she lifted her chin. 'Will you imprison me? Lock me up? That's the current solution to the suffragettes.'

He cursed. 'You will be locked up if you continue. You nearly committed a crime today. I cannot allow this any longer.'

'Allow.' She repeated the word with sarcasm. 'You have no rights over me.'

'I have rights.' He clipped the last word. 'My rights as your husband.'

'But you promised me a marriage of convenience,' she insisted. 'We made our terms.'

He swore, under his breath. 'You didn't tell me your life would be in danger.'

'I didn't know that would happen!'

'Those horses could have trampled you. The police were waiting to arrest you. If you were caught, you might have gone to prison. Do you understand?'

'Of course I understand! Do you think me a fool?'

'Yes!' he shouted. 'Yes, I think you're a fool for risking life and limb! Do you understand me? I forbid you to attend any more such protests.'

'You forbid it?' Her voice rose, too. 'Who do you think you are?'

'I'm your husband!' he roared.

'And my master?' she threw back at him, in equal rage. 'Have you forgotten our arrangement? Was it all a lie, a trick, to get your hands on my fortune?'

The bedroom became deadly quiet. She'd gone too far, a voice in her head warned her. But she lifted her chin. She couldn't back down.

Adam clenched his fists. 'That's a despicable suggestion.'

'You promised me I would have my freedom.'

He slammed his fist into his hand. 'You won't have your freedom if you don't have your life!'

Violet shook her head, furious. 'I know the danger. I'm prepared to take the risks...'

'You won't,' he said through gritted teeth. 'Not any more.'

'What will you do to stop me? Lock me in my bedroom? You know the terms of our marriage.'

'Those terms were a mistake.' He bit out the words. 'If you knew how much I regret...'

He swung away from her and glared out the window, into the night.

Violet stared at him in horror. His profile was set as hard as the bricks of Beauley Manor. Her heart began to thud.

'You regret the terms of our marriage,' she whispered.

Yet the way he'd touched her. He'd made her believe...

Adam turned back to face her. His expression was inscrutable. 'Of course I regret it. The terms we made were ridiculous. I don't know what impulse drove me to it.'

'You got the better side of the bargain.' She threw the words at him while his rang in her ears.

He regretted marrying her.

Adam's jaw clenched. 'So you regret the terms also.'

'I didn't say that.' Tears welled in her eyes,

but she forced them back, lifting her chin. She wouldn't cry. She was too angry to cry.

'Our terms must change,' he said. This is exactly what I wanted to prevent. What happened today must never happen again.'

He regretted making love to her, too.

In a stride he crossed to where she stood by the open doors.

'Do you understand me, Violet?' Adam seized her arm. 'You can no longer be a suffragette.'

She wrenched herself away.

'I'll always be a suffragette.'

With a crash, she slammed the connecting doors shut.

Violet turned the key in the lock.

Seated on the dressing-table stool, she shook with anger. She half-expected Adam to come crashing through the door. She'd never seen him so furious. She'd never been so furious herself.

All the sensations of the day and night churned inside her as she stared at herself in the mirror. In the looking glass, her cheeks were as white as the satin of her peignoir.

She stood and paced the room, trying to gather her thoughts. They were as jumbled as skeins of silk in her embroidery box.

Hopelessly entangled.

Her worst fears had come true. She'd told

Adam, before they married, that the bonds of love could bind a woman. She was caught in them now, those bonds of love.

Her fingers twisted as she paced up and down.

They had spoken such angry words to each other. He wanted her to give up the militant group, ordered her to do so in a way she'd never imagined he would. It was true he'd touched a nerve about their militant activities. She felt conflicted about it herself, but it had to be her choice.

She wiped her eyes with the back of her hand. She thought he'd understood. She could not allow him to make her decisions. Nor could she allow her feelings about him to sway her.

She shuddered. Loving him as she now knew she did, would she be able to defy him? In time, would she weaken? Surely she would never give up being a suffragette. But she'd never wanted to have to choose between love and duty. Was there room in her life for her passion for the Cause *and* her passion for Adam? Or would those bonds tighten?

He'd told her on their wedding day that he wanted to avoid entanglements. That physical contact must be kept to a minimum. She hadn't understood, completely, not then. Now she did. He hadn't wanted her to develop feelings for him.

Yet she had. She'd trusted him. Made love to

him. Given him her all. She shivered, as though his hands were once again caressing her skin. How could it be? The desire she'd witnessed in his face, at his hands, in his body…yet he'd said he regretted the terms of their marriage. Beyond the connecting door, she heard another slam shut. Adam had left his side of the bedroom by the door that led directly to the upper hall. She drew a painful breath. It would be intolerable to remain another day. She had to leave Beauley Manor. She had to break free from the bonds of love.

Was it dishonourable to leave? Feverishly, still pacing, she tried to reason. No. She had married him in good faith. He'd married for freedom from the burden of financial ruin for his family, his home. She for the freedom to follow her ideas, to support the Cause.

For her, that freedom was gone.

She had done her part. Her dowry could be used to rebuild Beauley Manor, to save it from crumbling into ruin. No creditors could take it. The gambling debts his father had accrued had all been paid.

Her duty was done.

Dragging herself to her feet, she pulled out her trunk.

It didn't fall through the floor. Not this time.

At the wardrobe she began to pull out clothes.

Dresses. Skirts. Blouses. Back and forth. All piled in the trunk. Back and forth. Back and forth.

She stopped, still. At the back of the wardrobe was her wedding dress.

She sank to the floor, the white-satin dress in her arms. With her finger she traced the pearl buttons, the ruffles and ribbons, the puffed sleeves.

Wilt thou have this Man to thy wedded Husband?

'I will,' she'd promised. Looking back, it was so clear. She had wanted to marry him. Some wiser part of her had been urging her along.

Her heart.

When had she known she loved him? The realisation had come to her mind so clearly as they'd dashed through London, hand in hand. Her body had known, before her mind. It had tried to guide her. Her feet had known, when he asked her to dance at the ball, as they waltzed together, across the floor. Her hands had known, as she'd reached for him, needing to touch him, in the river. Her lips had known, at that first kiss, before they were even wed.

Violet took a deep breath. She ran her fingers over the pearl buttons on her dress, as she thought of her other vows. They'd spoken of children. One of each. A boy and a girl.

A pang of sorrow ripped down her middle, from her heart to her stomach. She'd begun to imagine those children, that boy and girl, playing on the lawn at Beauley. It was as if they already existed, were part of the family.

It wouldn't happen now.

She had to leave Beauley Manor, and those barely acknowledged hopes and dreams.

She couldn't stay. She couldn't remain, not after what had happened between them. Not when her feelings had changed so much for him.

Their marriage of convenience was over.

What a scandal it would be. A bitter laugh escaped her lips. A scandal had brought her to him. The scandal of being a suffragette. Now she would have to face a worse scandal, the scandal of leaving her husband.

She held tight to the wedding gown. She had to leave it behind. She wouldn't ask for the return of her dowry. She would never do that. She loved Beauley Manor as much as Adam did now. It had become her home. Her cause, too.

She'd helped save his home. That was all she could do. Now she had to save herself.

He didn't love her, as she had grown to love him. He had merely been doing his duty.

Tears poured down her cheeks as she hung the wedding dress in the wardrobe.

She'd married Adam for duty.

She'd leave him for love.

On the flagstones, Adam stood at the bottom of the stairs, Beau at his side.

'Damnation,' he swore.

When the connecting door had slammed between them and the key had turned in the lock, he'd stared at it, dumbfounded.

How had the conversation between them turned to such chaos, spiralled so out of control? He wanted to go to her, hold her in his arms and explain what had driven him to his harsh behaviour.

After what he'd experienced in his childhood, witnessing the horrific scenes between his parents, he'd learned to avoid anything that could wreck his sense of security and stability. His feelings for Violet had blasted through all that.

He'd intended to use reason, cool persuasion, to convince her that giving up her militant activities was the best course of action. He hadn't reckoned on that powerful, almost primitive force surging through him to protect the woman he loved.

He exhaled. Of course he loved her. He'd fought that deep attraction from the start, the pull that went beyond the physical. No wonder he'd been intent on ensuring they kept their physical distance. Now that distance had been breached, releasing all the feelings that had blazed inside him for so long.

Instead of cool reason, he'd lit a spark of fury in her that had ignited his own. He knew he'd ended up handling it badly, but still…

Damnation.

He'd waited for the connecting door to open between them again. When she didn't appear, he'd eventually gone downstairs, into the hall, and reached for a bottle of whisky.

Beau barked.

'Only one, boy. Don't worry.'

His father had drunk many a whisky in the hall, Adam brooded. He wouldn't fall into that trap.

He slumped into a chair by the open fireplace. The flames had long burnt out.

The whisky flared down his throat. It warmed his body, but didn't soothe his mind. The emotions churning through him had aroused painful memories of his childhood, memories he wanted to forget.

He gazed through the window, into the awakening sky. Red fingers of light pierced the violet dawn. It would soon be morning.

He drank again, deeply.

He'd go down to the river. It was always a calming place for him, even if lately visions of Violet at the water's edge haunted him there. In a short time, she'd become part of Beauley Manor. It was really too late in the year for an early morning swim, but he needed it. By God, he needed it. He'd walk, in any case. Give them both time to cool off.

She was so foolhardy. So stubborn. Couldn't she see that he'd do anything to protect her from harm?

He finished the whisky, resisted another.

He had to make her understand. But he'd let her be, for now. That was the most straightforward approach. He'd sort it all out, in the full light of day.

Seizing a coat, he headed out the door and clicked for Beau. The dog came leaping out of the manor, barking.

'What is it, boy? Come along.'

Beau barked again, circled.

'Come on, boy.'

He had to regain control. He'd walk for as long as it took.

Violet heard a bark from outside the window.

Folding the letter she'd been writing, she slipped it under a silver candlestick on the dressing table.

At the window, she stared out into the breaking

morning and looked down to see Beau chasing behind Adam as he strode away from the house.

Violet wiped her hands across her cheeks. 'Goodbye, Beau.'

The dog barked again. Fainter, this time.

She put her hand on the glass.

Adam didn't look back.

'Goodbye,' she whispered.

Adam flung wide the connecting door. He didn't have to search the adjoining bedroom to know Violet wasn't there. He knew it. Instantly.

She was gone.

Lying on the dressing table was a white folded paper. He picked up the letter and read it once. Twice. Three times before the words sank in.

He crumpled the paper into a ball inside his fist, let it fall among some items she'd left behind. Candlesticks, pots and bowls. A silver-backed hairbrush.

Mere remnants. Her presence had gone. It was more than the sight of her, that presence, as she dressed for dinner, sat at her dressing table, or brushed her hair. More than her scent, that fragrance of violets that followed her and now haunted him. More than her voice, making speeches about the Cause, or laughing, as she talked to him and offered him violet creams.

More than her touch, even though yesterday afternoon she'd found the places in his body that gave him more pleasure than he'd experienced before. More than the taste of her, sweeter than a Coombes Floral Cream.

Her presence was more than all his senses could put together. It was something else, something more. A connection between them that made him stronger, more powerful, yet more at peace. A knowing that at the end of the day she would be there for him, a surety, a sanctuary, a safe harbour for his body and soul.

He'd never expected that marriage could become a haven. It had never appeared so to him. But their marriage of convenience had unexpectedly begun to provide an opportunity to explore what marriage might be. Partnership, as well as passion.

He unrolled the ball of paper, scanned it again. She'd been fair, more than fair. Generous, but that was Violet.

He was to keep her dowry, for Beauley to be saved. The paper crushed into his fist again as he swore. Didn't she realise what an insult it was to him that she thought he would want her money, if he didn't have her? Did she think him so dishonourable?

He would return her money as soon as he could and find another way to save Beauley.

Casting the letter aside, he glared around the room. The sight of a wardrobe door left ajar made him wince.

Gritting his teeth, he threw it open.

Empty. Except for a garment left behind that almost brought him to his knees.

A white-satin shimmer. Her wedding dress.

Pain slammed into his chest.

Then he saw it, on the floor by the bed.

Purple. Green. White.

He picked up the scrap of tricolour ribbon. It would be a mistake to try to hold her. That was no foundation for a marriage. No matter how much he loved her, he wouldn't force her to stay. He'd cornered her, by changing the rules, by trying to control her.

All he could do now was to honour his side of the agreement, no matter how it tore him apart.

He'd promised Violet her freedom.

He had to let her go.

Chapter Seventeen

'The slow sad hours that bring us all things ill...'
—Alfred, Lord Tennyson: *'Love and Duty'*
(1842)

Violet awoke and stared at the violet-sprigged wallpaper and lacy curtains that she thought she'd never see again.

The last time she had awoken to the sight of her old childhood bedroom was months before. Before her marriage to Adam. Before she knew for certain what she had always feared.

Women could not have love and freedom.

Perhaps a man could. Perhaps a man could find in a woman's arms comfort, not a cage. Not that she'd believed Adam would ever cage her.

She shivered.

That was why it had been so dreadful, so painful. Such a shock. She'd thought they'd set out the terms of their marriage of convenience as equals. But, no.

Women and men were not equals. Not yet. Until women had freedom, there could be no love. Not the kind of love Violet wanted in her life. Not the kind of love she thought she'd found with Adam.

She threw back the covers and paced the floor.

Would she ever get him out of her mind? Ever since she had arrived at her parents' home she had been unable to get his name out of her head. It throbbed, like a headache.

Adam.

Adam.

Adam.

Seizing her dressing gown, she wrapped it around her and went to the window, pushing back the curtains.

After leaving Beauley, the entire journey back to the north of England had contained an air of unreality. A dreary rain had matched her mood. Pulling up outside her parents' door in the carriage, she'd felt numb, only to find, inside, the news of her papa.

'Violet! Oh, we're so glad you're here!' her mama had cried when she appeared in the drawing room, where her papa was seated with a rug over his knees.

'Papa!' She had rushed to him. 'You're not well.'

'It's my heart,' he'd admitted, struggling for breath as he tried to get up to greet her. 'It's been playing up.'

'He's not been well for some time,' her mama had said, wringing her hands.

'Why didn't you write and tell me it was this bad?' Violet had choked back a tear. Her father was normally up and about, not sitting on a chair by the window.

'Didn't want to worry a new bride. The doctors tell me I'll be fine,' he'd assured her. 'It's not being able to get to the factory that's worrying me.'

'You're not to get upset, the doctors said so,' Mrs Coombes put in.

'Well, it's lucky I'm home,' said Violet.

'Why have you come home, Violet?'

In an instant she'd made a decision. She wouldn't tell them what had happened between her and Adam and that their marriage was at an end. It would only upset her papa further.

'I missed you both. I wanted to see you.' That much was true, at least.

'It's lucky I came back,' she'd added. 'I can run the business for you, Papa. Just watch.'

Work. Yes. That was the answer.

Violet checked her watch lying on the dressing table. It was only seven o'clock, but she would go straight to the factory. The workers were there at eight. She would be there, too.

Anything to get that name out of her head.

Adam.
Adam.
Adam.

'I don't believe it!' Jane exclaimed. 'Violet wouldn't leave Beauley Manor! Not without saying goodbye!'

'She's gone.' Adam couldn't trust himself to say any more.

Jane appeared about to cry. 'But we're sisters now, that's what she said. Sisters! What about the Cause? What about the rally? She was going to take me with her to a suffragette rally in London. What about the suffrage play? We had all kinds of things planned. It isn't possible!'

'It's possible.' Adam clipped the words. He found it hard to speak.

'Where has she gone?'

'Back to her parents, I believe. In Manchester.' He guessed that much.

'But wasn't she happy here at Beauley?' Jane asked, bewildered. 'She seemed happy. Oh, I shall miss her so much.' Adam bowed his head. He slammed his eyes shut as he struggled to gain control. His sister's emotion would not trigger his own. He would not allow it.

'Adam.'

He twisted his neck, expecting to see Jane. Instead he saw Arabella's hand in its black-lace glove, on his shoulder.

'I'll miss Violet, too,' she said. 'I'm sorry she's gone. She—made a difference here.'

Adam nodded, not trusting himself to speak.

So she'd even won Arabella's heart.

She'd broken his.

'Good morning, Miss Violet—ooh, I forgot. You're a married lady now,' one of the men who worked in the factory called out to her.

'Violet is fine.' Violet smiled. In truth, she preferred it. She didn't want to think about being married. She must not.

Weeks had passed since she arrived in Manchester. The sounds of Adam's name, echoing in her brain, had reduced from more than hourly to only a few times a day, if she didn't allow herself to think about him. That wasn't often. But being called Mrs Beaufort would only bring it all rushing back.

Work, she reminded herself, yet again. It would remove the pain, in time.

She liked to spend time on the factory floor. She'd always loved the factory, especially as a child.

Every step of the process of making chocolates had always fascinated her. Now she was seeking improvements in the procedure. Sometimes she took visitors on tours, to show them how their famed Floral Creams were made, from start to finish. The cocoa beans came from the Orient. They were ground into a buttery mass. At the factory, in huge vats, sugar and milk were added and cooked together to make a delicious-smelling warm liquid. When the liquid was evaporated, a crumbly chocolate mixture was created, put through a mill, then mixed with liquid and butter to the correct consistency for Coombes Floral Creams.

In another part of the factory, essences were made from fruit and flower petals to make the flavouring syrups. They stood in glass bottles, glowing in jewel colours. The syrups were mixed with sugar and cream, then kneaded by hand into smooth fondant. The fondants were then dipped by hand into the chocolate by women Violet had known since she was a little girl. A crystallised petal, dusted in sugar, was always the final element. After scrubbing her hands, she'd often been allowed to place the petal on the top of the completed chocolate sweet.

The process looked easy, but Violet knew how many times her father had failed at creating the taste that made their chocolate fondants so popular. He'd never given up.

That was the Coombes way, Violet reminded herself.

She stood and watched the swirling chocolate being stirred. The scent of cocoa and warm sugar rose in her nostrils. She put her hand over her mouth.

A young woman from the chocolate finishing area rushed over. 'Are you all right?'

Violet straightened and smiled delightedly. She threw her arms around her. It was Hannah Walsh, whom Violet had known all her life. They'd played together as children. Now Hannah was the mother of two children herself. 'I'm quite all right. Oh, how are you, Hannah? It's so good to see you. Are your family well?'

'Very well.' Hannah beamed. Her eyes were bright in her freckled face. 'I'm expecting my third.'

'Congratulations,' said Violet. 'That's wonderful news.'

Hannah hesitated. 'There's something we've all been wondering. If it's true, I mean. You're a suffragette now, aren't you?'

Violet lifted her chin. 'Yes, I am.'

Always. No matter what it cost her.

'Some of us here at the factory want to start a

women's group,' Hannah said. 'Many of us want the vote.'

Violet nodded. 'It's a matter for all women.'

'Will you help us?' Hannah asked.

'Of course.' Violet reached out and squeezed Hannah's hands. 'I also plan to hold a meeting for women workers here in the factory. I want to know your concerns and how your working conditions can be improved. I'd be proud to help.'

'You would?' Hannah sounded amazed.

'I would.' Violet had been thinking, during her long sleepless nights, about how she could bring some of the ideas from the Cadbury factory to Coombes. She hadn't yet been to the Bournville village, the factory in a garden the Cadbury family had created for their workers. It made her think too much of Adam. He'd said they would go there together. That wouldn't happen now. But it was no reason for her not to put some of her social reform ideas into practice at Coombes. All the workers would benefit.

'I want to establish two social reform committees,' Violet explained to Hannah. 'One for men and one for women. It will need support from the women in the factory to make it work. Will you help me, too?'

Hannah nodded firmly. 'We'll work together.'

According to her reading about Cadbury's, and other books of business, late into the night, such reform committees could improve morale and help achieve success, as well as bringing the concerns of women workers to the fore.

As she walked away from the chocolate vats towards the factory office in the corner of the building, another wave of nausea came over her.

She leant against the office door, shivering. She was never ill.

Was it because she missed Adam? Sick with longing. Sick with love. Surely that could not be the reason?

Adam.

She'd had no response from the letter she left for him. Perhaps he was relieved she had gone, she thought bitterly. How had she been so wrong, so mistaken at what she'd taken for signs of true affection between them? She'd thought that the touch of his lips, his hands, had meant so much more than it did. She'd thought it was real. True.

True love.

'What a fool you are,' she said aloud.

'Did you say something, Violet?' Her mother popped her head around the door of the factory office. She had taken to coming to help in the mornings.

'No, Mama,' Violet said. 'Nothing at all.'

* * *

Adam skimmed stones across the river.

One. Two. Three. Four. Five. Six. Seven. A stone for each of the weeks Violet had been gone.

He hadn't thought it possible for the manor to feel so empty.

Earlier that day, before he'd come out for a walk to try, without success, to clear his head, he'd worked at his plans for Beauley. He'd heard from a notable engineer. Adam's plans were good plans. Great plans. Plans that could ensure the manor's survival for many more generations. It was possible to save the manor from its marshy fate, from sinking into oblivion. Beauley had stronger foundations than they first thought.

Beauley would survive. The manor could be saved.

Adam picked up another stone, forced himself not to imagine Violet on the edge of the riverbed, peeling off her stockings to reveal those stupendous legs, and the laughter, the kiss it had led to and more.

Through sheer force of will, he could manage to divert his mind by day. It was at night, while he slept, that his mind played havoc with his memory, turning the recollection of the night they'd spent together into dreams.

He lobbed another stone, watched it splash and ripple.

Those dreams. They were enough to drive a man into the river to cool off.

He turned back to the Manor. He would go over the plans again. He was determined to save Beauley without having to use any of Violet's settlement.

'We'll build new foundations.' Her voice echoed in his head.

'Adam!'

He looked up to see his sister racing towards him.

'Adam! You must come. Quickly!'

Too many chocolates.

In front of the full-length mirror, Violet patted her stomach. She twisted to look at her waistline from another angle.

Yes, it was definite. Her waist had thickened.

Too many chocolates, she told herself again. That's all it was. She managed a chocolate factory, after all. She had done so for over two months now.

But she hadn't been able to face chocolate all that time, her brain uncomfortably reminded her. And with the illness she continued to experience in the mornings—

There was no denying it.

Trembling, she sat on the edge of the bed. A strange, cold perspiration filmed her skin.

Pregnant.

That was the word she had been trying to stop entering her mind. She certainly couldn't say it aloud.

It made sense. She'd missed her courses, twice now. The first time, she'd assumed it was the upset of leaving Adam, followed by the shock of finding her father ill.

She counted back dates. It was possible. More than that. It was probable. All the signs pointed to it.

'Pregnant.'

This time she spoke aloud.

Now she understood the illness she'd experienced, watching the swirling chocolate being made. That was when it had started. She'd experienced dizziness, too, and other odd symptoms.

Her brain wouldn't take in the information properly. She'd told Adam that she'd wanted to wait to have a family in order to give her all to the Cause. Yet now, after their first time making love, she was carrying his child.

Surely it was impossible. Yet a flutter in her stomach, a flutter as light as a butterfly wing, a flutter of excitement as well as trepidation, told her that something had changed inside her, physically.

But emotionally…

Her stomach began to churn, swirling like the chocolate in the vat. It was such a shock. She couldn't think straight. Yet she knew, immediately, no matter what the future held, that no child that came from the love she had shared with Adam could be regretted.

Yet how would she cope? She bit her lip. She was a woman alone now.

After dressing in a skirt and blouse, leaving her corset looser than usual, she had made her way in a kind of daze over to the factory office. She hung her coat on a brass hook. The weather had changed to rain and cold.

She put her hand on her stomach and removed it hastily as her mother bustled in.

They got to work. It was a relief from the other concerns whirring in her mind. She was struggling to comprehend it.

'You have a head for figures, Mama,' Violet said later, after they'd been working on the accounts for a few hours.

'I used to help your papa right at the beginning,' Mrs Coombes confessed. 'It was so enjoyable for me. Then your papa hired people to do the work and he wanted me to spend time being a lady.'

'I had no idea.'

'We were happier somehow, even though we had so much less money, when we were first married,' her mama said wistfully.

'You can be happy in that way again, Mama,' Violet said. 'Don't stop coming here to the factory when Papa is better. You can keep an eye on him, make sure he doesn't overdo it. And he loves your company.'

Mrs Coombes's eyes widened. 'Do you think I ought?'

'Papa would adore it. I'm sure.'

'That would be so nice. I've been lonely in the house without you, Violet. There's only so much embroidery one can do.'

'Why, we're more similar than I ever suspected, Mama,' Violet said, amazed. 'I'll make a suffragette of you yet.'

'Oh, no. I couldn't be a suffragette.' Mrs Coombes looked horrified.

Violet bit her lip. She'd been considering further her own activities as a suffragette. In spite of her fury at Adam, she'd been forced to an unpleasant conclusion. She had reservations about the militant activities of the lilac-letter group.

'There are many ways to support the Cause,' she said.

'I will always support *you*, Violet,' Mrs Coombes said, with a surprisingly acute glance. 'I hope you know that.'

Violet blinked back sudden tears. 'I know that, Mama.'

She couldn't say any more. It was still such a shock. She wanted to confide in her mama about her pregnancy, but she couldn't. She needed some time.

They returned to the accounts.

A few hours later, when Mrs Coombes had gone back to the house, the women factory workers streamed into the office, with Hannah Walsh at the front.

More than twenty workers, Violet estimated. More than she had expected to attend. She had Hannah to thank, she suspected. They were packed so tightly she couldn't see who was at the back.

Moving around the front of the desk, she prepared to address the group. She'd clothed with care. A simple white blouse with a soft collar and cuffs and full sleeves, and a grey skirt. A tricolour suffragette ribbon looped into the chain of her pocket watch.

Nerves flickered in her stomach and her hands were clammy, as they had before she had given her speech at the garden party. Then, Adam had been beside her.

The women were quiet as they waited for her to speak. Hannah gave her a broad smile.

'Welcome, everyone. Thank you for coming here today.' She paused. Nausea still plagued her, but she wouldn't let it stop her speaking. After a deep breath, she managed to continue. 'There are over two thousand workers here at the Coombes Chocolates factory. Six hundred of them are women. As some of you know, I am a suffragette. It is my goal to see women be able to vote for our government in our country. But it is also my goal to ensure the best possible working conditions for women here at Coombes.'

She scanned the group. On many faces there were expressions of surprise as well as interest. She wondered what they would say if she told them how much she had in common with many of them now, especially with her old friend Hannah Walsh, not only as a working woman, but also as a mother-to-be.

'I intend to establish two social reform committees,' she continued. 'One for women and one for men. The aim of these committees is to help to create a happy family life for Coombes workers.'

Violet cleared her throat. A happy family life, with both parents. It was something that she might not be able to give the baby she carried. But the ripple of her heart and stomach told her that whatever happened, she would love Adam's child.

She focused on the women in front of her. She would try to create happy lives for the workers of Coombes Chocolates and their families, no matter what the future might bring. It meant more to her than ever.

'I need your help,' she told the women. 'I ask you now to make any suggestions you can think of that might assist women to do their work at Coombes and have happy families, too.'

Most of the faces in front of her were blank.

A woman who worked in the packaging section raised her hand. 'I'm not sure what you mean, Miss... I mean, Mrs Beaufort. What kinds of suggestions?'

'Well, over at the Cadbury Chocolate factory...' Violet began.

'Ooh,' giggled Hannah. 'Don't you let your father hear you talking about Cadbury here at Coombes.'

Violet chuckled. There had always been a rivalry between the chocolate companies in the north, and there were a few. There were the Cad-

bury, Rowntree, Fry and Terry chocolate businesses, too.

'Cadbury's have excellent conditions for their
workers at the factory at Bournville village,' Violet said. 'I'd like to imagine we might achieve
the same. If not better,' she added, with a note of
rivalry, and a smile.

The women laughed.

'What exactly do you mean, Miss Coombes?
Do you plan to build a village?'

'I'm not sure that's possible,' Violet conceded,
'but there are lots of improvements that might
be made. Such improvements are not only to do
with working conditions, health and safety, but
also to do with education and social life. For example, at Bournville staff are encouraged to attend night school and are allowed to leave work
early twice a week to attend.'

'Women as well as men?' asked Hannah.

Violet nodded. 'Another of their innovations is
to provide warm rooms to dry clothes and places
to heat food at the factory.'

'It would be so nice to have a hot lunch in the
middle of the day, especially in the winter,' said
one woman, with a nod.

'I've heard some factories in the south have
nurses, who help when the workers are sick and
their families, too,' another woman commented.

'That's right,' said Violet. 'They are the sort of ideas that I'm looking for. Let me be clear: I'm not making promises, but I do want to hear your suggestions. Please. Call them out. Don't be shy.'

'Playgrounds for the children,' came a voice.

'Half-day on a Saturday!'

'Football and cricket fields. The lads will like that.'

'Let's have a garden. With a lily pond.'

'Perhaps—a nursery?' one woman asked. 'Would that ever be allowed, in a factory?'

'A school. Let's have a school,' said Hannah.

'We could get up a women's hockey team!' a young woman said enthusiastically.

By the end of the meeting, Violet was overwhelmed with ideas. Some of the women, including Hannah Walsh, had agreed to join a committee and get some of the ideas started. The women left, chattering and excited.

'Upon my soul!' A voice came from the back of the room.

'Papa!' Violet exclaimed. 'Have you been here all the time?'

Her father's face was ruddy. 'If you mean have I been here for your women's meeting, I certainly have. Did you think you could get anything past Reginald Coombes?'

'You ought to be at home, resting,' Violet protested. His recent turn had been one of his worst. It had kept him from the factory for weeks.

Mr Coombes lifted his chin. 'What, at home, out of your way, my girl? There's nothing wrong with me. Now, what exactly are you up to?'

In return Violet lifted her own chin. 'You know I always wanted to follow you into the business, Papa. I have so many ideas, so many plans. Times are changing, a new century is here. There are new ways of doing things. When women are given the vote...'

'They haven't been yet,' he objected.

'But they will.' Violet pressed on. 'It isn't only government that must change with the times. Businesses like Coombes must change, too. We have significant social obligations as well as commercial interests. This first step is the meeting I had today, for the social reform committee.'

'You think the Coombes Chocolates factory needs social reform. Is that so?'

She took a deep breath. 'Yes, Papa.'

'And do you want to know what the founder of Coombes Chocolates thinks about it?'

Violet quaked, but kept her voice steady. 'Yes, I do, Papa.'

'I think it's a wonderful idea.'

'Oh, Papa!'

She rushed into her father's waiting arms. He hugged her tightly. 'I'm very proud of you, Violet. Your new-fangled ideas about women's votes and reform committees—I know I've taken a while to come around to them. And I said some things to you in London before you got married that I've had time to regret very much indeed.'

'It's all right, Papa,' Violet choked. 'It's all right now.'

From his waistcoat he pulled a spotted hand-kerchief and passed it to her. 'Upon my soul.'

He patted her awkwardly on the shoulder. After she'd finished with the handkerchief, he blotted his own eyes. 'I wouldn't change you for a son. I couldn't be prouder of anyone than I am of you.'

'Thank you, Papa,' she managed to reply.

When her father had gone, with a last pat of her shoulder, Violet slumped down at the desk. In spite of her weariness, there was still another task she must do.

With a rustle, she drew a piece of Coombes Chocolates writing paper out of the desk drawer and took up her fountain pen. She had made her decision. She would write to the lilac-letter group and let them know.

She could no longer carry out militant activities to support the Cause. It was her decision, and hers alone, as it had to be.

It wasn't only because of her newly discovered pregnancy. During her sleepless nights, she'd been forced into scrupulous honesty. The truth was, she'd felt most uneasy about the lilac letter that had asked her to carry bricks and stones. It was partly why she'd been so defensive, so angry at Adam for challenging her about her militant means. She wished she could tell him so. But it was too late.

She'd never give up the Cause. She would fight for every woman's vote. But she would find another way.

First she had an even more important letter to write. She placed her hands on her stomach.

She could not keep her pregnancy a secret from Adam. Secrets had already cost them too much. He would have to know.

She would still be a mother, alone. But now, after the meeting with the factory workers, she felt more hopeful. She would cope. Necessity was the mother of invention, so the old saying went. With determination and ingenuity, the women workers at the Coombes Chocolates factory would find ways to do their jobs and care for their families.

So would she.

The fountain pen clenched in her fingers, Violet formed the first letters.

Dear Adam.

It thudded, louder than ever, in her head. In her heart. *Adam. Adam. Adam.*

She dropped the fountain pen and put her head in her hands.

'Violet.'

A voice came from the door.

She raised her head and gasped.

'Adam.'

Chapter Eighteen

'Could Love part thus? was it not well to speak,
To have spoken once? It could not but be well.'

—Alfred, Lord Tennyson: *'Love and Duty'*
(1842)

'How did you find me?' Violet gasped.

'I went to your parents' house.' Rapidly, Adam surveyed the Coombes Chocolates factory office. It was a small, busy room, packed with papers and files. A large leather-topped desk, where Violet sat, dominated the room. On one wall was a large-lettered inscription from the book *Self-Help* by Samuel Smiles.

Where there is a will, there is a way.

Adam stepped over the threshold. 'May I come in?'

'Of course.' Her tone was polite, but wary.

He took off his top hat, held it in his hands. 'Your parents told me I would find you here.'

They'd told him, too, that Violet was always at the factory office, working. Now he saw her, he understood the concern on their faces. She looked pale, exhausted. Dark circles were under her eyes. But nothing could dim their beautiful blue as he stared at her, drank her in.

She stood, the desk a barrier between them.

'I'm sorry to find your father so unwell,' he said at last.

'He's much better than he was,' Violet said. 'When I arrived I discovered he'd been having more difficulties with his heart. Another of his turns, but worse than before. He needed rest.'

'So you took over running the factory.' The Coombes had told him that, too.

'Yes. Mama has helped.'

'But you've done most of the work.'

Violet shrugged her shoulders. 'It had to be done.'

'And you always do your duty.'

'I try.' She lifted her chin in that familiar gesture he loved and missed. 'Why are you here, Adam?'

For you, he wanted to say. *I've come for you.*

'I need your help,' he said instead.

'My help,' she repeated flatly.

She wasn't making it easy for him. He gritted his teeth. 'As a suffragette.'

Her forehead creased. Puzzlement was in her blue eyes. 'As a suffragette? What can you mean?

You told me in no uncertain terms you would not allow me to be a suffragette.'

He clenched his jaw. 'I recall what I said to you. But circumstances have changed, drastically. I need you to make use of your suffragette connections.'

She leaned forward, placed both hands on the leather desk. 'Why?'

His fists curled around the brim of his hat. 'I need you to visit my sister in Holloway Prison.'

Her mouth fell open. 'What?'

'She's been imprisoned for criminal damage. She won't see me,' Adam said. 'She only wants to see you.'

The look on her lovely face. The instant compassion. He ought to have known she'd respond that way.

'Of course I'll visit the prison.' Violet moved swiftly around the desk. A waft of her tantalising violet scent came over him. 'I'm sure I can see her. I'd do anything for Jane.'

'That's just it.' Adam shook his head. 'It isn't Jane in prison. It's Arabella.'

Violet shivered. She drew her coat closer around her as she sat at the table in the bleak, dimly lit visiting room. It was little more than a cell, with a small window, and seemed dark, even though it was morning. The walls were a sickly cream, the wooden chairs and table scuffed and dully polished. A locked door faced her.

Holloway. From the outside, it looked like a medieval castle, with its turrets and bricks, towers and arched windows. From the inside, it looked like what it was. A grim prison.

A gate clanged nearby.

Footsteps echoed in the hall outside. The door opened. Arabella, dressed in grey, her hair scraped back, came into the room accompanied by a stern female prison guard with a bunch of keys at her waist.

Violet leapt to her feet and rushed towards her. 'Arabella!'

'Hello, Violet.'

'No contact with the prisoner,' the guard intoned.

'Thank you for coming to see me.' Arabella sat on one of the wooden chairs on the other side of the table. Her voice was fainter than usual and she appeared thinner, but there was a determination around her eyes and mouth. 'I have so much to tell you.'

'I wasn't sure I'd be able to visit you,' Violet said, shocked by Arabella's gaunt appearance. Her experience had clearly been harrowing. Yet she seemed happier, somehow. There was a different energy about her, more purposeful. It had proved more difficult to see her than expected. There were some privileges such as letters and visitors that were available only to certain classes of prisoners.

'Not all the suffragettes can have visitors,' Arabella said. 'I won't have any more, after this. I don't want special privileges. Many of the suffragettes don't get them. But I had to see you, Violet. I had to say—'

Her voice broke off.

'Arabella,' Violet cried. 'What is it?'

Arabella gave one of her sniffs. It wasn't haughty at all, Violet now realised. 'I want to tell you I'm sorry, Violet. When you first married Adam, I was unfriendly to you. Snobbish and unkind.'

'It doesn't matter any more.' How Violet wished she could give her sister-in-law a hug, but there was no chance of that, with the prison guard close by. 'Not in the least. It doesn't matter at all.'

'I was jealous,' Arabella admitted. 'You seemed so free, so independent, and I was not. I'm the eldest of our family. Did you know that?'

Violet nodded. 'Of course.'

'I'm five years older than Adam. Yet I've never been away from home, or done anything on my own. I haven't been to school, or university, as

Adam did. I can't contribute in any way to the good of my country. It struck me, after you left, that I'm treated like a child.'

'Not by Adam.' Violet found herself racing to defend him. He'd never tried to dominate his sisters. He'd always treated them with respect.

'Not by Adam, no,' Arabella agreed. 'But by society. By the law.'

She swallowed painfully. 'I began thinking, after you left Beauley Manor. Why do I accept it? Why do I allow my existence to continue this way? I'm a grown woman. Yet I have no rights.'

Violet exhaled. How well she understood.

'When you left Beauley, one of those letters came,' Arabella went on. 'The ones on lilac writing paper. I'd seen you receive them and you always seemed quite shaken by their contents. I guessed they were how the suffragettes corresponded with you. I opened it.'

'You opened my lilac letter?' Violet was astonished. It was so unexpected.

For a moment Arabella hesitated. 'I took your place as a suffragette.'

'So that's how you ended up in here!' Violet exclaimed, aghast. 'Oh, Arabella, what did you do?'

Arabella glanced towards the prison guard and back at Violet.

'Arson,' she muttered. 'I can't say more. Top secret. You know the rules.'

Violet fell back against her chair, horrified. *Fire.* It was well beyond civil disobedience, or anything she had imagined being involved in. 'I don't believe I'd have gone along with that. It could get out of control so easily. Someone might have got badly hurt.'

'It's a price that must be paid,' Arabella said, with a glint of fervour in her eyes.

'We'll have to agree to differ in our ways and means,' Violet replied, inwardly shocked by Arabella's forcefulness. For her, it was a step too far.

Arabella's thin fingers squeezed Violet's. 'I'd do it again. It's you I have to thank, Violet.'

'You want to thank me? Why?'

'The speech about the women's votes you gave at the garden party. You have a gift. It inspired me to join the Cause. It has changed my life. It has changed me.'

'I can see that,' Violet said, stunned.

Arabella glanced at the clock on the wall. 'We haven't much time. There's something else I must tell you.'

Violet leaned in. 'What is it?'

Arabella hesitated. 'Adam may have told you. He tried to protect me and Jane, but our childhood was quite—distressing.'

'He told me some of it,' Violet said gently.

Arabella shuddered. 'There were dreadful scenes. Terrifying to a child. I learned to keep my feelings under control and so did Adam. But he feels things, deeply. When you left him I thought his heart would break.'

Violet put her hand to her bodice. Her own heart began to thump.

Arabella coughed. 'He walked around Beauley Manor as if he were a ghost. He didn't sleep, he didn't eat. I'd hear him at night, pacing the solar. Jane brought home some Coombes Floral Creams to remind him of you. She thought it might make him happier. But Adam was so angry. He threw them away. He said he never wanted to see a Floral Cream again.'

'I can't believe it.' Violet's voice trembled.

The prison guard clanked her keys. 'Time's up.'

Violet's eyes welled with tears. 'Oh, Arabella. We have to get you out of here.'

'There's no need. I'll survive it. This is won't be the last time I'm imprisoned. I'll never give up the fight for the Cause,' vowed Arabella. 'You know what we say. Never surrender.'

Briefly, they embraced, while the prison guard looked the other way.

'Adam missed you so much,' Arabella whispered as she left the room. 'You had to know, Violet.'

Violet pulled her coat tight around her stomach.

Behind her the huge prison doors slammed shut.

She staggered. The visit had been exhausting, physically and emotionally.

'Violet.' She spun around to find Adam behind her, in his top hat and frock coat.

'I've been waiting for you,' he said. 'I've got the carriage.'

Violet opened her mouth.

'Please, Violet.' He spoke again before she could say any more. 'I must hear about Arabella. Come into the carriage. We need to be private.'

Wordless with relief, she followed him. She needed to be with him, just then. What Arabella had told her rang in her ears.

He quickly surveyed the street around the prison before he opened the carriage door.

'What is it?' she asked in an undertone.

'Reporters,' he said briefly. 'Looking for scandal.'

Pressure passed through his glove to hers as he helped her into the carriage.

He frowned before climbing in after her, seeming to note her pallor. 'You're shivering.'

'It was cold inside the prison,' she said.

Inside, Violet leaned back against the leather seat and took a deep breath. The touch of his hand remained a shudder through her.

Adam took the seat opposite hers. His knees brushed her skirt as he settled back into his seat.

He frowned. 'Are you all right?'

'Oh, yes!' Violet took another breath. 'It was emotional, seeing Arabella.'

'Perhaps these will help.' He passed her a large tin of Coombes Floral Creams.

Violet stared at Adam in amazement.

He ran his hand through his hair. 'I wanted to find a way to say thank you.'

Violet's throat choked. 'You don't need to thank me.'

He'd thrown some Coombes Violet Creams away, Arabella had told her.

Because he missed her. Longed for her. As she had missed and longed for him.

Adam exhaled. 'Tell me. How did you find my sister?'

'Surprisingly well,' said Violet. She set aside the tin of chocolates. She couldn't eat. Not now. Quickly she told him what had transpired between her and Arabella in the prison.

Adam closed his eyes and put his head back against the seat for a long moment. 'It's unbelievable. She's become a militant. Arabella.'

'I blame myself.' Violet confessed.

Adam shook his head. 'Arabella has made her choice.'

'She has certainly taken up the suffragette gauntlet now.' Violet hesitated. 'I'm not sure I can follow so far in her footsteps. I realised that, when I saw her in the prison. There are some militant actions that go too far for me. But she has embraced it completely. She says she's been treated as little more than a child. Never going away to school, or university.'

'I've been thinking about that myself recently,' Adam said to her surprise. 'Arabella is intelligent. She's always reading. It does seem unfair that she hasn't had the same opportunities as I have enjoyed.'

'So you do believe in women's rights.' Violet couldn't help saying, with an edge in her voice.

His jaw set like rock. 'I've always supported women's rights.'

She lifted her chin. She had to know. 'Then why did you tell me I couldn't be a suffragette? You forbade it, as my husband.'

He exhaled. 'Damnation, Violet. Didn't you realise? Seeing you in danger—it made me crazed. The thought of you being hurt, or worse. It was far too dangerous for you to be a suffragette. I felt I had to control the situation to keep you safe.

After that night we spent together, I never wanted you to leave my arms.'

'What?' Violet's hand flew to her heart. 'But you said you regretted the terms of our marriage.'

Adam scowled, then his face cleared. 'The terms. Not our marriage. I never regretted marrying you. Not for a moment.'

He seized her hands. His were strong, warm. 'How could you believe I'd be glad you were gone? That I wouldn't long to see your face, your forget-me-not-blue eyes? Your lips? To hear your plain speaking?'

Her throat choked. 'I thought you were sorry you married me.'

'I never expected to feel the way I did,' he admitted. 'I thought I could avoid...'

'Entanglements?'

He gave a short laugh. 'Indeed. I know now that I didn't want to avoid entanglements with you.' His eyes burned into hers so intently she flushed. 'It was the kind of emotional scenes I witnessed in my childhood I didn't want.'

'I was entangled, too,' she admitted. 'I knew I couldn't give up the Cause, but I couldn't fight my feelings for you. I didn't think it was possible to have both in my life.'

'I didn't make it easy for you. I realised that, when I found you gone.' His jaw clenched. 'If I loved you any less I could never have let you go. I loved you too much to force you to stay, if all you wanted was to be free.'

'I never wanted to be free of you...' She faltered.

His teeth gritted. 'Yet you left Beauley Manor without a goodbye.'

'I thought it was the only way. And—I thought you didn't love me.'

He became still. 'Ah.'

'It was intolerable.' Her voice turned to a whisper. Then she steadied herself. 'How could I stay? I couldn't bear you regretting our marriage. Looking at me over the breakfast table, dining with me in the evening. Lying beside me at night. Making love to me.' She bit her lip. 'All the while wishing you had never made our marriage of convenience.'

'Violet.' Adam pulled her into his arms. 'The only inconvenience in our marriage is that we never realised how very convenient it was.'

Adam's mouth found hers, as though recognising her with his lips.

Across the carriage they moved together, his body pressed into hers, his hands wrenching her closer as their lips found each other. Nothing mattered but his kiss, just then, and what he told her with his lips.

He loved her.

She loved him, too, she told him with her searching tongue, with something deeper than desire, more real, more powerful.

When he finally pulled away she stared at him in wonder.

'Violet.' He held her close. 'When you left, it was as if all the flowers in the garden had died. My senses failed me. Colours dimmed, I could barely taste food.'

'Arabella said you threw some Coombes Floral Creams away,' she said, as she nestled against him. 'You never wanted to see them again.'

'They made me think of you. *Violet.*' With his finger he caressed her lips. 'I believe I fell in love with you the moment you popped that violet cream in your mouth. You have the prettiest lips. They're shaped like a bow.'

His gaze made her flush. She felt the heat creep into her cheeks.

'You changed so much when you came to Beauley Manor,' he said. 'Your beliefs. Your banners. Your speeches. You were a breath of fresh air. You brought the whole Beaufort family into a new way of thinking, a new life. Leaving the past behind.'

He took a strand of her hair in his hand and wound it around his finger. 'Your commitment, your passion—it captivated me right from the start.'

Tears burnt her eyes. 'So you do understand how I feel about the Cause.'

'I always did.' He grinned bleakly, sent the dent in his cheek darting. 'But I didn't expect to feel the way I do about you.'

Adam reached into his waistcoat pocket.

He held out a small blue leather box. 'This is for you.'

Violet's eyes widened as she took the box. With fingers that shook, she snapped open the lid. Inside, nestled on white silk, lay the ring he'd chosen for her, a tiny flower, the leaves made of emeralds, the petals amethyst and, at the centre, a white pearl.

'It's a flower,' she said in wonderment. 'A violet.'

He'd bought it for her that day in London. He'd got the idea when he picked the last violet in the grounds of Beauley Manor, the day of the garden party.

He'd kept the ring with him throughout their separation, like a talisman.

Violet lifted the ring to the light. She stroked the jewels with a trembling finger as understanding dawned on her face.

'When we went up to London together, while you were on your way to Downing Street, I was collecting this ring,' he explained. 'I had it made for you.'

'The day you rescued me.'

'I'm not sure who did the rescuing,' he told her. 'You rescued Beauley. My family. Me. You've opened my eyes. My mind. You've opened my heart.'

'I thought it was my money you needed.'

'It turns out I needed you.'

He heard her stifle a sob.

'I needed you, too,' she whispered. 'But I prize my independence.'

'Your independence is what made such an impression on me. It's what I adore about you. Along with your courage. Your bravery. Did I say it was when you ate that chocolate fondant that I fell in love with you? Let me amend that. I think it was when you fell from the balcony.'

Violet laughed. 'It was quite a fall.'

'Indeed,' he drawled.

'Perhaps that may not have been the occasion,' he corrected. 'It may have been at our engagement. When you kissed me.'

She bit her lip. His body responded instantly, but he held back from kissing her again. 'Will you wear this ring? Will you marry me?'

Tears sparkled in her eyes, turning them sapphire. 'We're already married.'

'That was a marriage of convenience,' he said. 'I want to marry you for love.'

For a moment she was silent. His heart drummed.

'I'd marry you again,' she replied at last in a voice that made the muscles of his heart contract. 'For love.'

Time stopped, swirled.

'I'd give you the world, if I could,' he said at last, when he could find words.

She smiled. 'I only want the vote.'

'Will this do, for now?' Taking her fingers in his, he slid the ring on to the fourth finger of her left hand, next to her gold band.

Their fingers entangled.

'You didn't remove your wedding ring,' he said huskily.

She shook her head with resolve. 'Never.'

He cleared his throat.

She smiled, a sweet, yet teasing, smile.

She looked down at her fingers, then up at him. 'This new ring is lovely. But it isn't all I want.'

'What do you want, Violet?'

She slid across the seat, at the same moment that Adam leaned into her, until there was no distance between them. She lifted her mouth close to his.

'Are you hungry? Do you want a Floral Cream?' he asked, with a half-smile that set her heart thudding.

'While we were apart, I couldn't face chocolate,' she told him. 'The scent made me ill. But now, I crave it.'

'Then you must have a fondant.' His eyes still fixed on her, with one hand he reached for the tin.

Violet tugged him back on to the seat. It was her pregnancy that had made her unable to face chocolate. She would tell him, of course, but she wanted to set it right between them, first.

'Not yet,' she said. 'I'm craving something else.'

He glanced at his pocket watch. 'We can make it back to Beauley in time for tea.'

'I always hoped you would come to the solar for afternoon tea,' she confessed. She'd been so happy whenever he opened the door.

'Did you?' His glance was a caress, as if on her bare skin. 'I only came for you. But that wasn't my favourite time of day.'

'It wasn't?'

He shook his head. 'I had ulterior motives.'

Quizzical, she put her head to one side. 'I don't understand.'

He leaned to whisper once more. 'In our bedroom. I liked to watch you dress for dinner.'

She swallowed hard. 'But I kept the connecting door shut.'

Had he been watching her, unawares?

He grinned. 'I didn't spy on you, Violet, tempting though it was at times. I have more integrity than that. But when you were dressed in your evening gown, we often talked while you were at your dressing table. I used to think about what I'd do.' He leaned in, his mouth hot against her skin. 'To give you pleasure.'

'I want you to show me,' she whispered.

Chapter Nineteen

'... Duty loved of Love...'
—Alfred, Lord Tennyson: *'Love and Duty'*
(1842)

The gaslight gleamed. The fire in the grate flickered red, orange, yellow as Violet sat in front of the dressing table, reflected in the glass.

Watching him, watching her.

They had arrived at Beauley Manor in the carriage earlier that afternoon. She'd watched as the house rose up out of the misty autumn sky. The rose-red bricks glowed like fallen leaves in the late afternoon sunshine. As she had been when she first laid eye on it, on her wedding day, Violet had stared, spellbound.

'I thought I'd never see it again,' she'd told Adam.

They'd both been quiet as the carriage rolled up the drive, crunching over the pebbles, towards the house.

He'd gripped her hand as he helped her from the carriage, then lifted her into his arms. Her boots were transported off the ground as he swirled her into his arms.

Her skirt flew. She'd laughed, holding on to her hat. 'Adam!'

'I presume you waltz?' he'd asked teasingly, as he'd asked her the first time they danced at the ball.

'I've had lessons,' she replied, as she had then.

'Excellent,' he murmured.

Violet closed her eyes. In her mind she could almost hear the music of 'The Blue Danube.' Adam had whirled her across the pebbled drive. In his arms her feet glided over the stones as if she floated above them. His grip never wavered as he lifted her off the ground in another turn, before placing her on the pebbles.

Now, Violet's reflection in the mirror studied him as she held up a diamond-and-sapphire earring. 'I'm wondering whether to wear these. What do you think?'

Adam took the earring as if to hold it against to her ear. Instead he bent his head and caressed the base of her earlobe with his lips. Slowly, he began to make his way down her neck.

He slid his hands over her curves. Leant between her breasts and breathed.

'Violets.'

She pointed at the bottle with its purple ribbon.

He caressed beneath her ear with his tongue, his teeth. 'You.'

'Adam…'

In the looking glass he watched her creamy skin turn to rose pink. Her lips parted in his name as with his lips he found the path deeper, between the crevice of her low-cut evening gown.

With a tip of his finger he reached for the point of one of her breasts, caressing it beneath the cup of her bodice. Lifted it out of her corset into his mouth. Watched her gasp.

He spun the velvet stool, swung her to face him. Took those pink tips again in his mouth. She twisted, leant backwards and arched into the curved wood of the dressing table, sending the crystal tinkling as she half-fell against it. He knew how to please her now, to find the place on her skin that would bring her pleasure. But he wanted to give her more.

He still held the earring in his fist. Dropping the jewel on to the dressing table, it fell with a tinkle against the crystal.

In a swoop he took her around the waist, lifted her higher on the stool. With one hand he found the frilled edge of her fashionable underwear. Toyed inside the edge for a moment, saw her tense.

Lifting her higher, he slid the silk garment

away, over her stockinged legs. Tossed them aside, on to the wooden floor, where they fell in a rumpled heap.

Still watching her face, he pushed back her skirt, then, slowly, one by one, he lifted ruffled layers of her petticoats. With one hand he parted her silken thighs. Lowered his head and dived.

This time, when he lifted her and laid her on to the bed, it was different. Harder. Stronger. Deeper. She knew their rhythm now, as if they danced together. She moved against him as he slid into her.

She told him, with her mouth, with her hands, with her body, as he drove into her, the longing she'd felt for him, when they'd been apart.

Their desire. Equal. No longer two, but one.

Man and woman. Husband and wife.

She matched the rise and fall of his body with hers. Faster. Fuller. Inside her. Until at last he cried out her name into her mouth, as he surged into her, a wave, at the same time the wave filled her.

She fell back, gasping. Silent.

Until he reached for her, again.

Violet's body tingled as she stretched beneath the sheets.

The door opened with a creak.

Adam lifted the silver tray he carried. 'Gate-keeper, butler, cook and lady's maid. I thought you might not be averse to some tea and toast in bed.'

He propped the tray on the nightstand. Violet laughed as she looked at it.

He raised a quizzical eyebrow. 'What is it?'

'Doorstops.'

He grinned. 'Ah, yes. I remember.'

She sat up in the bed. Around her the room whirled. She fell back against the pillows, closed her eyes.

Instantly he was beside her. 'Violet. What is it?'

She put her hand to her mouth. 'I feel ill.'

He looked at the plate of toast. 'The sight of the doorstops.'

She began a chuckle that turned to nausea.

'I don't think I can eat,' she said, after a moment.

Adam jerked back his head. 'You missed dinner last night. Now you'll miss breakfast.' He frowned, concerned. 'Try a cup of tea.'

She sat up and poured some tea from the silver pot into a china cup. She sipped. It was Darjeeling, her favourite, but nowadays it tasted quite odd.

She raised her teacup. 'Is it too early to make a toast?'

He grinned quizzically.

'To Beauley,' she said. He'd told her the Manor was to be saved. 'And its firm foundations.'

He laughed. 'No more rotten floorboards.'

She made a mock frown. 'Does that mean separate beds?'

'Certainly not,' he murmured, his gaze on her lips.

She took another sip of tea. It was time. Her stomach fluttered.

Adam spoke before she did. 'There's another toast that must be made. I'm afraid I lack a teacup, but if we are toasting our respective Causes, then I must also make a salute. To suffrage.'

Violet laid her teacup in the saucer.

'We might still argue about it sometimes. And about other things too, I expect.'

He gave a bleak smile. 'While you were away, I realised that our marriage is nothing like that of my parents. And I can handle some chaos. The new foundations of our marriage will withstand a few arguments, I think.'

Violet knew she could trust Adam. He would support her unconditionally in her vocation as a suffragette now. There was no misunderstanding left between them on that matter. It was all settled between them, as she had hoped. It was time to tell him the news.

When she lifted her teacup her hand was trembling.

Concerned, he slid the cup away from her. 'You're not well. Would you care for something different to eat or drink?'

'No.' A sudden smile filled her, as though it were shining up through her belly, her heart, and up to her face.

The relief. The joy. To be able to tell him, face to face.

She took his hand, with its strong fingers, and laid it over hers, on her stomach. 'I wonder if I might not have been eating too many chocolates. I have been running a chocolate factory, after all. Do you think so?'

'You're perfect as you are, Violet.'

'I hope you will always think so. Especially in a few months.'

He frowned. 'Nothing can change my feelings for you. Haven't I made that clear?'

She laid her own hand on top of his. 'Surely you can guess.'

His frown deepened, became two forked lines between his brows.

'I'm pregnant,' she whispered.

Shock etched his face.

'Are you sure?' he demanded.

Violet nodded. 'I'm sure.'

Adam wrenched his hand away.

'Adam!' Violet exclaimed. 'What is it?'

He was on his feet, across the room. He stared out the window, into the garden, his back to her. She couldn't make out his expression.

Her fingers trembled as they formed a protective clasp over her stomach.

'Do you want our child?' she whispered, aghast.

During their terrible argument, he'd told her he regretted the terms of their marriage, even though he'd later explained his true meaning. She'd believed him. Surely it wasn't possible for him to be angry with her now.

He spun around. A muscle worked in his cheek. 'Of course I want our child. How could you imagine for a moment I would not? We have our home, we have each other. I want, more than anything, to bring new life into the world to share it with us.'

'Then what's the matter?' she asked, bewildered.

His jaw hardened. 'You must recall our agreement, when we made the terms of our marriage of convenience.'

She nodded.

'Violet.' He came back to the bed, seized her hands. 'You wanted to wait.'

She bit her lip.

'I still recall your words,' he said. 'You spoke of bonds of love in marriage that bind a woman.'

How well she remembered.

He shook his head. 'I ought to have considered this eventuality. It was my duty.'

'We're both responsible.' Their desire for each other had been equal. Shared.

Rapidly, she told him what she had learned at the Coombes Chocolates factory, when she held a meeting with the women workers to find ways to both work and have a happy family life. 'It's possible for a woman to have a family and a vocation. I'm sure of it.'

'All the same.' He cupped her face in his hands. 'I have no wish to bind you,' he said huskily.

'The bonds of love are no bonds at all, when two people are pledged as we are.' She brushed her lips against his fingers. 'You've taught me so much, Adam. How to build something that will last. I want to build a family, with you.'

His kiss told her all she needed to know, to be sure. A vow. A promise.

To freedom. To family.

'I wonder if it will be a boy or a girl,' she said at last, as he held her in his arms.

'We agreed to one of each,' he reminded her, with a grin. 'I'll hold you to that.'

Then he sobered. 'I would hate even more to see you in any danger, now you're with child.'

She shook her head. 'I told you. The militant way Arabella is following, I've realised now, is not my path.'

When she had been separated from Adam, she'd made her decision, alone. She would never give up the Cause. She would fight for every woman's vote. But she would find another way. Her own way.

'Mrs Emmeline Pankhurst is a mother and she's the leader of the suffragettes,' Violet said. 'It doesn't stop her. In fact, her daughters follow her footsteps in the Cause. If we have a daughter, perhaps she will do the same. Every woman must do what she can.'

'And every man,' Adam said.

'What do you mean by that?' Violet asked, curious. 'What are you thinking, Adam?'

'I'm not sure yet,' he said slowly. 'We shall see.'

Chapter Twenty

'Live happy; tend thy flowers; be tended by
My blessing!'
    —Alfred, Lord Tennyson: *'Love and Duty'*
                        (1842)

One year later, 1910

'Come with me,' Adam said.

'Where are you taking me?' Violet demanded, as she slipped her white gloved hand inside his.

Adam grinned. 'You'll see.'

He held her hand, tight, as they followed the path around the side of the Manor, Beau at their heels.

'But, Adam,' Violet protested, 'there's so much to be done before the garden party today. There's nothing around this side of the house. This is the area you told me not to come to. You said there is work being done that was important to rebuilding our foundations.'

'So there is. Here.'

He led her further on, to a high wall.

Violet ran her hand over the stone. 'This is new.'

'Yes. It's been made to blend with the old bricks of Beauley Manor, but it is new, brand new.'

'Is it going to be part of the Manor?' she asked curiously. 'Are you extending the building out here?'

He lightly touched her stomach. 'At the rate we are going, we'll need to extend.'

She laughed.

He pulled a key from his pocket and handed it to her.

'After you.'

In bewilderment, she stared at him. 'What?'

He pushed back some ivy growing over the wall. 'Here.'

Violet stared at the wooden door, with the brass keyhole. 'I don't understand.'

'You will. Open the door, Violet.'

He put his arms around her waist, stood behind her. With a sigh, she leaned back against him. How well she had come to know his hands, to trust his touch.

Violet turned the key in the lock. It was stiff, difficult to turn.

'Here.' He put his hand over hers. They turned it, together.

'Oh.' Violet breathed.

She couldn't believe her eyes. In front of her was a walled garden, but it was no ordinary garden. The flower beds, full of blooms, contained purple pansies and violets, and white lilac and white petunias, amid the green leaves.

Purple. Green. White.

'It's a suffrage garden,' he said.

Tears welled in her eyes. 'It's so beautiful.'

'Do you remember? You told me about the fashionable gardens in one colour. But I thought you would prefer three colours.'

Adam leaned towards Violet, so close his lips almost brushed hers. His cheek dented as he grinned. 'I know my preference. I'd prefer one colour. A garden full of violets.'

Violet felt her cheeks turn tell-tale pink. The intimacy grown between them astonished her. Only she knew what he meant by wishing for violets.

She stared about. There was a swing seat, garden benches and a large wrought-iron table and chairs. 'Why, I can have meetings in here, with the other suffragettes.'

'You can use it for whatever purposes you like. I had it planted for you.' He turned serious. 'I want us both to grow in our marriage, like this garden.'

'*"Marriage, like government, is a series of compromises. One must give and take, repair and restrain, endure and be patient,"*' Violet quoted.

'Samuel Smiles,' said Adam with a chuckle. 'I've become wedded to many things since I married you. The maxims of Samuels Smiles. Violet creams.'

She smiled. 'I hope so.'

'It's a secret garden,' he said. 'If you want it to be. But I hope you'll allow me to visit you here, sometimes.'

She held the key out to him. 'I'll keep the door unlocked. It's ours.'

He closed his fist around her hand, with the key inside it.

'I hope we'll be here together often,' she whispered.

Beau barked.

'And you, too, Beau,' she said with a laugh, as she gave the dog a pat.

She straightened, looked into Adam's dark blue eyes. 'No more closed doors. Not between us. We don't have any secrets.'

He gave a wry grin. 'Actually, we do.'

He led her to the garden bench. 'I have some news.'

She leant towards him, interested. 'What is it?'

'You will remember Mr Burrows, the M.P. for our area.'

Violet grimaced. 'How could I forget?' He had been so scathing about women's abilities, or the lack of them. Thinking about it filled her with an instant of rage. To think that a Member of the British Parliament believed that women were incapable of voting. But he wasn't the only man who held such views. In a way, she ought to be grateful to Mr Burrows. It was the day she'd found her voice.

'I was proud of you, Violet, the way you stood up to him.'

'You stood up for me, too,' Violet reminded Adam. It was one of the clues she'd had to her feelings for him and his for her. The way she'd felt having him beside her, standing up for her. It had been a turning point to how it could be for a husband and wife who shared both passion and ideals. 'What about Mr Burrows?'

'He's standing down as our Member of Parliament.'

'That's good. Perhaps someone with more forward ideas will take his place,' Violet said.

'I understand there is someone who has expressed an interest.'

'Who?'

Adam stood and took a bow.

The realisation dawned on Violet. 'What? Adam? You?'

'Indeed.' He smiled. 'You're looking at the new future Member of Parliament for our area, Mrs Beaufort. If all goes to plan.' He took her hands in his. 'I can no longer stand by and see injustice done against the woman I love, or any woman. You know I'd have supported you in the House of

Lords, but I want to be part of the change. I want to make the laws for this country, better, fairer laws. In the House of Commons, where one day I believe women will be granted suffrage, the right to vote.'

Violet's eyes welled. 'Freedom.'

'Freedom,' he affirmed. 'I'll need your help on the campaign trail. You have developed quite the reputation. I expect people will come out to hear you speak more than me.'

'I won't be planning to give up my campaigning for the Cause any time soon.'

A world where women and men had the same opportunities in life seemed unimaginable now. But in her heart she believed it would happen. She would never give up the fight. And there were other women, and men, too, who would never give up, either.

'That's good.' Adam checked his pocket watch. 'Because you're supposed to be campaigning right now.'

'We,' she corrected.

'Ah.' He brushed his lips against her neck before murmuring in her ear. 'My favourite word.'

Violet's cheeks warmed. Since they had reunited, they had become closer in a way that she had never imagined possible. Closer in their pleasure and their work.

She loved their days and their nights. Candlelit

nights, when the connecting door was opened between them, and their marriage came to life. Not only through words, but also through touch. Dusk and dawn, too, early, sun-gold dawns and long, violet-hued dusks, that meant they could slip away to their bedroom, yet still be in the light.

She felt freer, in the light. Being able to see him, his body, his face. He wanted to see her, too. She knew his expressions now, those most intimate expressions of desire that only she witnessed when they were alone. Passion. Craving. Need. And other emotions, too. Feelings they could share with each other. Feelings they no longer had to hide.

Adam put on his straw boater. It had a suffrage band around the crown of his hat. Purple, green and white. 'Shall we go together?'

Violet adjusted her sash. 'Together.'

Violet and Adam strolled across the lawn, wending between the chairs and rugs, nodding and smiling. 'Good afternoon. Good afternoon.'

'Good day.'

'Welcome to Beauley Manor.'

The sun blazed on to the garden. Roses, peonies, irises, delphiniums and foxgloves created a blaze of colour. White-wicker garden chairs and tables and seats dotted the lawn. The croquet hoops had been laid out and the local regiment band were playing a rousing tune.

Stalls had been set up for the ladies' bazaar, to sell handiworks to raise funds. One stall held suffragette items, tricoloured ribbon that could be added to hats and belts, striped sashes and bands, plus garments and underclothing in the suffragette shades.

Another popular new stall was a huge table containing Coombes Chocolates, donated by her parents. 'Chocolate Manufacturers to the King' proclaimed an enormous banner above the stall. Her papa had achieved his dream at last, and been awarded a Royal Warrant. She'd wondered if Adam had been involved in procuring the Warrant through his connections at Court, but he denied it.

'Coombes speak for themselves,' he'd said with a grin, popping a chocolate in his mouth before pulling her under the bedcovers.

In another part of the garden, long tables for refreshments were ready and the kitchen staff were smoothing out the long white tablecloths, laying out plates, teacups and teaspoons that glinted in the sun. The Punch and Judy puppet show was ready for the entertainment of the children, the clues for the treasure hunt had been hidden around the garden and the ribbons and prizes were ready for the running races. By the bandstand a white tent had been put up and a large wooden podium had been set up, ready for the speeches.

In aid of the Cause.

'Violet.'

They turned to see Arabella crossing the lawn, carrying a small white bundle. She passed the baby to Violet.

They looked down on the sleeping child. Sunlight danced around her, catching the gold on her small head.

'I could look at her for ever,' Violet whispered, holding her close.

Adam leaned down to stroke the side of the baby's cheek. 'Her skin is so soft.'

Violet smiled with respect at her sister-in-law, swathed in a purple, white and green sash. Pinned to Arabella's bodice was a silver hunger-strike medal, inscribed with the words 'For Valour' on the bar. It had been awarded to her by the Women's Social and Political Union in recognition of her efforts. She was thinner than ever, after another spell in prison. It had been particularly gruelling, but Arabella swore she would never give up her militant activities or surrender the Cause. She was held in high esteem by the suffragettes.

'Will you hold her during the speeches, Arabella?' asked Violet.

Arabella gazed at the baby with complete devotion. 'Of course.'

'And there's the suffrage play later,' Violet said.

Adam chuckled. 'I must say I'm looking forward to seeing Jane perform in the play.'

'I'm sure she'll be marvellous,' said Violet.

She passed the baby back to Arabella. 'Go to your godmama, Liberty.'

'Liberty,' Arabella repeated. 'It's an unusual name.'

Adam clasped his hands momentarily around Violet's corseted waist, so swiftly that no one else could notice. Yet the effect of his fingers was instant—warm, firm—through her dress. 'Her parents were married in unusual circumstances.'

'The best circumstances are those in which people make the best of them,' Violet said.

'Indeed,' said Adam. 'I've not heard that expression. Is it Samuel Smiles?'

Violet shook her head. 'No. It's mine.'

He grinned. 'You've grown wise.'

She grimaced. 'I've learned some lessons.'

'So have I,' he murmured in her ear.

'I'll find a chair near the front,' said Arabella. 'I want to be sure I can hear every word, Violet. It's almost time for the speeches.'

Bearing Liberty with care, she hurried away.

Violet glanced around the garden. She spotted

her mama, looking less terrified than she had in the past, conversing with Mrs Beaufort, Adam's mother. Both were attired in the colours of the suffragettes. Her mama's cartwheel hat sported huge purple and green feathers.

'Where is my papa?' she asked Adam.

Adam pointed to a hedge. A curl of cigar smoke came up from behind it.

'Oh, Papa.' Violet sighed.

'His health is so much better now,' said Adam. 'He hasn't had a turn for some time, has he?'

Violet shook her head. At least her papa was his old self again, if not better, with his new Royal Warrant.

'Are you ready to speak?'

'Yes.' Not just to speak out for herself, Violet vowed. For Jane, for Arabella. For her mama. For her mother-in-law. For the women of Beauley. For Hannah Walsh and the women at the Coombes Chocolates factory. For all women everywhere. For Liberty.

'It's my duty,' she said. Until all women could vote, and speak out, for themselves.

Adam pulled the brim of his hat down in front of them. 'How fortunate we are to have to do our duty.'

'I agree,' Violet whispered.

She reached up and kissed him.

Epilogue

'In that last kiss, which never was the last...'
—Alfred, Lord Tennyson: *'Love and Duty'*
(1842)

On the podium, Violet adjusted her hat. Her hands were perspiring; they felt clammy in her lace gloves.

Courage, Violet said to herself.

She adjusted her sash. It was striped in the colours of purple, white and green, of course, but it was longer than usual, to make room for her rounded belly. Perhaps it would be a boy, this time.

'Shall we settle upon one of each?' Adam's voice came back to her.

She looked up at him, standing tall beside her on the podium. His jaw was set firm above his necktie. She could see the lines of fatigue on his face after the long weeks of campaigning, but his eyes were bright blue as he glanced back at her, full of intensity of purpose, full of love.

'Adam Beaufort.'

He smiled as he stepped forward, back straight,

head high. Only she could see the slight clenching of his fingers.

Violet held her breath.

'Twenty-two thousand, six hundred and eleven votes.'

A roar of applause went up in the hall.

Adam whirled around and swept Violet in his arms, lifting her off her feet to kiss her.

'You did it,' she choked, through tears and laughter. 'You won the election!'

'There's still one vote I haven't won,' he whispered in her ear.

'Whose is that?'

'Your vote,' Adam said. 'It will happen, one day soon. I'm sure of it.'

'Women will have the vote,' Violet vowed. 'One day.'

As Adam held her in his arms, she knew it would.

* * * * *

Historical Note

Violet's story celebrates every woman who ever fought for the rights we enjoy today.

Deeds, not words: Today we might not be able to imagine what it was like to have no vote and few legal rights, but in Violet's time this battle had not yet been won. In 1903 the Women's Social and Political Union was founded by Mrs Emmeline Pankhurst and her daughters Christabel and Sylvia. They demanded that women have the right to vote and they were not prepared to wait.

'I invited a number of women to my house in Nelson Street, Manchester, for purposes of organisation,' wrote Mrs Pankhurst. 'We voted to call our new society the Women's Social and Political Union, partly to emphasise its democracy, and partly to define it object as political rather than propagandist. We resolved to limit our membership exclusively to women, to keep ourselves absolutely free from party affiliation, and to be satisfied with nothing but action on our question. *Deeds, not words* was to be our permanent motto.'

You can find out more from The Pankhurst Centre.

Activists and Militants: In the early twentieth century, frustrated by their lack of progress, the women's movement splintered into various groups with competing means to achieve the goal of suffrage, including those who used radical and militant means, from civil disobedience to property damage, arrest and even arson.

Some suffragettes supported these activities; others thought they harmed the Cause. Violet's story represents this turbulent period.

Find out more at the British Library: https://www.bl.uk/votes-for-women/articles/suffragettes-violence-and-militancy

Votes for Women! The suffrage play that Violet, Jane and Arabella discuss was written by Elizabeth Robins, an actress, playwright and ardent suffragette. Many pamphlets, books and plays were written by women to support and broadcast the aims of the Cause. The themes in *Votes for Women!* capture the mood and conflict of the day.

It was first performed in London in 1907 and

the script of the play was published by Mills and Boon in 1909, the same year as this story.

Chocolate Empires: The time period in which Violet's story is set was when great chocolate empires such as Cadbury and Fry had come to prominence. The confectioners generally provided excellent conditions for their workers, including women. In this, Violet's goals at Coombes Chocolates make her very much a woman of her times.

You can discover more about chocolate factories and their history at: https://www.cadbury.co.uk/our-story

If you'd like to taste a floral-flavoured chocolate fondant, try my recipe at the end of this book.

Shrinking Violets: Are violets shy? These bright purple flowers from the viola family, which includes violets and pansies, are colourful and easily seen. They got this poetic epithet in the nineteenth century, which describes their growing places in the shade and undergrowth. But violets are no wallflowers; they thrive in sunshine, too.

The Blue Danube: Violet and Adam dance at the ball to the immortal waltz 'The Beautiful Blue Danube' by Strauss. Take a twirl around the floor yourself. In this rendition by Andre Rieu and his orchestra, the female musicians wear beautiful ball gowns—and watch out for the white-gowned debutantes and their partners who appear on the balcony: https://vimeo.com/258077067

Love and Duty: Interwoven into the story is Tennyson's poem 'Love and Duty' (1842). Full of desire and conflict, it is the inspiration for Violet and Adam's choices which, fortunately for them, had a happy ending.

Between chocolate, duty and love may we never have to choose…

Violet Creams

A recipe for chocolate violet fondants, to share on International Women's Day (March 8th).

- *Fifteen ounces of granulated sugar*
- *Half a pint of water*
- *Two teaspoons of glucose*
- *Two tablespoons of violet syrup or violet liqueur*
- *Three tablespoons of double cream*
- *One ounce of icing sugar*
- *Eight ounces of dark couverture chocolate*
- *Violet food colouring*
- *Crystallised violet petals*

To make the fondant, put the icing sugar and water in a saucepan, place over a low heat and stir until the sugar is melted. Add the glucose and bring quickly to the boil. Let it keep boiling until it forms a soft ball if you drop a small piece into cold water. When it is at that consistency, turn off the heat. While the mixture is still warm add the violet flavouring and colouring as you desire. Let it cool and add the cream.

Pour the fondant mixture on to a damp marble slab or wooden board. With a flat-bladed knife fold the outside of the mixture into the centre, several times. When it is cool enough, using icing sugar on your hands, knead the mixture until smooth and creamy.

Let the mixture set for a minimum of three hours, then roll into any shape you fancy. Cover the shapes with melted chocolate and allow to set again after topping with a crystallised violet petal.